WATCHED FROM A DISTANCE

LOVE UNDER FIRE

WATCHED FROM A DISTANCE

LOVE UNDER FIRE

ALLISON B. HANSON

This book is a work of fiction. Names, characters, places, and incidents are the product of the author's imagination or are used fictitiously. Any resemblance to actual events, locales, or persons, living or dead, is coincidental.

Copyright © 2018 by Allison B. Hanson. All rights reserved, including the right to reproduce, distribute, or transmit in any form or by any means. For information regarding subsidiary rights, please contact the Publisher.

Entangled Publishing, LLC
2614 South Timberline Road
Suite 105, PMB 159
Fort Collins, CO 80525
rights@entangledpublishing.com

Amara is an imprint of Entangled Publishing, LLC.

Edited by Nina Bruhns
Cover design by KAM Designs
Cover photography by
MRBIG_PHOTOGRAPHY/iStock
oksixx/DepositPhotos

Manufactured in the United States of America

First Edition September 2018

For my writing soul mate, Misty Simon. I'm so glad I found you!

Chapter One

OUTSIDE DENVER, COLORADO

No one in the history of the world had ever been this nervous at a child's soccer game. U.S. Deputy Marshal Dane Ryan knew he shouldn't be here. He'd taken every precaution, but it still wasn't safe.

Not only was he at risk of being discovered, but he was sure the fake mustache made him look like a 70s porn star.

The mothers sharing the bleachers stared at him and murmured to each other. He was a stranger, and mothers protected their young with a vengeance. Especially from men who looked like they made a living playing the part of Hot Copier Repairman.

The truth was, Dane wasn't even watching the game in the field where he was seated. His interest was in the game in the neighboring field where the ten-year-olds played with slightly more skill.

His son, Tobey, was number twenty-one. Tobey needed a haircut, and the lace on his left shoe was coming untied.

Dane knew all those things, but he didn't know his son's favorite flavor of ice cream. Did he really like playing soccer, or did he feel obligated to join because his friends did?

At the other field Dane's wife, Caroline, sat next to her new husband, Randy, and cheered for their son's team. Technically, she was still his wife. Not his ex-wife. Although, since she'd been told he died in a fire, he couldn't blame her for moving on with her life. Legally, their marriage ended when his death certificate was filed five years ago.

Five years ago, when David Ryan ceased to exist, and Dane Ryan was born from the ashes.

Just then, Tobey scored a goal, and Dane yelled out. "Good job!"

Except, at the field where he was seated there was a time out for a crying child.

Shit.

He gauged the spectators. The lionesses were uneasy. He should go. This was too risky. Worse, it was becoming a habit.

He'd stayed away from his old life for years, but recently, while on medical leave recovering from being shot in the leg, he'd become restless.

Restlessness had given way to curiosity, and curiosity—along with a strong wave of missing what he'd lost—had brought him here. Three times.

It wasn't healthy. This wasn't his life anymore. He'd given it up so Tobey and Caroline would be safe. So they wouldn't have to uproot their lives and start over because of his mistake.

One of the women had pulled out her phone and had it pointed in his direction.

Time to go.

With one last look at his son running down the field, Dane let out a sigh and slid out of his seat. He needed to leave before his photo ended up all over Facebook. No doubt these women would recognize him if he came back. Which meant he couldn't come back.

He'd tried to stay away but hadn't been able to. Now he had a compelling reason.

He was dead. It was time to start acting like it.

His leg was stiff from sitting for so long, and the dampness from the late-April day didn't help much. The familiar pain throbbed though his left thigh as he limped away.

He paused behind a tree to see Tobey run over to Caroline and Randy. It was obvious his son was happy and loved. That was all Dane needed to know.

It was time to move on.

This time for real.

Chapter Two

Miles and hours away from the soccer field, Dane decided it was safe to stop for the night. He chose a hotel with a bar across the street, knowing he didn't want to be alone.

In his past life he had been a people person. He'd had clients and meetings. There had been daily interactions with people. As a U. S. Deputy Marshal assigned to Task Force Phoenix, he sometimes went days without speaking out loud.

After seeing the happy family that should have been his, he needed to feel connected to someone. If only for a night.

The usual twinge of disappointment washed over him at the idea of sleeping with a stranger. He could forgive Caroline for getting married and moving on. She thought he was dead. But Dane didn't have the luxury of that freedom. In his mind, he was still married. Regardless of how tense and strained that marriage had become before it ended with his fake death, he wasn't the type of man to walk away.

Tonight, he granted himself permission from his list of reasons. Not only was he no longer legally married, but he was not the same person Caroline had married eleven years ago. He had a different identity, a different job, and lived a much different life.

No longer the young executive who was eager to please, he was now a hardened thirty-five-year-old marshal who'd been trained to kill, and had used that training six times in the last five years.

Time had moved on, and they'd both changed.

As much as it bothered him, he knew deep in his heart that if he'd stayed, they wouldn't still be married. They'd been headed for divorce; he'd just been too stubborn to say it, and she'd refused to give up her pretense of living the perfect life. It didn't matter that they were miserable. If they appeared happy, they were.

The walls of the bar were covered with the normal sports memorabilia. It appeared hockey was the owner's favorite. The place was crowded, but naturally there were no lone women at the bar waiting for him to walk in. That would have been too easy.

He sat next to a group of people and nodded in greeting. A few minutes later, he had inserted himself into their conversation and was having a good time.

Feeling someone brush up against him from the other side, he turned to see a gorgeous brunette sit down.

"Was someone sitting here?" she asked when she noticed him looking at her. Dane had tossed the mustache as soon as he was out of town, but the residue from the adhesive pulled as he smiled.

"No. Help yourself." There was only one seat available next to him, which meant she wasn't expecting anyone to join her.

Digging through her purse, she smiled at the bartender. "Can I get a beer? The special would be great." She pulled some money out and stacked it on the bar in front of her, the international sign she planned to stay awhile.

In a matter of minutes, they were chatting easily, and she had shared her story—divorced, not looking for anyone. Lena Scott was focusing on her career in design, and she was in town for a meeting. It had gone well, but now she was second-guessing everything because they hadn't called her back yet. She took a sip of her beer and looked at him expectantly.

Right. She wanted him to share. Normal people expected a person to reciprocate. He swallowed down the urge to tell her the truth, and pushed the lies out of his mouth.

"I'm in sales. Just passing through." That was the extent of his story. He kind of blanked out while studying her eyes. They were multi-colored. Gold, green, blue, and gray all mixed together in a kaleidoscope of colors.

"Are you married?" she asked.

He shook himself from the hypnotic trance so he could focus.

"No. No, I'm not," he answered with a smile.

Things were definitely looking up.

Chapter Three

Lena Scott smiled back at the man sitting next to her, tamping down her acute nervousness.

She'd expected this to be easier. There'd been a time, years ago, when meeting a guy in a bar hadn't made her panic. It had been easy to start up a conversation and find a common interest. All over the world, millions of people spent their Saturday evenings playing out this tried-and-true method of seeking out companionship.

Unfortunately, she wasn't really here for companionship. She had a very different motive, and it was that motive that caused her voice to shake when she'd asked him if he was married.

She let out the breath she was holding when he answered in the negative. It wouldn't be the first time a man lied about having a wife when meeting a woman in a bar, but she believed him.

About that part, at least.

The rest, she wasn't certain. Sales? She didn't get that vibe. The way he'd brushed over her questions to turn them back on her convinced her he wasn't who he was pretending to be.

Not that she should judge. She wasn't in Colorado for a meeting. She wasn't a designer. And she wasn't going to sleep with him, despite the attraction that spiked when she looked into his warm brown eyes.

At another time, she might have been interested in the lean muscles, the dirty-blond hair, and bright smile. But she had a job to do. One she couldn't afford to mess up. Getting to know him would only make that job more difficult...but she wasn't ready to move on to the next step. She needed time to mentally prepare.

She turned up her smile and leaned closer, using her body language to promise all the things she wouldn't be able to deliver.

Chapter Four

Dane spent the next hour talking and laughing with the beautiful woman. Lena was just what he needed to help him feel alive again. Being dead took its toll.

"I'll be flying out tomorrow," he said when it was going on midnight. It was time to seal the deal and move this somewhere more private.

He hoped she wouldn't mind if he stayed the night. It somehow seemed more respectable if he stayed rather than ran away like a thief in the night.

"What time is your flight? I'm leaving tomorrow, too," she said after biting her bottom lip.

She was a bit of a puzzle. She seemed to know where this was going, but there was something—shyness maybe?—that made him think she didn't do this very often.

"Eight," he answered honestly. Throughout their conversation there had been several times when he'd been able to tell her the truth. He'd enjoyed sharing those small facts. It made this next step slightly easier.

"Eight forty-five," she said with a smile.

"Maybe we could have breakfast together before leaving for the airport," he hinted with a grin.

She pressed her lips together and kept her gaze on the empty glass in her hands. He noticed her hands were shaking, but she gripped the glass tighter and smiled.

"What happens in Denver, stays in Denver?" she offered quietly.

"That's right."

"Okay."

He could tell by the dip of her head she was nervous. She must not make a habit of meeting men at bars and taking them back to her room. That made this even better.

His leg throbbed when he stood, causing him to suck in a quick breath as the shooting pain subsided. He'd broken down and taken a pain killer when Lena was checking her phone, but it hadn't taken effect yet.

"Ready?" he asked.

"Are you okay?" She looked down at his leg.

"Yeah. Old injury." *Injuries*, he corrected silently. He didn't offer the story since it was too unbelievable, even to him.

First, he'd been shot in the leg by his boss's daughter. She'd been afraid at the time, and Dane was the first person to move toward her. A few months later, he was bitten by a dog in the same leg. And just three weeks ago, he'd been doing surveillance and fell off a roof. The same leg got ripped up on a fence. He was cursed.

"You kind of got a sexy John Wayne swagger thing going on," she said with a laugh that made his body stir.

"Thank you, ma'am." He tipped his imaginary cowboy hat and grinned.

This was going well. He liked a woman with a sense of humor. Caroline had been funny when they were in college, but real life had stripped it away.

"If you like the swagger, wait until you see the sexy scars." Depending on the angle, they resembled an old woman with a pipe or a tree being stepped on by a giant chicken foot.

She laughed again. "You really know how to sell it."

He reached for her hand and tugged her into him. Their lips met, and she let out a soft sigh as she melted against him.

One thing that hadn't changed about Dane in all these years, he was still a romantic. He enjoyed the thrill of a first kiss, and the way a woman's eyes lit up when she was interested. The anticipation of slowly stripping a woman and revealing each treasure of her body.

Maybe that was the reason he didn't care for the normal bar hook-up. It lacked the natural exploration. It felt manufactured and fake.

This kiss, however, felt real.

Excitement and anticipation tingled down his spine.

His earlier concern of whether or not he would regret doing this was gone. It still might end up being a bad idea, but at the moment he no longer cared.

He wanted Lena.

He managed to release her so they could continue to her hotel room. Inside, he closed the door and pressed her up against it to kiss her lips and move down her throat.

"Let's have a drink," she said as she maneuvered away from him. He backed off, knowing she might be having second thoughts about being with a stranger.

As much as he wanted their encounter to proceed to sex, he would be content to simply be with her. To hold her and not feel so alone.

She tossed her purse on the first bed and went to the mini-fridge to pull out a bottle of whiskey and a can of cola. As she unwrapped the first of the plastic cups, he remembered he wouldn't be able to join her.

"None for me, thanks."

"I thought you were a Jack and Coke guy."

"I was up until an hour ago when I switched to plain Coke. I took a pain killer before we left so I would be able to…move." He winked at her.

"Oh." She looked at the fifth of whiskey in her hand and set down the cup.

He stepped closer and wrapped his arms around her waist. He didn't want her to need a drink for courage. If she wasn't completely on board, he'd happily back off. While he wasn't expecting anything long term, there was a chance for something more than a one-night stand. He lived in D.C. She lived in Charlotte. They were at least on the same side of the country and near major airports.

Maybe they could make something work if things went in that direction.

"If you've changed your mind, we can just talk. Or I can go. Whatever you want."

"It's not that. I mean, I want to. It's just—"

He put his hands up to stop her. She bit her lip. This was more than just nerves. This was all out anxiety. She might think she wanted this, but something was not right.

"It's okay, Lena. I don't want you to regret this in the morning." He turned to leave. "How about if I meet you downstairs for breakfast?"

He was nearly to the door, but she hadn't answered. He could almost feel her indecision in the air. He wasn't going to pressure her, though he was going to try for another kiss before he left.

He was thinking about that kiss when something smashed into his head. A burst of light shot through his vision.

Then darkness descended, and he fell to the floor.

Chapter Five

Dane was moving. The darkness was still there, but the cloud around his brain had subsided enough that he was awake. And definitely moving.

Realizing he was in trouble, he relied on his training to mentally prioritize a crisis list. First and foremost, he was tied up, and didn't know where he was. The thin hood covering his head caught on the stubble of his jaw when he turned his head.

He wasn't sure who had hit him or if Lena was okay. He could still smell her perfume, but he wasn't sure if she was close or if it came from his clothing.

"Lena?" he whispered, his voice raspy.

"*Shh.*" She was next to him. Close.

"Are you hurt?" he asked, keeping his voice low. He moved to reach for her and remembered his hands were tied behind his back.

"N-no."

"What happened?"

Maybe she had seen the intruder. She might have

information that could help him get them out of this.

"Are you hurt?" she asked rather than answer his question.

"My head feels like it was hit with a baseball bat, and my arms are cramping up. But I'm not damaged."

"That's good."

"Is he awake?" a male voice said from farther away.

"No. Not yet," Lena lied. "How much longer?"

"We're almost there. Maybe ten minutes."

"Can you turn this up? I love this song," she requested.

The men obliged and Shinedown filled the vehicle, making his head throb.

"Do you have a family?" she asked, her breath right by his ear.

This was a different question than the one she'd asked before. Originally, she'd asked if he was married. He assumed she'd asked to determine if he was available. But her question now stirred a different fear in him.

"No," Dane answered, thinking about the little boy who couldn't be in his life and the wife he never really knew.

"That's good," she said. And he knew he was fucked.

A few minutes later, the sound of the tires changed from the hum of pavement to the crunch of gravel. When the vehicle bucked under him, a small hand on his arm braced him from rolling over.

The vehicle stopped. Doors opened and closed and the distinct sound of the rolling of a van door before someone grabbed his feet and yanked him across the rough carpet of the vehicle.

His leg was so stiff he stumbled and would have fallen if a large body hadn't caught him and pushed him back up.

"Easy," Lena said. "You don't have to be a dick."

"Right, we wouldn't want to hurt him." The man chuckled darkly.

Dane had been focusing his thoughts on a plan of escape, and how to help Lena until he heard that ominous laugh. Now he had to prepare himself for what would happen next. Pain. And lots of it.

He knew he was only still alive for the purpose of ransom or information. And since he didn't have anyone who would pay two nickels to get him back, he assumed they were planning to extract information.

That usually meant torture.

He'd been trained to manage pain and taught how to shrink inside his own mind to protect himself. He wasn't sure what they planned to do with Lena, but from the sound of three individual sets of footsteps he knew she was walking under her own power.

Was she in on this? Had she set him up? As he replayed her conversations with the men, it seemed likely. But he'd looked in her eyes last night and seen nothing but honesty and interest. He wasn't normally wrong about these things.

His ability to read people had helped him in the business world, and it had kept him from danger on more than one occasion in his new profession.

It was the oldest trick in the book, using an attractive woman to lure a man into danger. He sniffed at his stupidity. He'd been so desperate for companionship he hadn't been paying attention.

She'd come into the bar after him. She'd allowed him to approach her instead of being aggressive. She'd waited hours for him to suggest they go back to the hotel so as not to appear too eager to get him alone.

How bored she must have been making small talk when all she wanted to do was bash him over the head and collect her fee.

"How's our new guest?" a different male voice asked, once he'd been brought into some kind of structure.

"Lena says we're supposed to take it easy on him." The men chuckled again.

Dane was tall and lean. Not thick with muscle like his task force brothers. Even with his eyes covered, he could tell the two goons that towered over his six-foot frame were like boulders. He wasn't going to be able to fight his way out of this.

They left him alone sitting against a wall for what felt like hours. He used his breathing to measure the time more accurately and decided it was not that long.

Eventually they came back.

His captors probably thought it would be easy to break him, but they would be disappointed. He wouldn't tell them anything.

His bound legs dragged behind him as they heaved him into a cool room and dropped him into a chair. The hood was ripped from his head and fluorescent light burned his eyes.

He blinked the room into focus, and his gaze fell on the small boy bound to the chair in the middle of the room. Tears streaked through the dirt on his face, and he looked up with the same dark eyes Dane saw every day in his own mirror.

Oh God, no.

"Dad?" his son whispered, and Dane knew he would tell them anything they wanted to know.

Chapter Six

Lena wanted nothing more than to be dismissed, but she knew she couldn't leave. They would want her to stay, if for no other reason than to force her to see and hear the pain she'd caused this man.

It wasn't her fault he was here. If she hadn't agreed to bring him in, they would have found another way to get to him. She was insignificant. How many times had Viktor Kulakov told her this? Enough that she'd finally realized it was true.

She wouldn't leave, though, even if she were granted that chance. If she stayed, she might have some small opportunity to help him.

It hadn't taken her long to realize Dane wasn't a sleazy criminal. He hadn't leered at her when she sat down at the bar. He hadn't pressured her to come back to his room after one drink. He'd been kind and sweet. He'd asked her questions about herself and waited patiently for her answers. Though the answers were all lies, she felt like he'd cared.

Then he'd kissed her, and she realized what she'd done.

She'd allowed herself to be happy for the first time in months. She'd actually fallen into her own trap.

As she'd walked hand-in-hand with him to her hotel room, she'd desperately tried to come up with some way to get him out of this without incurring Viktor's wrath.

Coming up with nothing, she allowed her heart to freeze over so she could do what needed to be done. Not for the first time, she wondered how long her heart could stay at that temperature before irreparable damage was done.

She stayed in the corner of the dingy room, trying not to be noticed. She had turned into a mouse over the last months. Hiding and scurrying away whenever danger approached.

Before her nightmare began, she'd managed a busy salon in Miami. She'd been strong and decisive. The stylists who'd worked for her respected her. No one would respect her now. She didn't even respect herself.

She would have been content to stay hidden in her corner, but another vehicle had arrived. Another one of Viktor's men came in carrying a little boy. The way his small body dangled over Murphy's arm, she thought he was dead, but then he kicked out and grunted against his restraints.

Murphy placed the boy on a chair in the other room, and she watched as Weller and Butch picked up Dane and dragged him into the same room.

What was going on? She'd listened in as they made their plans, and she'd not heard anything about them involving a child.

When Dane's hood was ripped off it had taken a few seconds for him to notice the boy in front of him. He'd gazed at the child and she saw the exact moment his heart burst into pieces—when the boy called him Dad.

"What's this?" Lena was propelled into the room by some remaining shred of courage.

"You did your job well," Viktor said from his spot beside

the boy. "You can wait out in the other room if you wish."

She stepped closer, her gaze fastened to the little boy tied to a chair, fear evident on his oddly familiar face. He'd called Dane *Dad*. Apparently, Dane had lied when he told her he had no family.

No. No. No. This wasn't the plan. This wasn't supposed to happen.

"You soulless witch," Dane spat at her. The warm, dark eyes that had gazed down at her the night before when they'd kissed had transformed into cold obsidian.

A chill shuddered through her, and she stepped back as if he'd hit her. What had she done?

"Lena?" Viktor's address brought her back under control. Even his voice—filled with smooth concern—was nothing but a lie. The man was slippery as a serpent. He didn't care about anything except money and power.

Slowly, Dane moved his scowl to the man in front of him, and Lena wanted to run away so he couldn't look at her like that again. But despite what she'd told herself earlier, this *was* her fault, and she needed to stay in case there was something she could do to help.

She also needed to make sure Viktor didn't doubt her. It would help her later.

Lifting her chin, she met Viktor's cold eyes. "I'll stay." He'd already taken everything else from her. She wouldn't walk away and allow harm to come to this child. She wasn't a monster. Desperate maybe, but not a monster.

"Suit yourself." He shrugged and turned his attention to Dane.

"I guess I don't need to make introductions, since Tobey seems to remember you."

Dane's voice was calm. "I don't know who you are."

"Viktor Kulakov." Viktor held out his hand to shake, then chuckled as if only then realizing Dane couldn't oblige.

Viktor liked to play with his prey. It was possibly his worst feature.

When the color fell from Dane's face, Lena knew Dane recognized the name.

Crossing his legs, Viktor brushed a piece of lint from his slacks. "I'm a man of business."

Business was an apt description. Though drug smuggling and human trafficking didn't get people mentioned in Forbes.

"I heard you'd been arrested."

Viktor steepled his fingers and let out a breath. "It was an unfortunate misunderstanding."

She was sure that meant some slimy lawyer had gotten him off.

Dane said nothing.

"Your son is a smart lad, Deputy Marshal Ryan."

She shot a surprised look at Dane. He was a U.S. Marshal? Her actions suddenly took on a whole new dimension of punishment. Great. Because she hadn't been in enough trouble as it was.

Dane didn't rise to Viktor's bait regarding his son. He remained calm, though she could tell he was seething with controlled anger. She admired his strength, but knew it wouldn't help him. At one time she'd been strong, too.

"I understand it's been some time since the two of you have been together." Viktor looked up at the rest of the group. Weller and Butch loomed over Dane, muscles bulging. "Let's give the father and son a moment alone to catch up, shall we?"

Lena knew the gesture was not from the goodness of his heart. Viktor Kulakov had no heart. This was a tactic. Viktor was setting the hook, to ensure the deputy marshal's cooperation.

Dane spared another glare for her as she left the room. She wanted to apologize. She wanted to tell him she hadn't known who he was. Hadn't known this was going to happen. But she was worried if she did, he might actually forgive her.

The last thing she deserved was forgiveness.

She was just outside the room when Viktor nodded to Weller, and the behemoth smacked her across the face. The fiery crack dropped her to the floor as she blinked the stars from her vision.

"Don't ever question my actions again. You put me behind schedule, and I hate when my schedule is disrupted."

She nodded, and the mouse retreated to the corner once again.

Chapter Seven

"Dad?" The word burned through Dane, along with a torrent of emotions. Love and fear being the most prevalent. "Am I dead?" Tobey asked while looking around the room.

"No." Dane reached for the boy, but his arms were still bound.

"But you're in heaven, and now I'm with you."

Dane smiled, realizing why his ten-year-old was confused. At another time, it might have been funny that anyone thought Dane would have ended up in heaven.

"I'm not dead, Tobey."

"But mom said—"

"Your mom thinks I'm dead. Everyone thinks I'm dead. It's a long story, and I'm so sorry I had to leave you, but I did it to keep you and your mother safe. I love you, and I didn't want to leave. Do you understand?"

"I didn't want to leave, either, but a man walked up to me at the park and grabbed me."

Caroline must be losing her mind. And rightfully so. Tobey was in the worst kind of danger. None of the men wore masks. That meant they weren't planning to let him walk out of this, even if Dane cooperated. The only way to guarantee survival was to get them out of there.

He tugged again at his restraints which were securely tied to the cold steel chair. The muscles in his injured leg spasmed in reply to the movement. Even if he could manage to free himself, he wouldn't be able to run fast enough to carry Tobey away. He didn't know where they were or how far he would have to run to get help.

Basically, he was screwed. Unless…

As much as he would gladly rip Lena limb from limb for her role in this, she might be his only hope. She'd seemed genuinely surprised to see his son brought in. He knew better than to trust her. She'd played her part perfectly and could still be manipulating him by playing good cop.

Even so, he was too desperate to give up the thought.

"Are we going to die?" Tobey asked.

The last time Dane had spoken to his son, Tobey had been almost five. He'd chattered about kindergarten and counting to a hundred. That was the Tobey in Dane's mind. At the soccer field, he'd seen how much his son had grown physically, but he wasn't prepared for the maturity and directness of his questions.

He'd never had the opportunity to be a father to a ten-year-old. He didn't know what to say.

"No," Dane answered, hoping like hell it wasn't a lie.

"If we don't die, will you come live with us again?" He frowned. "Mom is married to Randy now."

Right.

"I don't think that will work. But I am going to get us out of this, and we'll figure something out, okay?" No need to worry about how to get out of an uncomfortable reunion with his wife at this stage of the game.

"Are you a super hero?" Tobey asked.

"No. If I were a super hero, I would have used a super power to break us out of here, and we would be chatting over a bowl of ice cream."

Tobey smiled slightly, and Dane felt like maybe he did have some super powers, after all. He'd been able to make a scared little boy smile in the middle of a crisis.

"Look, I don't know what's going to happen next, but I want you to know this. I love you. You are the most important thing in my life, and everything I've done and will ever do is to keep you happy and safe. Okay?"

Tobey nodded. "Mom told me you died because you needed to do the right thing."

Dane swallowed so he could speak. "It was something like that."

It was good to know Caroline realized it had been the right thing. She hadn't agreed with him when he'd wanted to go to the FBI to blow the whistle on his employer's illegal activities.

She'd wanted him to stay out of it so it wouldn't disrupt their perfect world. She hadn't realized their perfect world was already crumbling under their feet.

When Dane's employers threatened his family to keep his mouth shut, he knew he had to do something. Unfortunately, that something had led him to faking his death and walking out on his strained marriage and his only son.

"I'm glad you're not really dead."

"Me, too." He winked at Tobey and got another smile. "You've been very brave. Don't worry, okay? It's going to be fine."

How it would be fine, Dane wasn't certain. But he had given up his life to keep this child safe once before. He wouldn't hesitate to do it for real this time.

Chapter Eight

Guilt twisted Lena's stomach as she stood outside the door listening to the father and son discuss their future. Because of her, they may not have one.

She needed to do something but wasn't sure what. Her hands were tied. There was nothing she could do that wouldn't make her own situation worse.

Viktor was an evil bastard, but he was smart and he always hedged his bets. She hated feeling useless and weak, but that was exactly what she was.

"I trust you've had a nice visit," Viktor said as he interrupted the father and son reunion, his enormous guards flanking him. Lena stayed back, looking for some opportunity in which she could overpower three large men with guns and save the day.

It was ridiculous. If she could do that, she wouldn't be in this mess. And neither would Dane. Or Tobey. She swallowed down a lump of anxiety.

"Can we talk somewhere privately? I think it's obvious I'm not going to go anywhere," Dane asked Viktor, sounding completely calm.

"Of course. Weller, please bring Mr. Ryan into the living room."

"Dad?" Tobey's voice went up with worry.

"It's going to be okay. I want you to close your eyes and think about playing soccer. Don't worry."

"I love you, Dad."

"I love you, too, buddy."

Butch escorted Dane out of the room. He stared down at her where she hovered by the door.

His glare went right through her. "You are a despicable excuse for a human being. I hope you rot in hell."

"I'm already in hell," she whispered, but he'd already been pulled away.

Chapter Nine

Dane needed a plan, and he needed one quick. How could he possibly overpower three men and Viktor Kulakov? They were all bigger than him. All armed. Then there was Lena. Who knew where her loyalties lay? Even if he fought his way through the guards, she'd probably shoot him dead to protect Viktor.

He needed to be smart, but at the moment his only thoughts were of the meeting with his son. Tobey loved him. And now he was counting on Dane to get him out of this.

Dane needed help, but there was no way to get in touch with his team.

Supervisory Deputy United States Marshal Josiah Thorne wasn't expecting him to report to his new assignment until next week, and no one else would be looking for him. He didn't even talk to the people in his apartment building.

The largest of the three beasts moved closer. Braced for the first strike, Dane tensed, feeling his thigh muscle protest. But the man just untied Dane's bonds and stepped back.

"You're probably wondering why I've brought you here."

Viktor smiled, a gesture that would in no way be confused with kindness.

"I figured you'd get around to telling me sooner or later."

"I need your help with a loose end." The man was probably in his late forties. His nails were manicured and his hair was perfectly in place. His tanned skin held only the most distinguished of wrinkles.

"Does this loose end have a name?" Dane guessed.

"It's so nice to be able to conduct business like men instead of barbarians." The man's cold, gray eyes flashed toward the other room.

"Let's get this over with. Tell me who's on your list. I'll find out where they are, and once I know Tobey's safe, I'll give you their location."

"Actually, I had something more expedient in mind. I'm being watched and so are my men. It took a great deal of resources to allow us to be present for this little adventure. After that inconvenient and unwarranted arrest, I'm not at liberty to hunt down the person who is causing me great personal distress. I'd rather have you bring the person to me. Once you hand him over, I'll release your boy."

Dane snorted. "Sure, you will."

"You insult my honor."

"My apologies to your honor." He made no effort to make his apology sound sincere in any way. This man had no honor. His use of children as pawns was evidence of that. "Who is it?"

"Well now, that's a where the first problem lies. I knew him as Robbie Vanderhook, but soon found out that was a lie. When I...ended his employment, it was because I found out he was a DEA agent named Robert Gates. But once again, I was deceived. It seems he's much better at hiding his true identity than you are."

The man glanced toward the room where Tobey was being

held. It was true, Dane's past wasn't buried as deep as some. But that was because he only had one enemy—his former boss, Tim Reynolds—and that enemy believed him dead. Reynolds was a crook, and dangerous when threatened, but he was definitely a little fish compared with Viktor Kulakov, who was the ruthless leader of an entire crime syndicate.

And Dane had led Kulakov straight to his old life by visiting Tobey when he should have stayed away. Tobey was in danger now because Dane had been greedy and wanted to see his son.

Viktor let out a breath. "At this point we've found three other identities, and I've become bored with this silly game. I wish to cut to the chase, as it were, and have a professional sort out the details." Viktor waved his hand as if this was nothing more than an inconvenience.

Dane's brows pulled together, more out of surprise than not knowing who the person was. In fact, he knew the man well—he was married to Dane's best friend, Angel Larson—make that Williamson now. Dane knew the man by his real name, Colton Williamson.

They were friends, and Dane was the godfather of the man's son.

Dane glanced toward the room that held his son. "I'll be happy to figure out who he is and bring him in." Along with the rest of Task Force Phoenix to take down these ass-hats and save Tobey. As much as Dane didn't want to leave Tobey behind alone, he knew the best chance to save his kid was to get away from there.

"I'd hoped you would be accommodating." Viktor steepled his fingers in front of his lips, which were turned up in a cruel smile. "Thanks to Mr. Vanderhook, I've learned from my mistakes. Trust is not something I give freely. It must be earned, and that takes a very long time. Unfortunately, we do not have time to get to know one another on that level."

Couldn't the man just get to it?

"I know you will come back if the boy is here. However, I'm sure you won't be alone when you do. To make certain everyone sticks to their task without deviation, I'm going to send Lena with you. She must check in every so many hours. If she reports you've misstepped, the boy dies. If she says you've run, the boy dies. If she fails to report in at the correct time, the boy dies."

"And if she kills me?"

"I trust her to make the right decision." Another eerie smile. "Lena!" he snapped, and the woman rushed into the room.

"Yes?"

"Accompany Mr. Ryan on his quest to extract a dear friend. Be quick about it. Time is of the essence."

"What about the—"

Her question was cut off by Viktor's glare, but Dane was certain she was asking about Tobey.

"You take care of retrieving Vanderhook, and I'll take care of dear Tobias." He raised a brow. "Unless you want to change the terms of our arrangement."

"No," she uttered quickly.

Dane wondered what kind of arrangement they had and decided he didn't care. The two of them and their arrangement could both go to hell. The quicker the better.

"Can I say goodbye?" Dane asked.

Viktor tapped his index finger to his lip twice and smiled. "No. You should be off. As I said, time is of the essence."

Rat bastard.

Viktor turned his reptilian gaze on Lena. "Call me directly in eight hours, no texts. You'll be given the time to call back at the end of each contact. Make sure you don't forget. One missed call and…well…as I said before, no need to be barbaric."

Chapter Ten

Lena flinched when Butch pressed a set of keys into her palm and sneered. "Don't bitch up my ride. Bring it back with a full tank of gas or I'll gut you."

She didn't understand. "How am I supposed to—"

Viktor held out a credit card scissored between his index and middle finger. He was so elegant, and yet so deadly. "For travel necessities."

She snatched the card from his grasp and turned for the door. Better to get this over with so she could get back to her own problems. She didn't look to see if Dane was following her. She heard his footsteps on the dry wooden floor of the ratty house. When those steps hesitated at the front door she turned.

"He'll be okay," she whispered. "As long as we do what we're supposed to."

Reluctantly, Dane moved on and climbed up into the passenger side of Butch's raised Jeep. At five feet six, she was not exactly short, but she had to hop up to the running board to get in.

Dane said nothing as she backed up and started down the bumpy lane toward the main road.

"So, do you know where we're going?" she asked as she made a left onto the paved road. She wasn't sure she'd picked the right direction, but she'd had to decide at the end of the lane.

She liked to have a plan, even if nothing ever went according to those plans.

Dane didn't speak. She waited a full minute before she glanced over. He was staring out the side window.

"Do you know where this Robbie guy lives?" she tried again. Nothing. "I get that you're pissed at me, but we have to work together to get this guy so we can free your son," she explained with more detail, hoping it would shake him into speech.

It worked.

"Pull over," he ordered and pointed to the side of the road. "Now."

She did as he said, not sure what would happen. Surely, he wasn't planning to run away or overpower her. If she didn't call Viktor at the correct time, he would hurt Tobey. She had no doubt about that. Viktor was a viciously dangerous man.

Without another word, Dane jumped down from the Jeep and headed for the trees along the quiet road. She hopped down to go after him, but by the time she made it around the back of the jeep, Dane was bent over vomiting into the weeds.

Her heart clenched at the sight. The tough deputy marshal was worried sick over his kid. This man loved his child very much. And she was partly responsible for that child being in danger.

She stepped closer and put a hand on his shoulder in what she hoped was a comforting gesture. She wasn't surprised when he shook it off and turned away from her.

"I'm sorry," she whispered and the man went off like a bomb.

Chapter Eleven

"You're *sorry*? You're fucking *sorry*?" Dane's hands shook with rage. He had to force himself to step away so he wouldn't risk strangling her. How *dare* she?

"You have threatened my life and might be responsible for get+ting my son killed, and you're *sorry*? How can a person be so heartless? Don't stand there and tell me how sorry you are when this is all your damned fault!"

"I didn't know they were going after Tobey," she said. "I didn't even know Tobey existed."

He took a step closer and she backed away. "Sure! You just happened to ask me if I had any family when we were in the van. That slight mention of what was to come. Just stop talking to me. You're nothing but a lying piece of shit! I can't even stand to look at you without wanting to kill you with my bare hands."

She didn't argue back, which was what he'd wanted. He was so furious he wanted to get it out. And why not at her? This *was* her fault. She'd lured him into danger with her sexy body and warm, deceitful smile.

He'd been weak and stupid, and she'd taken full advantage of it. And now Tobey was in danger because Dane had been so lonely. *Fuck!*

He stepped away to retch again.

Blaming her only forced him to see his own failures. If he hadn't gone to see Tobey, whoever had been watching him wouldn't know he still had a family. Dane had led the wolves right to their door.

After ten more minutes of stomping and raging at the trees, he realized he needed a plan. A good one.

Lena had gone to wait in the Jeep. He limped back and hoisted himself up into the seat, letting out a breath at the pain.

"I have the pain pills that were in your pocket. Would that help?"

"Don't be nice to me. I hate you." At the moment, he wished Viktor had sent Butch or Weller on this adventure instead of Lena. He didn't need the reminder of how weak he'd been. But Viktor wouldn't send one of his protectors away since he still felt threatened. He would keep the muscle close by.

She sighed. "For what it's worth, I hate me, too. It doesn't mean you need to be in pain for no reason."

His head was throbbing, along with his leg. "*You* hit me." He realized it must have been her. The room was small. There hadn't been anyone else there.

She nodded. "I was planning to put a sedative in your drink, but when you said you had taken pain medicine, I worried about an interaction."

Because he was no good to them dead.

"I hit you with the bottle. I'm sor—" She stopped before she got the word out. With a frown she turned the key and the Jeep roared to life.

"Go south." He rested his head against the glass of the passenger window and tried to focus on a plan to save Tobey. He understood now why marshals weren't allowed to work their own cases. His ability to make rational decisions was compromised by the overriding need to get Tobey to safety at all cost.

He wasn't thinking like a marshal. He was thinking like a desperate father.

He wondered how Thorne had done it. Long ago, his boss had walked away from his daughter. He'd kept watch over her through the years, and sent his team in whenever she'd needed help. When Samantha witnessed a congressman shoot a woman in an alley, Thorne had sent other people to her rescue while he remained in the shadows.

Dane didn't want to stay in the shadows hoping someone else would save his kid. He wanted to take care of it himself. He wanted to rush into that broken-down house, kill all of them, and carry Tobey away to safety.

But that plan was unrealistic. Not only was he outmanned, but they most likely were already moving Tobey to another location so they couldn't be ambushed.

Dane needed to think. He pointed to a truck stop and Lena pulled in. It was almost two in the afternoon, and he hadn't eaten since the night before.

The rumble in his stomach reminded him of a flight attendant's demonstration and the importance of securing your own air mask first before assisting other passengers.

Dane needed to get himself together first, so he would be able to help Tobey.

Chapter Twelve

Lena was glad to stop. She'd had to pee for the last forty-five minutes, and her stomach was growling so loudly she'd turned the radio up to cover the noise. While she was technically the one in charge, she didn't want to push him into another rage.

Well-deserved as it was, it wasn't helping their cause.

She didn't hesitate as he went to the men's room without a word to her. Instead, she hurried off to the other side of the building to use the ladies room. He wouldn't run. She didn't know what he was planning, but she knew that much. He wouldn't do anything to risk his son's life. But he was a marshal. He'd definitely be planning something.

Dane's blond hair was darker when wet and his serious eyes sought her out in the diner. She raised a hand and he came to sit across from her.

"I got you coffee," she said, pushing the cup closer.

"I don't drink coffee." He didn't even look at her or bother to glare. She had fallen below hatred into complete indifference. To him, she was nothing. "Especially not after you've touched it."

She assumed he was accusing her of tainting it with something rather than a general case of cooties. She let out a breath of annoyance, though she had no right to be annoyed. She had admitted her plan to drug him so she didn't blame him for being leery.

He picked up the menu and studied it until the waitress walked over.

The older woman smiled at him and he smiled back, the sight a cruel reminder of what Lena had destroyed. She'd gone to the bar specifically to lure him to her hotel room and drug him so Butch and Weller could get whatever Viktor wanted from him.

When they'd driven him to that abandoned house, she'd expected they might rough him up to get information out of him. She had assumed he was just another criminal associate of Viktor's. Dane seemed rather tough and she thought he'd survive the ordeal. Little did she realize exactly who she'd lured into a trap.

She'd rationalized it in her mind because she didn't have a choice. She honestly hadn't known they were planning to use the man's son against him. But she should have guessed.

Dane ordered a ton of food, and when the waitress left, the smile fell from his face. "I'm surprised you didn't order a plate of white mice."

Yes, yes. She was a snake. Whatever.

Frustration got the best of her. "I hope you're not using all your brainpower on clever little jabs at me." She leaned in so the other diners wouldn't hear her. "I know I'm shit. Trust me, there is nothing you can say to make me hate myself more than I already do. I truly didn't know they were going to use your kid. Like I said, I didn't even know you had a kid."

"You didn't ask until it was too late. You didn't want to know. Now your conscience is clear." He crossed his arms over his chest.

She let out a breath and looked around to make sure no one had noticed their altercation. She rubbed her forehead and tried to calm down.

Was that true? Was that the reason she hadn't asked until it was out of her control? If she'd asked at the bar and he'd told her about Tobey, would she have been able to lure him into her room and club him over the head with a bottle?

She couldn't do anything about the past. She needed to focus on what was next. "Please tell me you know where this guy is. We can go get him, turn him over to Viktor, and get Tobey back."

Had she thought she missed his smile? She didn't like the one on his face now. It was twisted and spiteful.

"In addition to being a cold-hearted bitch, you must be the stupidest goddamned person on the face of the earth if you actually think that's what will happen. Tobey has seen Viktor. I have seen Viktor. We are as good as dead."

She swallowed as that sank in. Dane had a point, however morbid. She'd seen enough movies to know the bad guys normally wore masks in hostage situations. Presidents, bunnies, or just a run-of-the-mill ski mask, they kept their identity a secret so the victim couldn't describe them to the police. Not covering their faces meant they didn't plan to leave behind living victims.

Her breath caught in her throat at the thought.

She had seen Viktor, too.

Chapter Thirteen

Dane ate everything on his plate as Lena picked at her silly salad. Everyone knew you ate hearty during a crisis because you didn't know when you'd get the chance to eat again. She obviously wasn't trained for this kind of thing.

His comment about him being as good as dead had made her face go pale with fear. No doubt she'd finally realized she was just as expendable as Dane was.

Nourishment had fueled his brain, and he was thinking through several plans. Unfortunately, the scenarios he came up with also came complete with a deadly ending if the plan went wrong. He already knew he would be too cautious to actually follow through on any of them. No way would he risk Tobey.

He wasn't going to be able to do this alone. He needed someone on the outside to call the shots. He needed his team.

But how would he get word to them without Lena knowing? He didn't have his phone. They'd kept it, along with his wallet and keys. He should have asked to borrow someone's phone in the restroom. But he'd been too furious to think of it at the time. Talk about being an idiot.

He needed to get Lena to trust him, but he'd already lashed out. Badly. He should have played it differently. Now he'd have to backpedal. After calling someone a soulless bitch and telling them you wanted to kill them with your bare hands, it would be a little difficult to change tactics at this point. Not to mention impossible. He wasn't that good of an actor.

As she paid for the meal with Viktor's card, he stood and waited for her to walk out of the restaurant first. It didn't matter that she wasn't a lady, he could still be civilized.

They were back on the highway heading south, and he hadn't come up with any way to convince her to jump ship to help him. What would it take? Money? He had some, but not as much as Kulakov.

The afternoon came and went in silence. The sun went down and it began to rain. She kept her eyes on the road, her fingers clenched around the steering wheel so tightly her knuckles were white.

Maybe offering to drive would endear him to her. But surely, she wouldn't let him drive. She would lose all the control if he were allowed behind the wheel. Except for the fact that he didn't know when she was supposed to call Viktor next.

He debated for another hour whether it was worth it to ask her for anything. Pride kept his mouth stubbornly closed. He didn't want to give her even the smallest inkling of power over him.

At eleven-thirty she pulled off the highway. "We need gas. And food. And I— I need a break, okay? I'm so exhausted, I'm worried I'll fall asleep and kill us."

It was the first time she'd snapped at him, despite the way he'd treated her.

He nodded and swallowed down the impulse to feel

guilty. She didn't deserve to be treated with respect. She was a monster. A criminal. But he needed her.

"Damn it," he muttered and got out of the car to go pump the gas. His mother—God rest her soul—would be repulsed by his terrible manners. If he did end up in heaven at some point, he'd rather not have to explain his poor behavior to his mother.

"Go clean up and get us a table," he demanded as he took the nozzle from her. He nodded in the direction of the truck stop restaurant with a frown.

"I only need a few minutes and a gallon of coffee."

"We're done for tonight." He wouldn't be able to help Tobey if they drifted off the highway and crashed into a tree.

"I'll be okay to keep going. I just—"

"I'm *not* okay," he cut off her argument. As chivalrous gestures went, his needed some work, but at least he would get the woman to rest.

Chapter Fourteen

It wasn't easy for Lena to go inside the restaurant when Dane had the keys to the vehicle. She'd already used the credit card and put it in her back pocket with her phone. But that wouldn't help her if he decided to run off without her.

Calling Viktor to tell him she'd failed wasn't an option.

Could she blame Dane for leaving her here? She let out a sigh and ordered her meal and a burger for him. She was so hungry she would be able to eat both. Plus, if Viktor checked the receipts, it would look like a meal for two.

How long would she be able to convince Viktor everything was going smoothly? If he asked her to put Dane on the phone, it would be game over. She had too much at stake to risk angering Viktor Kulakov, but she refused to condemn an innocent child for her stupidity.

"Get it together," she whispered, letting her head rest in her hands. She could have slept sitting at the table. Maybe she did. Because when she lifted her head, Dane was sitting across from her tapping a straw out of the wrapper, and their food was there.

His gaze stayed on hers as he popped the straw in his drink

and sucked down a swallow. She pressed her lips together to hide a stupid smile. He didn't trust her. Not remotely. But this was something, at least.

They ate in silence, and she paid the check leaving a bigger tip than normal because she was too tired to figure out the math.

He stood with a groan as she signed the bill. Enough was enough. She found the bottle of pills in her purse and grabbed his hand to pull him closer. "This is ridiculous," she snapped, shaking one of the capsules into his warm palm. "Take it."

"Do you think this is going to win me over?" he asked, his voice low.

"No. I'm just tired of seeing you in pain when you don't need to be."

"And who's making sure Tobey isn't in any pain right now? Huh? I have no right to take something to dull the pain when Tobey could be hurting, or worse."

"I can assure you, he's being well taken care of."

"Oh, yes. Viktor seems like the most amazing host. He's planning to *kill* him. Why would he treat him civilly?"

She let out a sigh and looked Dane in the eye. "Because he wants to make sure you still have hope. If he mistreated Tobey, you might reach a point where you'd be content to let him go to end his suffering. Viktor would lose his power over you." She shook her head. "No. He will make sure your son is treated well. Right up until the moment he gives the order to kill him. Until then, you still have a chance."

She hadn't said it just to make Dane feel better. It was true. Tobey still had a chance. And so did she.

Chapter Fifteen

Lena's words—calm and sure—sliced right through him, and nearly had him choking up his dinner. Thankfully, she was right. He still had a chance to save Tobey.

Viktor Kulakov was a master of manipulation. He knew that much from what Colton Williamson had told the team. Colton had worked for the DEA and was undercover in Kulakov's organization for two years before being shot six times and declared legally dead. That's how he ended up joining Task Force Phoenix.

Kulakov would use Tobey to keep Dane in line, and it would be much more effective if Tobey was left unharmed… right up until Viktor no longer needed him.

Dane wouldn't give Kulakov a reason to use Tobey to motivate him into compliance. He would make sure Viktor thought he was working on finding Colton. But while he was doing that, he also needed to find Tobey so he could get him out of Viktor's clutches. Before it was too late.

And with that thought, he was back to his original question of how he would do that with Lena watching him.

She put the key in the ignition, but he stopped her before she could start the engine. He let out a sigh and decided to just go for it. He didn't have time to feign friendship, and doubted he'd be able to make it believable, anyway.

"Do you have my wallet and phone?" he asked.

"Yeah." She pulled her giant purse from the back seat and dug through it until she found his wallet and handed it over. His ID, credit cards, and cash were all gone. He now had two condoms and a gym membership. Not helpful in his current situation.

He rolled his eyes and tucked the useless accessory in his back pocket as she handed over his cell phone.

"Who are you going to call?" she asked.

"My team. I'll need a minute." He reached for the door handle, wanting privacy.

"Wait." She grabbed the phone back. "What are you going to say?"

He'd expected a flat out no, so he offered a truthful explanation. "I'm going to tell them what happened, and see what they suggest I do." Because he still couldn't come up with a viable plan on his own. He was too close to the situation. He needed help.

"You're not going to go get this Robbie guy?"

"That *Robbie* guy is a good person. He was a decorated marine before he joined the DEA. His father and four brothers were all cops. The only reason Viktor hasn't gone after his family is because he's so well hidden. He's in witness protection because he was willing to give up his old life to put Viktor behind bars."

Dane wished Colton would have been successful in putting Viktor away.

"*That Robbie guy* is married to my best friend, and they have a baby. While you might be vile enough to put a child at risk, I'm not. So, no, I'm not just going to go get this Robbie guy. He's a real person. A good person." Dane ran his hand through his hair before adding, "Besides, I don't know where he is."

She handed over the phone. "Make the call in here. I know you hate my guts, but we're in this together. Whatever we have to do to make this right, we'll do."

He stared at her for a long moment, not seeing anything but sincere regret. He knew better than to trust her.

"Make the call here, or don't make it at all. It's up to you," she said. She might have sounded like she was in control of the situation if her voice hadn't shaken twice as she delivered her order.

Rather than push her on it, he took the phone and made the call.

Chapter Sixteen

It began to rain as Lena sat in the parking lot staring out the windshield, wondering if she'd made a huge mistake. Twenty minutes later, Dane was still on the phone with someone from something called Task Force Phoenix, recounting every detail of his ordeal.

He didn't leave anything out. Not even her role in the horror story. To her surprise, he didn't embellish the tale with nasty names. He kept it simple, referring to her as the woman who'd hunted him down and hit him with a bottle. She considered that a step in the right direction. And much better than soulless bitch.

She couldn't blame him for his choice of words. From where he was sitting, she probably seemed that way. And truth be told, she was starting to feel like she really had lost her soul. Or rather, it had been taken from her. Each day that passed, she felt another piece of her soul stripped away, leaving behind more numbness.

Last August, her world had been turned upside down and tossed around like a dingy in a storm. And now she'd landed here in this parking lot with Dane. Maybe if she'd told him the truth from the beginning, he would have been willing to help her instead of hating her.

Other than a few muffled comments, she hadn't picked up anything from the other end of the call. What were they planning, and how would it affect her and her situation?

"Okay. We'll meet you there. I can't fly, I don't have any ID. We'll be staying at the Super Motel west of Kansas City. Can you send supplies tonight?" He nodded, and gave them the name of the hotel across the street. "Great. I'll see you in a few days."

He hung up and pointed to the hotel. "We're staying there. Go get us a room with your fancy platinum card."

She drove the few hundred feet to the other parking lot, and got out to go into the office. Dane didn't move.

Even if he ran off, she wouldn't give him up and put his son in more danger. But Dane didn't know that. Letting him believe she would tell Viktor was the only way to ensure his cooperation. It also kept him from killing her.

After securing a room with two queen-size beds, she took a breath and stepped out of the motel, hoping he would still be there.

She wasn't even surprised to find the Jeep empty.

Chapter Seventeen

After his surveillance of the property, Dane headed back to the Jeep. When he came around the building, he spotted Lena standing by the vehicle, her phone in her hand and worry on her face. He picked up his pace and yelled to her, hoping she wasn't sounding the alarms of his escape.

"Yes. Okay. Goodbye," she said into the phone as he walked up. "It was my scheduled time to call in."

"I thought you figured I'd escaped."

"You have no money, no ID, and your friends are sending supplies to this hotel."

She was smarter than he'd given her credit for. Evil and smart. A bad combination. "When do you have to call in next?" he asked.

"I can't tell you that." She bit her bottom lip. At another time, the gesture would have interested him. But he'd fallen for that trick before. He'd like to think he was intelligent enough to learn from his mistakes.

"Right." He frowned. For a brief moment he'd allowed himself to hope he wasn't alone in this ordeal. But, no. She was the enemy. Despite looking like the sexy girl-next-door, she was rotten inside. He would be wise to remember that.

She led him to their room. Neither of them had any luggage. They would need to stop for clothes and necessities the next day. They would be driving for a few days and they didn't need to make things even more uncomfortable by neglecting important things like hygiene.

For now, the only thing he wanted was a bed. The pain killer had helped, but he was still sore from sitting all day. A groan escaped as he kicked off his shoes and socks. After washing his face in the bathroom, he wrestled off his jeans and winced as he fell back on the bed, stars crowding his vision for a moment.

He heard a sharp gasp from his roommate and figured it was because he had stripped down to his boxers. Fuck modesty.

He tugged off his shirt and threw it in the direction of the chair as he slumped back on the pillow and let out a deep breath. He had almost reached sleep when he heard the microwave come on.

Not caring enough to see what she was doing, he kept his eyes closed and tried not to think about where Tobey was or what was happening to him. He'd never be able to sleep if he did.

He felt the cooler air of the room hit his skin as the sheet was pulled away from his body. He shot up to a sitting position, then gasped in pain.

"Damn it. What do you think you're doing?" he yelled at the woman who had exposed him. She was still dressed, but her gaze was on his lower body.

Seriously? There was no way he was having sex with her. Not happening.

His cock stirred in protest of his conviction. *No way*, he thought again, for good measure.

"You're hurting. I want to help." She held up a wet towel. She folded it and placed it over the damage on his leg. He sucked in a breath from the scalding temperature.

"Son of a bitch, that's hot."

"It will help. Give it a minute." She went into the bathroom.

He'd had heat therapy before and it was helpful. He might have thought to try it, himself, if he hadn't been thinking about so many other things.

A few minutes later, she stepped back into the room and removed the towel that had cooled. She sat on the edge of the bed and opened a tiny bottle with the hotel logo on it.

"What are you doing?"

"I'm going to massage your muscles so you can sleep easier."

"No. I'm good. I don't want you touching me." He pulled away, but she didn't move.

"I have a certificate in massage. Let me help you."

"I thought you were a designer," he scoffed as she squeezed the lotion into her palms and rubbed them together.

"And you said you were in sales, Mr. U.S. Marshal. I think we both know we're capable of lying when we have to." She put her hands on him and he jumped from the contact. She concentrated her efforts on the outer muscles rather than just the areas that had been injured.

It felt good. With each stroke of her hand, he could feel another fiber of his body unwind and stretch out. He made a happy moan and wished he could take it back.

He didn't want her to think he appreciated her help. Or needed it. Except, it was too hard to focus on hating her when she was making him feel so good.

He opened his eyes to see her leaning close to his leg. She'd taken the ponytail out, and her long, brown hair fell around her, blocking his view of her face. The ends of her hair brushed against his leg as she moved.

Then he saw another movement—against his will his cock had hardened and now it lurched to get her attention.

It worked. She sat back, her gaze on his unruly member.

Shit.

"That's enough. Good." He swallowed and jerked the sheet up to cover himself, but the flimsy fabric did nothing to help. Especially when he twitched again.

"It's normal," she said as she kicked off her shoes and crawled in her own bed with her clothes still on. He might have suggested she use his T-shirt so she'd be more comfortable, but he didn't want her to think he wanted her to take off her clothes.

"It definitely wasn't because I was thinking about you," he grumbled, not sure why he felt the need to call even more attention to the situation.

"Of course not." She reached up and clicked off the light between their beds.

He lay there in the darkness thinking about how different things might have been if she hadn't worked for Kulakov. If they'd had a chance to be the people they'd pretended to be at the bar.

His leg felt better. Her touch had been amazing, and now he was able to rest easier.

After debating for a few seconds, he let out a quick breath and did the right thing. "Thank you," he managed, though he couldn't help it came out somewhat grudgingly.

"Don't mention it," she answered, and he thought he heard a smile in her voice.

At the memory of her pretty smile, his body reacted again.

Christ.

Chapter Eighteen

The next morning, Dane woke to the sound of the shower. It was only five a.m. and he wished he could sleep a little longer while he could still manage it.

It would be another long day on the road. To his surprise, his leg didn't feel too bad. He reached over to the night stand between the beds and turned on the light. His meds were sitting there, and he opened the bottle to get one out.

He didn't know what do to about Lena. He wanted to hate her for what she'd done, but it seemed to take more effort than he cared to expend. She'd done something nice for him last night, despite his animosity toward her.

He felt like he needed to do something to put them back on the same level. He didn't like feeling indebted to anyone. Especially evil vixens with massage certificates.

He was drawn from his dilemma by a strange sound coming from the bathroom. The water in the shower was still running, but he heard something else. A soft whimper.

Was she hurt?

He was out of bed before his leg was ready to hold him.

Stumbling, he righted himself and moved for the bathroom. His hand was on the knob ready to push in the door, when he heard the sound again and realized what it was.

She was crying.

He let his hand drop and stepped away. He didn't know what to do. If he had feelings for her, he might have gone in and offered a hug or some futile words. If they were friends, he might have tried to cheer her up by making a joke.

In this situation, he thought the best thing he could do was to give her some privacy and send her silent wishes of comfort.

When she came out, he shifted and pretended to wake. She wouldn't know he'd heard her crying in the shower where she thought the sound of the rushing water hid her sobs. That was the best he could do.

Though he did wonder what kind of sorrow had caused her tears.

Evil women didn't usually cry. Did they…?

Chapter Nineteen

Dressed in the same clothes from the day before, Lena felt slightly better being clean underneath. She'd needed a moment alone to deal with...everything...and now she felt better prepared to face the day. Even if she knew today was destined to be every bit as sucky as every other day for the last eight months.

They'd just made it to the door of the restaurant for breakfast when her phone rang. The familiar photo and number caused her heart to flutter with equal amounts of joy and dread.

"I have to get this. Go on ahead. I'll be right in." She took a steadying breath and smiled before connecting. "Hey, baby."

Chapter Twenty

Dane watched Lena as she paced by the side of the restaurant. She waved and smiled into the device as if she didn't have a care in the world. Seeing her laughter made him hate her all over again.

Here he was with his guts tied up in knots, worrying about his kid, and she was making gooey eyes at her boyfriend. Hell, maybe she had a husband. She didn't wear a ring, but she might have taken it off while she was deceiving Dane.

She'd taken his phone back, but from the clock on the wall above the counter he could see she'd been on the call for fifteen minutes when she hung up.

She transformed right before his eyes. The second the phone was tucked into her back pocket, she slid down the wall of the building to sit on the wet pavement. Her head fell to her knees and her fingers clenched painfully in her shiny, brown hair.

The man in him urged him to go to her, to offer something to ease her obvious pain.

The marshal in him sat back in his seat and frowned.

While he wished he could say he was happy to see her suffer, he wasn't. But that didn't mean he was able to offer her comfort, either. What had brought about the abrupt change?

Nope. He didn't care. He focused on his breakfast.

It was some time before she slipped into the booth across from him. She smiled even though her face was red and blotchy, her dark lashes spiky with tears.

"I got you pancakes. They're cold now," he said, not mentioning her breakdown. He didn't want to know what upset her. He didn't want to care.

"Thank you," she said with a thick voice. He watched as she wolfed them down.

Twice, his mouth opened to ask if she was okay. It was an automatic response to tears. But he swallowed down the urge.

"So, you gave up on massage therapy to take on a life of crime?" he asked before taking a sip of his orange juice.

She shook her head. "This wasn't a choice." She tossed her napkin on her plate and looked out the window. "I was a manager at a salon. I loved it. I'd finally found something I was good at." She shrugged and took in his empty plate. "Are you ready to hit the road?" And just like that, the storm clouds that had collected in her eyes dispersed and she offered him a shaky smile.

He didn't know what this woman's story was, but it was becoming clear there was more to her than he'd thought.

Chapter Twenty-One

The alarm on Lena's phone went off when they were leaving the restaurant.

"It's time to call Viktor. I'll meet you back at the room," she told Dane with a calm she didn't feel. Every time she was forced to speak to Viktor was another moment she felt powerless and weak.

She walked around the building, feeling the sun on her face as she took a breath to prepare herself to speak to Satan himself. It was such a beautiful day, she hated to ruin it so early in the morning.

"Lena, how are you?" he asked as if he really cared.

"Fine."

"I trust you had a nice chat with Mackenzie this morning."

She swallowed down the blinding pain at the reminder, as well as the urge to scream at the man. "How is Tobey?" she asked instead, not sure if she would believe him if he granted her an answer.

"Fine, fine. I just checked in with my associates, and they assure me he is comfortable."

Comfortable. By whose standards? Viktor Kulakov would probably say her ex-husband was comfortable, even though she was pretty sure he was sleeping with the fishes, or whatever Viktor did with people who didn't pay him the money they owed him.

"How is our friend?"

"Pissed off, but I'm dealing with it."

"Keep watch, Lena. He will probably try to get you to side with him. He'll pretend to be your friend so he can get you to drop your guard. I need Robbie Vanderhook, or whatever his real name is. You need to make sure Dane finds him."

She almost laughed at the idea of Dane Ryan pretending to be her friend to get her cooperation. She actually wished he *would* pretend not to hate her. Maybe just a little. One look into his hard eyes, and she knew he would have killed her by now if he didn't need her to make these phone calls to Viktor.

"And if I help, you'll give—"

"We'll discuss it once you bring me Vanderhook."

Discussing wasn't the same thing as doing. "But you said—"

"Let's not play this tedious game. We both know you're in no position to negotiate or make demands. Bring me what I want, and I'll give you what you want. That's how it works."

Except, he wasn't to be trusted. "How can you be sure Vanderhook is even still alive?" she asked. She'd heard the story of his untimely demise. Weller had assured Viktor he'd shot him six times and he'd been as good as dead when they left him there.

"I have my ways. Find the man and bring him to me. Call me back at three p.m."

"Yes, okay."

She set the alarm to go off before the next phone call, and tucked it in her back pocket. She felt the familiar tightening of her throat and hot tears filled her eyes.

Instead of giving in to them, she took a few deep breaths

and looked up at the blue sky. Crying never helped. She didn't know how much longer she could keep going like this.

Every time she got her hopes up and thought this nightmare would come to end, Viktor needed her to do some other impossible task.

She had no leverage, which meant things weren't bound to change anytime soon. She glanced up at the hotel and let out a breath. Viktor had warned her not to trust Dane. That he might try to get her to side with him.

She'd laughed it off, but now she wondered if maybe that wasn't her only option. Not the befriending part, because she didn't think that was possible. But siding with him might be a step to ending this repetitive cycle she was caught in. She needed to do something. And he was a marshal, wasn't he?

In the room, he was sitting on the edge of the bed waiting for her. There wasn't anything to pack.

"What did Kulakov say?" he asked.

"He said Tobey is comfortable."

The only answer was a glare and a snort of disbelief. Right. Why would he believe anything she said? Especially when she was passing on information from a diabolical madman.

When they checked out, there was a box waiting for Dane. He tucked it under his arm and headed for the Jeep.

She wasn't sure how to approach him about switching her loyalties. He probably wouldn't believe her even if she had the courage to bring it up. He didn't trust her, and she didn't see that changing anytime soon.

She put the key in the ignition, but waited as he opened the box and pulled out a manila envelope with IDs, credit cards, and a new phone. There may have been other things in there, hell he might have pulled out the Hope Diamond and she wouldn't have noticed.

Because all her attention was focused intently on the gun he pulled from the box.

Chapter Twenty-Two

Dane felt so much better having a weapon. Not a sentiment shared by his travel companion, if her sharp intake of breath was any indicator.

"If I wanted you dead, you'd be dead already," he reminded her. He didn't need a gun to take out a hundred-and-ten-pound woman.

"Then why do you need a gun? You won't get close to Viktor with it. Butch and Weller will just take it."

"Relax. I'm not going to shoot you. I need you." He needed her to keep making those phone calls so no one hurt his kid.

He pulled a GPS unit out of the box and secured it to the windshield once he'd turned it on and selected the first saved location.

"Follow the directions it gives you," he told her.

An hour later, he spotted a sign for a department store and tapped her on the arm to get her attention. "Take this exit. We need new clothes and supplies."

She signaled and took the exit without any fuss. As far

as guard dogs went, she was of the Chihuahua variety. She walked behind him into the store and followed him to the men's section.

Inside the store, she seemed reluctant to leave him.

He rolled his eyes. "Look. We're going to have to trust each other at least enough to know the other person isn't going to run off. Of the two of us, I'd be the one who's screwed if you leave. If I were to bail, you would just look bad to your boss."

"Yes, because Viktor Kulakov is the epitome of patience and understanding when it comes to the failures of his employees," she muttered.

He knew that. Colton Williamson had been shot six times in the chest and left for dead because Viktor had been unhappy with him. No, Kulakov didn't hold back when displaying his disappointment.

"Fair enough. I promise to meet you at the checkout in ten minutes." He held out his hand in a gesture of goodwill.

She frowned for a moment, then took it. "I promise not to leave without you."

He didn't know what motivated her. He'd seen her with Viktor and it was clear they weren't in a romantic relationship. She'd also said she had no choice. What did that mean? Was she trapped, too?

He would work on figuring out why she was working for Kulakov and, if possible, attempt to win her over to his side. He just needed to wait for the right time.

As promised, they met at the appointed time at the front of the store. Standing there as she approached, he was once again struck by how pretty she was.

He hated that he still found her attractive. It didn't matter how nice she looked on the outside when her soul was a dark, slimy pit. If it weren't for her, he wouldn't be in this mess.

He knew that last thought was somewhat unfair. She

wasn't running the show. This hadn't been her idea. She'd actually seemed upset when she saw Tobey. And if she weren't here, he'd be shopping with Weller or the other lump who worked for Viktor.

Having her here instead might prove to be his good fortune. She didn't seem skilled as a guard, and he knew he could overpower her if needed, even with a bum leg. But force wouldn't get her to share any information he might need for his mission to save Tobey.

He would have to find a way to win her trust.

Chapter Twenty-Three

It had taken every bit of strength Lena had to walk away from Dane to go select her clothes and supplies. Instead of getting easier, it was more difficult each time they split up.

When would this plan of his kick in? Not that she had a clue what the plan was. She knew his team was involved in some way. Would they be waiting for her in the parking lot? Would she be arrested?

She had been given the task of making sure Dane brought in Robbie Vanderhook. But they were apparently friends. And she had no way to force him to do it. Now that he was armed and in touch with the authorities, she was completely at his mercy.

And mercy was not something Dane had a lot of when it came to her.

Stowing their purchases in the car, they stopped for fast food before getting back on the highway. She glanced over to see he had a bit of ketchup on his full bottom lip.

She remembered kissing his lips. His kiss had been soft, but strong. Like he would do what he wanted, but make sure she was taken care of, too.

God. She shouldn't have been thinking about sex. At this point, she was surprised she even remembered how it was done. It had been a while. Other things had taken precedence. But now, sitting next to this man, things were tingling in places she'd thought had died years ago.

While it was nice to find out she was still a woman with normal desires, it was impossible to have those desires for someone who hated her with a fiery passion.

And crap. Now she was thinking about passion.

Chapter Twenty-Four

Dane stared out the Jeep window as they passed a truck. He needed to do something. He was going stir-crazy. He pulled out his phone. "What's your number?"

After her reluctance to leave him in the store, he thought it might be a good idea if they exchanged numbers in case they accidently became separated.

"You're asking for my number?" She grinned at him in the same way she had that night. "I'm not sure I'm ready for that. I'm not really looking for a relationship right now."

Her joke brought a slight smile to his face, despite not wanting to react.

Keeping her eyes on the road, she dug her phone out and pulled up the number in the settings. Clearly, this wasn't her personal number since she didn't know it by memory.

He entered it in the contacts of his new phone. Then he also sent it to Angel along with a text.

Angel was his best friend, and a whiz when it came to computers and phones. She could make it look like someone was calling from Portugal if she wanted to. She could also make it look like they were heading west when they were actually going east.

He sent the text, let out a sigh of boredom, and stared out the window again.

"Do you want to drive for a little while?" she asked.

"What?" He turned to look at her. Surely, she was playing him.

"Did you want to drive? To be honest, I'm getting sick of it. I could use a break."

"You're going to let me drive." His voice was as flat as the highway they'd been on all day.

"I know you don't trust me, but I've made a decision to trust you. One of us needs to go first. I don't think you're going to plow us into a tree. Nothing good would come of that. You need me to call Viktor. You're not going to do anything to make that impossible. So, yeah, do you want to drive for a little while?"

"Okay."

He wasn't sure if it was a trick, or if she was that desperate to be relieved of the duty, but he climbed into the driver's seat and pulled back onto the road. With both of them driving, they would be able to cover more ground.

"Thank you," he muttered as he merged onto the highway.

He changed the radio station and turned it up. He almost felt relaxed. It was easy to imagine this scene in a different way. He and Lena heading off for a weekend getaway. Her hand in his, and them singing along with the radio.

But that would never be possible. She'd ruined whatever they might have been when she betrayed him. He flipped off the radio and kept his gaze locked on the road in front of him.

When the sun had long abandoned them, and his stomach growled in protest, he decided it was time to make his move. They would need to stop in the next few hours for the night. He had a plan, and he was going to have to trust part of it with the woman curled up against the passenger window.

It was time to find out how loyal Lena really was to Viktor Kulakov.

Chapter Twenty-Five

The smile Lena had tricked out of Dane at lunch was a distant memory. Dane was back to being his stoic, angry self as he pulled over and flipped through the flyer he'd picked up at their last stop. If ignoring her were a sport, he would have a gold medal.

Every time she thought she might be breaking through the stone wall, she had the door slammed in her face again. She'd allowed him to drive, and still he couldn't do more than grunt out a grudging thanks and go back to treating her like something stuck to his shoe.

Fine. She got it. She was trash. He hated her. But did he need to put so much energy into it? No matter how much he didn't like it, they were in this together. They needed each other.

She was almost ready to ask him where they were going, and what the plan was, when he spoke first, making her jump in surprise.

"Can I see Kulakov's credit card?" he asked.

"Why?" She'd been paying for everything so far.

"You'll have to trust me."

She laughed once, then pulled her brows together. "Wait. You're serious?"

"Yeah."

"You think I'm going to hand over the card so you can run off with it? I'd be stranded with no choice but to tell Viktor you got away. I get that you hate me, but at least have the balls to kill me yourself."

She shook her head. She'd already trusted him enough for one day. She'd let him drive, and it hadn't won her any points. This give-and-take couldn't be one-sided.

"I'm not going to run off with the card. If you'll remember, I need you to keep making those calls to Kulakov so he doesn't kill my son."

She swallowed and looked away. He'd hit her in the soft spot. She didn't like being reminded his son was in danger and she was the only thing keeping Tobey safe.

With a quick exhale, she pulled the card from her back pocket and held it out. Whatever he was going to do, she just wanted all this to end. She was too exhausted to keep fighting on both fronts.

"Okay, I'll trust you. Please don't force me to do something I will regret for, what would undoubtedly be the very short, rest of my life."

He simply snatched the card from her fingers and made a call to secure a hotel room with two queen-size beds. When he had completed the reservation, he handed the card back to her.

"That was it?" Her jaw dropped. "That was the big mystery? You called in advance to get our room?"

"Yep. Do you want to drive now?"

Something was wrong. She was certain he'd called a hotel in Nashville, but they were still heading east. She glanced at his profile as he sat in the passenger's seat glaring out the window. What was he up to?

If she thought he'd actually tell her, she might have worked up the courage to ask him. A half hour later, he abruptly pointed to an exit and ordered her to take it.

She was almost past it, so she ripped the wheel to the right and took the ramp faster than she should have. He cursed and grabbed the dash. The tires squealed on the pavement, but they stayed upright and moving.

At the stoplight at the end of the ramp, he told her to turn left and directed her to a hotel at a different chain than where he'd secured the room.

"Stay here. I'll be right back." He jumped out of the vehicle without asking for Viktor's card. So, why...

When he was almost to the entrance of the hotel, she gasped in awareness.

He was making it look like they were staying in Nashville when they were really hours away. If he planned to do the same thing the next night, they could be thousands of miles away from where Viktor would think they were.

She was impressed. It was a clever plan.

But what would happen to her when they got wherever they were going...?

Chapter Twenty-Six

Going against every rule of etiquette he'd ever been taught, Dane removed his bag from the back of the Jeep and left Lena to carry her own. It had been difficult not to continue to drive when she looked so tired.

It was becoming more of an effort to be rude to her than to just act normal. His anger had faded slightly when she'd handed over the card without first demanding to know what he was doing with it. She'd said she trusted him.

The way she'd practically begged him not to force her to do something she would regret, made it clear she didn't want to have to report anything to Kulakov that might put Tobey in more danger.

He'd become convinced she felt guilty about what had happened, which could only mean she really hadn't known the plan ahead of time, as she'd said. She was simply following orders.

Orders she didn't agree with.

"You didn't ask why we're here instead of the hotel where I booked the room."

He'd seen her looking at the ad in the hotel flyer when he was dialing the number. He'd expected her to pretend she didn't see, or act like she didn't notice.

"You don't want Viktor to know where we're really going," she said as she followed him to their room. "When we don't show up in Nashville, they will automatically charge the card and it will look like we stayed there."

Her ability to figure it out was notable. But it left him confused as to why she hadn't questioned or stopped him.

"You haven't asked me where we're going, either," he said when they were inside the room and the door was secured behind them.

She shrugged and let her bag slip down her arm to the floor. "You've made it pretty clear you don't trust me. I wasn't going to waste my time asking you when I know you won't tell me."

"I had planned to tell you if you asked," he said almost defiantly.

"And would you have told me the truth?"

His lip pulled up on the one side and he shook his head. "No. I wouldn't have."

"Then I guess I'll find out when we get there. Unless you're planning to off me before then."

She'd implied he was planning to kill her on more than one occasion. Did she honestly believe he would do that? *Could* do that?

Okay, so maybe at first he had wrestled with the idea, and he'd even told her he wanted to, but they were past that now. He knew he couldn't do it. And not just because he needed her to contact Kulakov at the scheduled times.

"I'm not going to kill you or leave you behind," he promised as he looked her right in the eye. "As you've said, we're in this together. At least for the time being. If we get to a point where things get too intense, I'll make sure you're left with an adequate excuse to protect yourself against Kulakov's wrath."

She gave a humorless laugh. "Do you really think there is such a thing? If I lose you, Viktor will kill me. And then he'll kill Tobey. We need to stick together. However much my company repulses you, you can't leave me. I won't tell Viktor where we are. You have my—" She stopped and shook her head, probably realizing her word didn't mean shit to him. The way she was about to give it to him freely, however, did mean something.

Maybe it wouldn't take much effort to get her on his side, after all.

Chapter Twenty-Seven

As much as Lena just wanted to fall into bed, she wanted a hot shower even more.

"Do you mind if I use the bathroom first?" she asked politely. If Dane wanted to hate her, she wouldn't put up a fuss, but she was going to kill him with kindness in the meantime.

"No, go ahead."

He'd tossed his bag on the first bed, so she took the second one.

She took longer than necessary in the shower, enjoying the hot water flowing over her tired body. When she stepped back in the room, he wasn't there. Then she noticed the keys to the Jeep and his phone were still on the desk, and relaxed. Anyway, she was much too tired to worry about it. If he wasn't back by morning, she'd figure out what to do then.

Her head hit the pillow and her world spun out into oblivion.

At some point, a hard body slid in behind her.

Dane's warm skin smelled of hotel soap, and she let out

a shocked sigh when his hand moved around her waist and worked under the shirt of her pajamas. She took a moment to wish she hadn't gone for the winky-face emoji pajamas and had instead gotten something a little more sophisticated. At least she'd shaved her legs.

When his thumb found her nipple, she forgot about the pajamas and focused on the intense sensation. She couldn't remember the last time anyone had bothered to touch her breasts.

Two years ago, when she and Brandon were still together, he hadn't bothered anymore. He'd simply done his thing and rolled off her to fall asleep.

By contrast, Dane was quite skilled in the art of satisfactory breast manipulation. She let out a moan, and stretched so he could reach the other side.

His lips touched the side of her neck and moved up to her ear. "Is this okay?" he asked. Whether he meant being in her bed or what he was doing to her nipple, the answer was the same.

"Yes. Please."

Unable to stop herself, she shifted so her backside was pressed firmly against his hot arousal. "Oh God," she murmured, hoping she remembered how to do this without embarrassing herself.

Instincts kicked in and she rubbed her body against his, wanting to feel the strength and safety of his body. She should touch him. She wanted to, but wondered if she was allowed…

Reaching behind her, she found him naked. She wrapped her fingers around his hardness and gripped him tightly. He moaned his pleasure against her shoulder.

His hand slid from her breast, across her stomach, and under the waistband of her pajama shorts. She squirmed in delight. Lower and lower, until his fingers reached the spot where she ached most. She writhed against him. God, it had been so long. How she'd missed the touch of a man. And this one was so incredibly skilled...

"Please," she begged, not caring if she sounded desperate. She was beyond pride as she tilted into his hand until he was touching her in just the right spot. "Yes. There." She tried briefly to control her breathing, but gave up when his fingers entered her.

"Do you want me?" he asked.

At another time, she might have replied with something witty, but at the moment she could only squeak out her answer. "Yes. Please. I want you so bad."

Then, right as things were really getting good, someone shook her arm, dragging her from a sleep so deep she would have sworn it was real.

The light between the beds snapped on, and Dane was standing over her with that annoyed look on his face. He shook her again, even though her eyes were now open.

"Wake up. You're having a bad dream."

She almost cried at how wrong he was. It hadn't been a bad dream.

It had been terribly, amazingly wonderful. She squeezed her eyes shut again.

But it wasn't real.

Chapter Twenty-Eight

Dane turned off the light and shifted onto his side so his back was toward Lena. Not that she would be able to see his erection in the dark, under the sheet, but still he felt the need to hide it.

Having her find out he'd responded to her moans and cries for more, would undermine his role as the indifferent asshole he was attempting to portray.

Even worse was knowing he'd responded to her even before she'd started moaning and writhing on the bed.

When he'd walked into the room, she was already sleeping. He couldn't help but notice the way she'd kicked the blanket off one side, and how her leg continued, bare and smooth, up to the short shorts of her new pajamas.

The winky-faces mocked him. Especially the ones blowing kisses with a heart.

He'd taken a cool shower, and not just because the hot water had started to run out.

Now as he lay there trying to sleep, he could only think of being with her at the bar. Talking and having a good time.

The anticipation of sleeping with her as they walked to the hotel, and that kiss. The kiss that had melted through the cold ice around his heart.

It had been perfect, right up until she'd knocked him on the head with a bottle and he'd woken up in hell.

That was the part he needed to focus on. The *real* Lena Scott.

Chapter Twenty-Nine

Lena managed to fall back to sleep, but it had taken a long time. She was embarrassed…not to mention frustrated.

Would it have been so horrible for him to touch her? He was a man. In her experience, they weren't all that picky when they went without female attention for very long. Any female attention would do in a pinch.

He must have been attracted to her on some level. She'd been able to lure him to her hotel room with the promise of nakedness.

Apparently clobbering him on the head had the effect of a perpetual cold shower, because other than the erection the night she'd massaged his leg, he hadn't responded to her with anything but disgust.

When she woke again, she heard the shower running. That was odd, since he'd showered the night before. Why would he need to take another…?

Oh. A cat-like smile stretched across her cheeks. Maybe she had affected him, after all. She moved to the door to listen and thought she'd heard a muffled groan. She had no way to know if it was due to a release of pleasure, or if his leg was bothering him.

She decided to let herself think it was pleasure. That was more fun. Flopping back in bed, she smiled up at the ceiling. This was a new day. With new potential.

As her thoughts whirled around all the possibilities for the hours ahead, her phone rang. Instantly, the smile fell from her face, replaced by the false, brittle substitute she'd created over the last months.

Chapter Thirty

Dane had woken with a hard-on the likes of which he hadn't experienced since he was eighteen. Trying to think it away hadn't worked. In fact, that had only made it worse. The early sunlight was coming through the sheer curtains and he'd been able to see the outline of Lena's body.

He'd noticed the spill of brown hair across her pillow, and the way her tank top had pulled to the side and was inches from exposing a nipple. That nipple had been hard, most likely from the air conditioning in the room. But he liked to think it was because she'd been dreaming of him again.

Not that he was sure she'd been dreaming of *him* last night. She hadn't said a name in her sleep, and he'd thought maybe she had a boyfriend. Even the resulting ridiculous wave of jealousy had done nothing to subdue his erection.

After an hour of watching her in the darkness, and aching at the sight, he'd given up and gone to the bathroom to relieve his misery in the shower.

The relief lasted about three seconds. What was it about the damned woman that turned him on so much?

He took another shower.

Once he was somewhat under control of his body again, he got out of the shower and gave himself a stern look in the mirror and opened the door to the bedroom to go out.

She was talking on the phone. Or rather, video-chatting.

He stopped, and hovered by the door to watch and listen. She didn't look up. She hadn't noticed him. He didn't dare move, so he wasn't close enough to see who she was Facetiming with.

She was smiling at the screen. He frowned. He barely knew her, but well enough to know this was not her real smile. Even the strained smiles she'd reserved for him were not like this painful, twisting parody of features.

Despite the distress on her face, she somehow managed to sound happy. "I see it. It's so pretty. Did you make that?" she asked in a voice that indicated she was talking to a child.

His frown deepened.

"Yeah. I colored it myself. Dis is you, Mama."

He froze. *Mama*? Lena was a mother?

Anger erupted anew. He'd hated what she'd done—putting Tobey in danger—but somehow, knowing she was a mother herself made it that much worse.

And here she was, making kissy sounds into the phone and waving at the screen. As if she was at work at the salon rather than on a road trip to kidnap a man and turn him over to a killer.

What kind of person could do such a thing?

"I love you, baby. Be good."

"I'll see you soon," a little girl's voice answered.

"Yeah, sweetie. Real soon, I promise." She was still smiling, but it had transformed into something ugly and terrified.

"Bye, Mama."

"Bye, baby."

She held the phone to her lips and closed her eyes for a moment as if steadying herself. When her eyes opened, she gasped with shock at seeing him standing there.

Or maybe it was at the look on his face. He was livid and wasn't holding back his hatred.

"It must be nice getting to say goodbye. I wasn't allowed," he said bitterly.

"It's not—"

"Please don't lie. I'm not even that surprised. One thing I would like to know is, how do you look in your daughter's face and not see Tobey?"

"You don't understand." She stood and opened her mouth to spew her defense, but he wouldn't let her speak.

He was incensed. His body literally shook with pent-up rage. The night before, he'd told her he wasn't going to kill her, but now he wasn't sure if that was true. He tasted copper in his mouth, and his muscles readied to leap on her and snap her damned neck.

"I understand perfectly," he ground out. "Your child is safe and happy, while mine is tied up somewhere, scared and alone. I don't even know if he's being fed." Damn it. His voice cracked on that last word.

Tobey was older now, but when he was little there would be days when he ate everything he could get his hands on, and other days he wouldn't be hungry and he'd just pick at his food.

Instantly, her eyes went from despair to anger. Tears filled them and she sprang at him, poking her finger at his chest. "Damn you, Dane! *Damn* you and your self-righteous judgment. I'm sick of it! You don't know *anything*!"

"I know you tricked me into a situation where my son might not survive, while you get to chat every day with your kid."

She shoved his chest. "I haven't seen my daughter in *eight months,* other than on the phone. I'm only allowed to talk to her when Viktor worries I'm not committed enough to his projects. You probably think it's a gift having contact, but it's like a knife in my stomach every time the screen lights up with her name. The very first thing she asks is 'When are you coming to get me?' and it *kills* me to have to lie and say 'soon.'"

He swallowed down the pain that thought produced.

Tears tumbled down her cheeks. She brushed them away with the back of her hand but more took their place. The tears did nothing to dampen her fury. "I'm in the same situation as you are. Maybe worse," she said with a sob.

"How could it possibly be worse than someone threatening your child's life?"

She gave him a tearful, pitying look. "Viktor uses the possibility of your son's death to motivate you. But he's promised a different fate for my daughter. He sells people, Dane. And he has a lot of clients who will pay dearly for a little girl."

Shit. Horror and disgust swamped over him, and he let his arms fall to his sides.

She flinched backward at the motion, and he felt his stomach surge again. This time, with revulsion for himself. He'd treated her abominably.

Christ Almighty. He should have figured it out. The clues were all there. At the very least, he should have *asked* her why she was loyal to Kulakov. When Dane had seen them together, she'd seemed more afraid of the man than respectful. But Dane had been so caught up in his own problems he hadn't even considered that she might have been forced to do Viktor's bidding.

Sympathy, guilt, pity, and regret all swirled through him.

God. They were both living the same nightmare.

Moving slower, he stepped forward and cautiously

wrapped his arms around her.

He couldn't change what he'd already done, but he could offer her his support from now on. It was the least he could do.

He gently kissed her hair, and murmured. "Tell me what happened."

Chapter Thirty-One

It was time to get things out in the open, and Dane hoped he hadn't scared Lena so badly she wouldn't feel comfortable to tell her story. He didn't have to wonder for long.

She seemed relieved to have someone listen. Did she not have anyone else to talk to?

She let out a deep breath and nodded before speaking. "My ex-husband, Brandon, took a job with Viktor Kulakov when Kenzie was three. He and I were already having trouble in our marriage. I didn't know what he was doing for Viktor, and I didn't care. He made good money. When we divorced two years ago, all I was concerned about was that he could pay alimony and child support. But then he stopped. Each time he came to see Kenzie he looked worse and worse. Eventually, I figured it out."

"Drugs?" Dane asked. He recognized the signs.

She covered her face and nodded. "Yeah. He asked me for money and even stole some out of my purse when I was putting Kenzie to bed. His eyes were unfocused, and his speech was off. He told me he owed his boss a lot of money."

"Did he say how much?" Dane asked.

"Fifty thousand dollars." She shrugged. "Even if I'd wanted to help, I couldn't. I made good money managing the salon, but not *that* kind of money." She waved her hands as if to ask who did.

There had been a time when Dane had that kind of money sitting around. But then he'd realized it was dirty, and tried to make amends. Instead, he ended up fake-dead.

"I didn't see Brandon for a few months. I didn't know what had happened. I thought maybe he was dead. But then he showed up at Kenzie's daycare when I was at work and took her. Someone new was working, and Kenzie had called him daddy."

Lena's lip trembled, and Dane wondered how many times she'd punished herself for not preparing for that possibility. Hindsight was a smug son of a bitch. He knew from experience it was easy to see where you went wrong when you were looking backward.

"Viktor contacted me immediately. Told me if I went to the police, he would sell my daughter to recoup the money he'd lost." Her voice broke, and only a monster would have not responded to her pain.

Dane sat on the bed and pulled her onto his lap. He held her while she cried noisily into his neck.

In the package with the gun and the GPS unit, there had also been a copy of Colton's file on Viktor Kulakov. He was a drug smuggler who had branched out to include human trafficking. Many a missing persons case had ended at his doorstep, but he was slippery and clever. When the federal prosecutor hadn't been able to make any arrest stick, a DEA undercover agent—Colton Williamson—had been sent in to gather evidence. Even after Colton had infiltrated his business and could testify to what he'd seen, the federal prosecutor didn't feel they had enough proof to put Kulakov away for a long time. He was holding out for more so they could put him in prison for the rest of his life.

Colton had set it up that a container of Kulakov's drugs was seized just after a deal. He was supposed to be caught red-handed. Instead, he'd somehow found out, and had Colton shot six times.

The incident was just one of the many reasons Kulakov was nervous and itching to find Colton. For revenge…and he didn't want any loose ends.

Dane knew from his own experience with his bosses that rich men could get away with murder. They had enough power to get people to do their bidding. Like lure a U. S. Deputy Marshal to a hotel room so he could be kidnapped.

"This is why you're cooperating with him?" Dane asked after the sobs subsided, and she nodded. He handed her a tissue from the stand between the beds, then another, and another.

She held up her hands in helpless surrender. "I don't know what else to do."

She looked up at him, her multi-colored eyes blazing with tears, more green now than the other colors. "I know you said I wasn't allowed to apologize, but I really am sorry," she whispered. "I don't have many choices, but you have to believe me, I wouldn't have endangered Tobey to save Kenzie. Especially knowing I might not save her anyway. It's been so long, and I'm not that stupid. I realize I might not ever hold her again, but I can't just turn my back and not try to save her."

He held Lena close and rubbed her back. "I understand now, and I'm sorry this terrible thing is happening to you. Of course you have to try. That's what parents do; we can't help ourselves."

He couldn't seem to hold her tight enough. She was breaking apart despite his efforts. She'd been alone with this heartache for months, with Viktor constantly ordering her around. How scared she must have been.

She deserved a good cry. She deserved to have something to hold onto.

Hope.

"Listen to me." He gave her a little shake to get her attention. "We're going to save both of them. Do you hear me?"

She stopped sniffling but didn't reply.

"Can you trust me to get us out of this?" he asked, unsure if he would be able to agree if he was in her shoes. This was her child, and so far, she hadn't been able to trust anyone.

It took a full minute, but eventually she nodded and looked up at him. "Right now, I don't have many options. At least you're one of the good guys. So, I'll trust you."

He wished her trust were based on something more than a lack of options, but he'd take it for now. After the way he'd treated her, he was surprised she trusted him at all.

"I'm sorry," she whispered again.

He let out a sigh before saying the one thing he never thought he'd say to this woman. "I understand. I don't blame you."

Chapter Thirty-Two

It felt good to be held. Dane's arms were warm and strong. His clean smell made Lena relax and snuggle closer. For a moment, she felt as though everything was going to be okay.

She didn't know what plan Dane had in mind, but she knew she had to do something more than simply follow Viktor's orders and wish for the best. That course wasn't yielding any results.

Viktor's promises to return Kenzie were all lies, and Lena was genuinely worried she would lose her daughter forever. Now that there was a chance to get her back, Lena realized she had slowly started to give up hope.

She didn't think she could hate herself any more than she already did, but disgust ran anew. What kind of mother gave up on her child?

One that is broken, her heart answered.

Another wave of tears hit, hot fire on her cheeks. She should have been embarrassed by the huge wet spot on Dane's shirt. She didn't even know how long he'd been holding her while she cried.

His hand rubbed circles on her back, and occasionally she felt his breath in her hair as he cooed words of peace to her.

"It's going to be okay," he said. "I'm here. I'll help. We'll get them back. We're in this together. You're not alone anymore."

His words—spoken to soothe—were what broke her. She'd had her child taken away, and she had been too weak to do anything about it. There hadn't been anyone she could turn to for help.

Brandon's parents, who'd treated her like a daughter even after the divorce, would have wanted to help, but there was nothing they could have done. Worse, they would have insisted on calling the police. A surefire way to get on Viktor's bad side and have him follow through on all his threats.

She wanted to believe Dane's words, she wanted to hope that she would see Kenzie again, but she wasn't sure she remembered how to hope.

When she got control of herself at last, she slid off his lap and stood. The room felt too small. She felt too restless. Her secret was out. She didn't have to deal with it alone, but she didn't know what to do with all the feelings jumping around under her skin.

Dane stood and rested his hands on her shoulders. His touch quieted the noise in her head. Strangely, she felt stronger when his hands were on her. For the first time since her daughter was taken away, she didn't feel quite so weak.

Thank God.

She wasn't alone.

Chapter Thirty-Three

The alarm on Lena's phone rang, interrupting whatever might have happened next. Dane didn't know whether to be grateful or…well, confused.

"It's time for my call to Viktor." She wiped the tears away and let out a determined breath. "I never knew I could hate someone this much."

He understood completely. He'd hated her that much at one time. But no longer.

She dialed the number and held it to her ear. "I'm here."

Dane could hear Viktor's silky smooth voice. "How is our guest?"

"Upset and angry."

"Is he closer to finding Vanderhook?"

"I think so. He's not telling me anything." She glanced up at him, and he frowned at the truth of that statement.

"Has he tried to escape?"

"No." She rolled her eyes. "But I'm not letting my guard down."

"Very well. Call me at ten."

"Oka—" Before she had the chance to hang up, Dane seized the phone from her and addressed her boss. She reached out to take it back. As if she could stop him from doing anything.

"Dane!" She winced.

"Viktor," Dane said, unfazed by her alarm, "I want to hear Tobey's voice. I want to make sure you haven't done anything to him."

Lena squeezed her eyes shut, and whispered, "Oh God."

Viktor surprised them both by answering, "Stay by the phone. I'll have them call you."

He couldn't believe Viktor had relented so easily. There had to be an angle. Or maybe he just wanted to remind Dane who held the cards, the way he did with Lena.

Dane kept the phone and paced around their room. She followed along behind him, not saying anything. The tension was building to dangerous levels when the phone rang.

"Hello?" His voice cracked with tension.

"Dad?" Tobey's voice was loud and clear.

Oh, thank God!

"Tobey, are you okay?" Dane wasn't sure he'd ever felt such relief before. But hearing Tobey's voice just about broke him.

"I'm good. Do you know when I'll get to go home?" he asked, and Dane felt the shooting pain Lena had described.

How did she do this every day? How did she answer this unanswerable question? Tobey was older than Kenzie, so Dane decided to go with the truth.

Or as close to it as he could without upsetting his son even more.

"I don't know just yet," he said, "but it shouldn't be that long. Are you okay? Have they fed you? Are you safe?"

"I'm okay. They get a lot of pizza. I didn't think I'd ever get tired of eating pizza, but maybe I am, a little. There are a few other boys here, too. I get a top bunk. We get to play video games all day long. Don't tell Mom. Oh. I guess you can't tell her. Because you're dead."

Despite everything, Dane smiled at his son's reasoning. He was safe, fed, and even having fun. Or as much fun as a person could have when being held captive.

Dane's heart relaxed a little more.

"Your secret is safe with me," he said. "Play as many games as you want. She won't find out." But he would find a way to tell Caroline their boy was safe. "I love you. I'll see you…soon," he said, and realized he'd said the same thing Lena had told her daughter.

"Bye, Dad. Love you, too."

He handed Lena the phone without bothering to disconnect the call.

She seemed to be waiting for him to break down, but he didn't. He felt slightly numb.

His son was safe. For now.

"He's okay?" she asked, her voice small. She moved to touch his arm, giving it a light squeeze before pulling away again.

Just as well. He wasn't sure if he wanted her to touch him. Yes, he'd just held her in his arms and comforted her, but he wasn't ready to be comforted himself. He'd been so angry at her before… But he knew she felt terrible. And knowing Tobey was doing okay, and knowing the reason she'd gotten Dane into this…well, how could he not forgive her?

However, given the volatile situation, and his unbidden attraction to her, it was probably best to keep his distance.

Using his own phone, he called someone who could help him with his next task.

"Hello?"

"Angel, I need to get a message to someone, and it has to be untraceable."

"My specialty is usually the reverse of that. I'm the one who traces the untraceable."

This was true. No one could hide from Angel. She was the master of tracking someone down. But she was also pretty good at hiding things. Last year when she was on the run, she'd virtually dropped off the planet…and fallen in love while she was at it.

"What level tracking would the receiver have at hand?" she asked.

"Local law enforcement. It's a missing persons case."

She let out a sigh. "Dane, are you contacting your wife?" Angel had always been too smart for her own good.

"Yes. I need to let her know Tobey is safe."

"Is he?"

Dane didn't want to think about that. "For now. I just spoke with him. He's being taken care of."

"Do you think Caroline will believe a random message from an untraceable source?" Best friends didn't bother to hide their skepticism.

"You're a mother. Wouldn't you want any bit of good news you could get?"

"I wouldn't believe it. Not unless I spoke to him myself." There was a pause and she gasped. "Wait. You just spoke to him? Do you have the number?"

"No. It was a blocked call."

"Blocked." She snorted as if it was not that big of a deal. "What's the number of the phone you took the call on?"

Dane rattled off the numbers.

"How are *you* holding up?" she asked. This was not business. This was Angel caring about him.

"I'm not," he admitted, noticing Lena had gone in the bathroom to offer him some privacy. "I feel like I'm going to fall to pieces any minute. But I know if that happens, I won't be able to help him, so I force myself to keep it together a little longer."

"I can't even imagine what it must be like." Sympathy poured through her voice.

"It seems like it shouldn't be this bad for me. I mean, I don't see him, or talk to him. Not like Caroline and Randy do. But even though I wasn't able to be with him, I still knew he was at home. Safe and loved, you know? I feel so useless."

"Don't worry about being a hero. Let the team work on coming up with a plan while you work on getting to the meet site."

"Okay. Thanks."

"Text me the message you want sent to Caroline, and I'll make sure she gets it. I don't know if I would believe it, but it would give me hope. Maybe it will help Caroline, too."

"I hope so. She must be a mess."

And rightfully so. Separating a mother from her child was the worst kind of torture. He glanced over as Lena walked out of the bathroom.

"I'll start working on tracing the number so we have a lead. Be careful, okay?"

"I will. Give John a kiss from his godfather."

"Will do."

Lena was sitting on the edge of her bed with her chin on her knees when he tossed his phone on the nightstand next to hers.

"Are you okay?" he asked.

Her eyes moved in his direction, but her posture remained the same. "You mean am I over my little drama?"

He let out a sigh and looked up at the ceiling. "No. You and I are in a situation that no parent should ever be in. I'm trained for high-stress missions, and I'm still not sure if I'm doing the right thing."

"I want to apologize again," she whispered, "but I'm not sure if you'll accept it."

He sat on his bed across from her and nodded. "Go ahead. Get it out."

"I'm sorry I lost it. I'm sorry I cried all over you. I won't let it happen again, I swear."

He'd expected another apology for Tobey. Not for crying on his shoulder.

So much for the not touching thing.

He went to sit next to her. He put his arm around her, and she allowed her head to fall to that place on his chest where she'd cried her heart out. She didn't cry now. She'd probably cried herself out earlier. She seemed to be in a better place now.

"I accept your apology. Can you accept mine? I've been nothing but rude and hateful. I didn't even stop to consider you might be dealing with something as bad as I was."

"I understand. I don't blame you."

"Thank you," he said, and held her out so he could look her in the eyes. "I want you to let it go, this whole situation with Viktor. I want you to stop blaming yourself for everything. You're doing your best. That's all anyone can ever do."

She nodded, but he didn't think she'd be able to give up the guilt. He wouldn't.

"Get dressed. We have some kids to save," he said, and she smiled.

The real smile.

Chapter Thirty-Four

Like the day before, Lena took turns driving with Dane. But unlike yesterday, today she felt hopeful for the first time in months.

They'd spent the whole day talking about their kids. It felt nice to talk about Kenzie. All this time she hadn't spoken to anyone about her daughter. There hadn't been anyone to tell.

Telling her story that morning had relieved some of her burden. She hadn't realized how tiring it was to carry it around until it was gone.

She was exhausted now. But it was a good exhaustion. They'd been driving all day *toward* something. Toward a resolution. Toward a chance.

Dane used Viktor's card to reserve a hotel room in Texas, while they actually stopped for the night in Virginia.

"Thank you for today," she said as she sat on the edge of her bed. Her hair was still wet from the shower and dripped on her leg like the tears that were coming again. It seemed like they'd never stop.

But these weren't tears of pain and despair. They were tears of gratitude to this man who had given her a chance to do something, and an opportunity to talk about her child.

She wiped the tears away. "I wish to God you weren't going through this, but I'm so glad you're here. I know that doesn't make sense." She shook her head, embarrassed by her words and the fact she was crying again. She was just so overwhelmed with hope.

He sat next to her on her bed, and she went eagerly into his open arms. She didn't let go of him even when the tears subsided. She felt safe in his arms. She'd been holding it together for so long, she'd forgotten what it felt like to have someone help. By silent consent, he didn't let go of her, either. Instead, he kicked off his shoes, pulled her back against his chest, and flipped the covers over both of them.

She felt him kiss the top of her head as she was sucked under by the weight of sleep. Her last thought was how perfectly his body fit against hers.

She wasn't alone anymore. There was someone here to help carry the weight.

She continued to drift into the deepest sleep she'd had in months.

When she woke, it was almost six. She was well rested, and Dane was still in her bed. They'd shifted during the night and he was lying behind her, his chest to her back, his arm draped across her waist, and his arousal pressed against her backside. It was much like the dream she'd had.

She tensed. Which woke him, though he didn't move away from her. She could tell he was awake by the change in his breathing and quickened rate of his heart against her shoulder blade.

Why wasn't he moving away?

The only answer was a slight movement of his hips as he pressed closer, and the lurch of his erection in response.

Very slowly, she let out the breath she was holding, so he wouldn't know she was awake. She knew this was just a normal morning reaction. He didn't actually want her. There was no way he could see her as anything but the woman who had endangered his life and been too weak to help his son.

His hand moved from her waist to her hip, and his cock throbbed against her again. She couldn't help the soft moan that escaped her lips. She was a woman, but she hadn't allowed herself to feel like one in so long.

Would it be so bad to have a moment of pleasure in this unending hell?

Without consciously answering the question, she pressed back against him and another soft sound left her lips.

His body went rigid where it was pressed to hers, and she expected him to push her away.

Clearly, this was not the right time, but she wanted to feel closer to him. She needed a moment to feel normal and alive for just a little while. Maybe sex would help her to forget the pain for a bit.

When he pulled away from her, it was to roll her onto her back so he could look at her. "You awake?" he asked.

She could tell his question was asked to verify consent rather than the state of her consciousness. She'd probably made similar sounds in her sleep the other night when she was dreaming about him.

Dreaming about this—him in her bed, touching her and looking at her like a man looked at a woman instead of the way a deputy marshal appraised a criminal.

"Yes," she answered and moved toward him.

Her leg brushed up the outside of his, her knee resting at his hip as she leaned up to kiss him. Any moment he would stop her, and she would let him. But until then, she would greedily accept any attention he gave her. Any distraction.

His lips softened to hers, and his hand came up to capture

her face and tilt it so he could delve deeper. In a flurry of need, they pulled and tugged each other's clothes off.

She didn't know why this was happening, she didn't know what would happen afterward, but she wanted it. She wanted him. She wanted to pretend for a little while that her life wasn't a complete disaster. She wanted to believe she remembered how to be a woman, and how to be happy.

"Lena," he said her name in a low whisper.

Her only answer was, "Please."

She didn't want to hear all the reasons why this was a bad idea. There would be time enough for regrets later. She couldn't walk away now. She needed this too much.

He bent closer, resting against her. The hard warmth of his body came down to cover hers, and she felt safe under him. A small grunt of pain reminded her of his injured leg and how it bothered him more in the mornings.

Not wanting him to be uncomfortable, she rolled him over so she was on top and he wouldn't need to tax his leg. But he wouldn't have it.

He swung her onto her back again and grinned. "Let me be the man," he said before taking her mouth again. His teeth caught her lip, but his tongue quickly swept out to ease the nip. He moved across her jaw and down her neck to her aching breasts.

She'd somehow forgotten all these sensations…maybe some she'd never felt before. Now she greeted them openly, knowing he was too far gone to stop now. Whether he truly wanted her or simply the release, he would continue.

Another moan—louder this time—left her as he moved to her other breast. Again, he used his teeth and tongue in a satisfying combination as his fingers trailed down her stomach and reached between her thighs.

She was wet and ready for him. As if her body knew what to do, even if she couldn't quite remember. It had been so long.

And even before her divorce, she'd given up on enjoyment from a man.

Dane's fingers stroked her perfectly, and she cried out when he removed them. She'd been so close.

She opened her dazed eyes and whimpered as he reached out for his wallet and retrieved a condom. Once he was covered, he nudged her legs apart and joined them in one movement.

Her gasp of surprise echoed in the small room.

"Are you okay?"

She nodded, unable to speak.

Passion promised oblivion, and she already felt the initial stirrings of her body taking over. An exquisite pressure began to build as he moved.

A groan of pleasure escaped her lips, driving him on, harder and faster. He seemed as lost as she was. Her orgasm came on embarrassingly quickly, but he was not far behind.

She blinked up at the sunlight slanting across the ceiling as his weight rested along the side of her body. Their chests heaved in an effort to catch their breath and she smiled, then closed her eyes, enjoying just one more second of pleasure before allowing the fear and dread of reality to sneak back in.

That second was over much too soon.

Chapter Thirty-Five

Dane might have thought what had just happened was a dream, except for the pain in his leg and the trickle of sweat running down his back. He didn't dream with such detail. Damn. He should work on that.

In the past when he'd had sex dreams, he'd woken hard and throbbing. He didn't climax. And he never dreamed about what happened afterward.

The fact that Lena was still in his arms proved it was real.

He'd had sex with Lena Scott. The woman who'd bashed him over the head with a whiskey bottle. The woman who was enslaved by Viktor Kulakov. The desperate mother who would do anything to save her daughter. Except maybe risk the life of his son.

Pulling her closer, he kissed her hair and wondered what kind of damage he'd done. Had she truly wanted this? Or had she given herself in sacrifice to earn his forgiveness? He wouldn't put it past her to go along with sex to please him.

Had he taken advantage of her guilt? Damn it to hell.

She'd been amazingly responsive, and he'd felt her

pleasure grasping him, pulling him toward his own. He'd been relieved she finished so quickly. With his leg tweaked, he didn't have the longevity he used to claim. He could only hope he hadn't destroyed what trust he'd managed to nurture between them.

Neither moved, even after their breathing had leveled out to normal. They couldn't stay like this forever. One of them would have to speak. They needed to continue on their trip. Time was of the essence.

"Should one of us say it was a mistake?" he asked, his voice rough.

"Do you think it was a mistake?"

"I'm sure it was…but I don't regret it. At least not yet."

"Let's just lie here for a few more seconds. I'm sure we'll start to feel guilty any moment now." Her body moved against his in soft laughter, and he smiled up at the ceiling, not regretting a damn thing.

They were both consenting adults. They were dealing with a shit-ton of pain and anxiety, and had needed the release sex provided. All perfectly acceptable. Except he wanted her again, and he knew he had another condom in his wallet.

The first time could be excused as them losing their minds from all the pressure. But why was his body responding to her warm breath on his skin, and the way her leg was twined with his?

She raised her head and looked at him, the smile melding into a different look. Apparently, it wasn't enough for her, either.

The last time he'd wanted to push into her, to be in control of their pace, but now his leg protested, and he was happy to position her over him once he had the other condom on. She sank down on his length with a moan of pleasure, and he enjoyed the opportunity to take her fears away, if only for a little while longer.

She rode him slowly, teasing him with a naughty smile. He snaked his hands along her thighs to her hips and pulled her down on him when she was not expecting it.

The room filled with the sound of her husky laughter… and his heart filled with a different desire. Not just lust or need. He understood his desire to protect her. What he didn't understand was this brand-new feeling that took over as he touched her face and pulled her lips to his.

Their situation and all the emotions had created a bond between them. An accelerated reaction that would have taken months to form naturally.

She paused, looking down at him with a strange expression. He wanted to ask if she felt it, too, but to do so meant putting whatever it was into words, and he wasn't able to do that.

A single tear rolled down her cheek, and he reached up to brush it away.

"I wish I had just been a woman at the bar," she whispered.

He smiled. "Me, too." He sat up so he could kiss her.

The change in position caused her to gasp in pleasure. Using his hands, he guided her up and down in a vigorous pace, until she broke around him, her hair covering his face as he held her close and rode out the spasms. When they subsided, he pushed up into her the half dozen times it took to finish, then he collapsed back down to the mattress.

His leg was killing him, but his heart and mind were soaring.

For the moment.

Chapter Thirty-Six

"Am I a bad mom?" Lena asked when she'd caught her breath enough to speak.

While she didn't regret being with Dane, the guilt of her brief happiness was starting to tarnish her memories of their passion.

"No. You're not a bad mom." He kissed her cheek and brushed a stray piece of hair from her face. "There's nothing we can do for either of them right now. There's no shame in wanting to feel good if you have a chance."

Surely, this wasn't right. She shouldn't be allowed to have even this brief respite from the pain.

He stood and stretched "I'll grab us breakfast while you get ready. Can we leave in a half hour?"

Nodding, she watched his glorious body unwind. She noticed the scars on his leg and fought the urge to wince.

"I know, it's ugly," he said.

"I wouldn't say that. It looks painful."

"It wasn't fun."

He hadn't told her what had happened, but she could

guess, based on his occupation.

"You were shot?"

He smiled. "Yep. And bit by a dog, and I fell off a roof and got caught on a fence."

She choked out a laugh of sympathy. "Are you making that up to get pity?"

He pulled his shirt down over his lean chest. He wasn't ripped, but he had definition. Including those lines she could still see at the waist of his low jeans.

"I don't need your pity. But I'll take a kiss." He leaned down and stole one. "You can pity me tonight when we're in bed again. For now, I need to find food, and we need to get on the road."

"Okay." She bit her bottom lip, feeling shy about their plans. She'd assumed this was a one-time thing. A release of tension.

He winked at her before grabbing up his phone and heading for the door. "Be back soon."

She carried her phone into the bathroom and turned on the water to wash her face. The woman in the mirror was smiling at her. A mischievous, happy expression she hadn't seen in years. Not since she was still in love with Brandon, and Kenzie started sleeping through the night.

After washing her face and brushing her teeth, she smiled, rejuvenated and ready to take on the world.

She dressed and tossed her things in the bag, so she'd be ready when he returned. According to the GPS, they would arrive at their destination by five o'clock this evening. He hadn't told her who would be waiting there. Maybe he would share the details today.

She was humming a happy tune when her phone rang its own happy tune.

She swallowed and pulled the device from her back pocket. She saw her daughter's smiling face on the screen.

Every ounce of joy fell away as she swiped to answer.

"Hey, baby. How are you?"

"Hi, Mama. Are you coming to get me today?"

The familiar pain seared through her heart as reality crashed in and stole her tiny moment of joy.

Chapter Thirty-Seven

Dane felt like a high school kid as he paced by the condom selection for the third time. Unlike when he was in high school, his hesitancy had nothing to do with whether or not to try the ribbed variety, or any worry that his father might walk into the store while he was paying for them.

His concern today was whether or not he should even buy them. To do so would mean he intended to keep sleeping with Lena. Part of him—most of him—wanted to buy the big box and head back. But there was another part of him that thought it was a bad idea.

This wasn't a honeymoon, or even a vacation. This was a desperate mission to save two children. Possibly more, since Tobey's new roommates were most likely also missing children.

It wasn't the first time he'd found himself torn between duty and pleasure. How many nights had he come home to his family and taken refuge in his wife's arms, back when his money-laundering boss had made vague threats if Dane didn't go along with their plans? He knew from talking to a couple of his current team members that it was a common need with soldiers, as well.

After a battle it was important to feel alive again. Sex made a man feel alive.

Dane hoped it had made Lena feel better. If only for a little while.

He picked up the bigger box and went to the counter. He wasn't sure if he'd have occasion to use them, but he wanted to be prepared.

They were ready to fight for their children's lives. There was no reason they couldn't help each other relieve the tension until the time came to act. Until they had a plan of attack, they could use sex to expend the restless energy.

He frowned when he walked into the hotel room and saw her sitting cross-legged on the bed, talking on the phone. Now that he knew her better, he knew exactly how strained that smile was, and sensed the struggle it took for her to keep it in place.

Anyone else might not realize the happy woman with the cheerful laugh was a fraud, but Dane knew. He could feel the stress coming off of her and reached out to touch her knee, hoping to offer her some strength to hold on until the end of the call.

"When are you coming to get me?" he heard the little girl ask, and watched as Lena pressed her lips together. He knew this was the hardest part. The lying.

"Soon," he whispered to her. She nodded at him and smiled.

"Soon, baby. I'll be coming for you soon."

"Love you, Mama."

"I love you, too, baby. So much."

He expected her to weep when she disconnected the call, but she looked up at the ceiling and nodded once. As if making a decision. "I feel like maybe that time it was the truth," she said.

He sat next to her and pulled her closer. "I think so, too."

As they ate their bagels, he noticed her phone sitting on the nightstand.

"Give me your phone," he said, holding out his hand. "Please."

She handed it over without even asking what he wanted with it. He saw that as progress. She trusted him with the lifeline to her daughter.

"This is the number that calls you to speak to Kenzie?" he verified, pointing.

"Yes. But don't call it. I won't be allowed to talk to her. I can only speak to her by Viktor's order."

He wasn't surprised. No one did anything without Viktor's approval.

"I'm not calling the number. It's okay." Holding her phone out, he used his own phone to text the number to Angel with a simple message.

DANE: TRACK THIS NUMBER PLEASE. WE'LL NEED A LOCATION.

A few minutes later, he received an answering text.

ANGEL: ON IT.

He realized if he wanted Lena to trust him, he needed to communicate better.

"I'm having the number tracked so we can figure out where he's holding our kids," he told her.

She paused as if putting a piece of the puzzle together. "They're not keeping Tobey with Kenzie." She blinked a few times then shook her head.

"How do you know?"

"Because I heard Weller tell Butch he was going to spend some time in his homeland."

Dane frowned as she continued.

"I didn't know what that meant, but I just remembered.

Butch is from Canada. I have no idea what province or where. I guess it's not a very helpful clue."

"It's still a clue." He rested his hand on her shoulder and smiled. Then he thought of something. "How do you know Kenzie isn't in Canada?"

"I can see palm trees through the window sometimes when she's talking to me."

"Could she still be in Miami?" He remembered that was where Lena said she had her salon.

She shrugged. "There are an awful lot of places with palm trees. That clue is about as helpful as the one about Canada."

"Every little thing helps us get closer to finding our kids. Once we find them, we'll be able to save them." He wanted so badly to rush forward to that part, but he knew successful missions needed to be carefully planned and thought out.

He couldn't just rush in and take Tobey without repercussions. Even if he knew where he would be rushing to. Every contingency needed to be planned for.

"I hope you're right," she said with a weak smile.

"I have a plan, but it means you'll need to trust the rest of my team to help. What do you say?"

"I can't keep lying to my daughter, and I have no idea how to get us out of this." It only took a second for her answer. "I'm definitely in."

He held out his hand and she took it, shaking it firmly.

They were in this together. Both their children were in danger. But now they were a team.

Chapter Thirty-Eight

Dane offered to drive, and Lena handed over the keys easily. Whether it was right to trust him or not, she was tired of going through this nightmare alone. She didn't have the strength to keep going the way she was. And she didn't have the resources to plan a counter attack.

Not that he'd said that was what they were doing…but she hoped so.

She wanted nothing more than to walk into Viktor's home with a dozen soldiers and walk out with her daughter. Maybe she watched too much television.

Whatever Dane's team planned to do, at least it was *something.* She was sick of doing nothing, afraid to make a move and be caught. Her daughter would pay the price if she messed up. But now there was a team of professionals gathering to help them take out Viktor Kulakov.

She glanced over at Dane and smiled. She was so energized and excited, she leaned across the seat and kissed his cheek.

"What was that for?"

"For helping me get my daughter back."

"We're going to do our best, but it won't be easy," he warned. "There are no guarantees."

She was aware. She knew he didn't have special powers. She'd seen the scar on his leg, proof he was a mere mortal. But he was her hero.

"I understand. But if it doesn't work, at least you've given me hope."

He smiled over at her, took her hand, and gave it a squeeze. "We can't do anything without hope."

What a difference it was to travel with him now, compared to a few days ago when he'd hated her. Her lips pulled up wryly at the memories from their earlier encounter.

"You're smiling," he said.

"Am I? I must be thinking about the chocolate shake I'm planning to get for lunch."

"Right." He laughed, the sound warm and comforting.

She liked this man. The fun, happy guy-next-door she knew could morph into a fierce deputy marshal in a flash… or a kind, giving lover. He was the hard outer shell with the soft, gooey center.

A few hours later they needed to stop for fuel. She froze in the midst of running the card and looked up at him.

"We forgot about the gas," she said.

"What?" He reached out for her arm.

"You reserved our hotel room in another state, but we've been paying for gas with this card. Viktor will know we're not heading south any longer."

"You think I'd miss something like that?" He shook his head and smiled easily. "I'm a professional. And you, my lady, insult me."

His joke allowed her to relax. He wouldn't be teasing her if there was danger. "But how…?"

"I text Angel with the information, and she goes in and

changes it. The charge will show up on Viktor's card from a different location."

She made a face. "I'm impressed, but also a little freaked out by your capabilities."

He shrugged. "Not mine. Angel is scary good at this computer stuff."

"Angel?" She smiled. "Is she a real angel? Is that how she's able to see all and know all?"

He laughed at her joke. "No. She's a spunky little thing who has been through hell. I hope you'll get to meet her someday. You'll like her."

"She won't be at the meeting?" Lena was nervous about walking into a room full of marshals. She wasn't exactly on the right side of the law at the moment, with the kidnapping and all. Granted, she wasn't a criminal by choice, but would they care?

"No. Angel and her husband have a new baby. She's not active anymore. Except when I need her." He smirked.

"I'm glad you're both on the good side."

"Sometimes it's difficult to tell which side is good, and which is bad."

She couldn't agree more. She was technically on the bad side, but she sure didn't belong there. "There's no good in Viktor Kulakov," she said.

Even though her daughter was being well cared for, and even had a nanny, Lena knew it wasn't out of the kindness of Viktor's heart. She wasn't deceived into thinking her daughter was safe just because she had a few new dresses and craft time.

"No. There's no confusion on that one," Dane agreed. "He's pure evil. He needs to be stopped."

"Why hasn't he been arrested? He's done so many illegal things. Isn't there anyone who can put him away?" Even just what she'd seen would be enough for an arrest, she'd think.

"The man Viktor sent us to bring back. He can put Viktor away. The D.A. is just waiting for the right time and more hard evidence."

"The right time would have been years ago," she said fiercely. "Before he was able to harm so many people."

"We'll find out more about the case against him at the meeting tonight."

She took her eyes off the road long enough to look over at him. "I'll be welcome at this meeting?"

He nodded. "Of course. You have information that could be helpful. And you have a big stake in the game. Why wouldn't you be welcome?"

"Because I technically work for Viktor."

"You never *worked* for Viktor. You don't have a choice. And as I said, sometimes it's difficult to tell which side is good and which is bad."

Chapter Thirty-Nine

Dane pulled the Jeep into an empty campground an hour after they'd planned to be there. Later in the summer this place would be filled with the hustle and bustle of campers, but for now it was nearly deserted.

He drove past a row of small cabins and stopped in front of the main lodge. He took Lena's hand when she got out of the car. She held onto him tightly until they got to the door of the lodge. Then she let her hand slip from his.

She'd been quiet for the last hour, and he understood why she would be anxious about meeting a whole team of U.S. Deputy Marshals. She probably expected a lot of black suits and dark glasses, but that wasn't how his team worked.

Task Force Phoenix was made up of people from all walks of life who had one thing in common—they were all starting over with a new life. Some of them—like Angel—had made a choice to start over, while others—like Dane—had been forced to start over because their old lives were no longer safe.

They all looked like normal people. Maybe a little more

muscle than the average guy—especially Justin—but they could easily pass for construction workers or bartenders or bodyguards, or pretty much any other profession. And they acted like regular people, for the most part. Other than ducking questions about their pasts.

Lena would see they didn't mean her any harm, and she'd soon warm up to them. Or so he hoped.

He didn't reach for her hand again. Instead, he opened the lodge door and followed her inside. The main room was large and filled with tables. The long table closest to the door was surrounded by people he knew.

Including a few people who shouldn't have been there.

Samantha McKendrick sat next to her father, Supervisory Deputy United States Marshal Josiah Thorne. Sam's husband, Garrett, leaned over her to point at a map in front of them. Across from them, Angel was jumping up with a baby in her arms and a smile on her face. Her husband, Colton, moved his chair to face the newcomers, and Dane gave him a nod.

He was about to make introductions, but was distracted when Sam gasped and rose from her seat.

"Oh, no!" she cried, and moved to come help him. "You're still limping. Because I shot you. I'm so sorry, Dane."

He waved her off. "Don't start. It's not your fault." She had only done what any normal person would do when threatened.

"Kind of her fault," Garrett said with a cough, next to her.

"I didn't realize I'd caused so much damage." Her hand covered her mouth in distress.

"Relax," Dane told her. "The limp is not just from the gunshot wound. It's Angel's fault, too. Her dog bit me in exactly the same spot."

"You're blaming the mother of your godson?" Angel said with a frown he hoped was feigned.

Christ Almighty. The women in his life! If they weren't shooting him, they were guilting him to death.

"Besides, I fixed you up," she added with a bratty little sister smile. She hadn't been able to heal him completely. But he still wasn't blaming anyone.

"I'm fine," he insisted. "I'm just a little stiff from the long car ride."

Sam gave him a wilted smile and went back to sit beside Garrett, who rubbed her arm.

Angel deposited baby John in Dane's arms, and the baby reached out with a fierce little fist and made a disgruntled noise.

For the last five years, these people had been his surrogate family, doing their best to fill the void in Dane's life. He smiled down at the infant he was cuddling, happy to reaffirm his team was about much more than encrypted codes and handguns.

Looking up, he realized everyone was staring a Lena.

Ah. Right.

"Everyone, this is, uh, Lena Scott."

Chapter Forty

As happy as everyone was to see Dane, Lena had felt totally out of place as one by one they noticed her standing behind him. It was obvious they were all good friends. And she was an intruder.

Not just an intruder, but someone who'd played for Team Viktor. They had no way of knowing she'd been forced into it.

One of the men—a giant—narrowed his gaze on her. "Lena Scott? Isn't she the one who knocked you out so Kulakov's men could grab you?" he asked.

Lena swallowed and stepped back. She should have realized they *would* know that. Dane had told his boss everything that had happened that night.

She wasn't going to win them over with that story.

"Yes," admitted Dane. "But she is being coerced into helping Kulakov."

A warm, fuzzy feeling stole through her at his defense of her.

She glanced around the table...and spotted someone she'd seen before. She let out a quick breath of surprise. She'd thought the man seemed familiar when he'd turned to face them, but she assumed she was getting him confused with some tough guy from a movie.

But that wasn't where she knew him from.

Robbie Vanderhook was sitting right in front of her. Smiling.

No. Not smiling. He was beaming with pride as his wife reached for their baby from Dane.

Lena had seen the man—Colton was his name, according to Dane—in photos Viktor had given her to identify him. The man looked different now, but she knew it was him. The difference was the light of happiness in his eyes.

A kind of happiness she had nearly forgotten existed during the last eight months.

Except for those few precious hours with Dane.

Without a moment's hesitation she realized what she had to do.

As Angel took the bundle of burbling baby back into her arms, Lena pulled the gun from the back of Dane's jeans.

And leveled it on the only man who could get her child back.

Chapter Forty-One

Dane was just about to tell everyone Lena was a friend when she swiped the Beretta from his waistband and leveled it on Colton.

Fuck.

This was not the way to make friends. Not with this crowd.

Sure, they liked to joke around about shooting one another, but for the most part it was frowned upon.

"What the hell are you doing?" Angel snapped.

Colton jumped up and put himself between her and the gun. Dane grabbed Angel's arm and pulled her back to safety at the same time Garrett stood to push her out of the way, over by the door.

"Lena, this isn't the way," Dane said calmly, as he would when easing a skittish horse.

Colton held out his hand to Lena in greeting, as if he hadn't noticed she was holding a gun on him. "Hello. You're Lena, right? You know me by another name, but I'm Colton Williamson."

That had not been a wise thing to do. It was obvious from the gasp by the door that Angel agreed.

Lena twitched, and Dane realized what Colton was doing.

"This is my wife, Angel. And our baby, John," Colton said with a smile.

Lena's chin quivered and she pressed her lips together. "I… I'm sorry, but—"

Dane should have realized the temptation would be too great. Kulakov had promised to turn over Kenzie if Lena brought Colton in. Dane knew she was too smart to believe it would go that way, but she wasn't thinking straight at the moment.

She'd recognized an opportunity and was desperate enough to try it. Dane knew, because a similar feeling had shivered down his spine when Colton first smiled at him.

He shook away the thought, embarrassed and disgusted with himself for thinking it, even for a second.

Angel, Colton, and John shouldn't have been here. Destroying a family was not the way to save another one.

"It won't work," Dane whispered in her ear. "Think about it. You know you can't trust Kulakov to do the right thing. Even if you could get away from here with Colton—which will never happen—Viktor will kill Colton, then he'll kill you, and sell Tobey and Kenzie to the highest bidder."

She made a noise of despair, and he knew he was getting through to her.

"You can't win playing his game. You have to be smarter. We'll find another way. One that will get your daughter back safely, and allow all of us to go home to our families."

Everyone but him.

Dane wouldn't have that opportunity. He no longer had a family. Not really.

"It's true. You know Viktor Kulakov," Colton said slowly.

"I still have nightmares about the man."

Lena swallowed loudly but didn't move.

Dane would have been able to unarm her in a few swift moves. Not to mention, the Beretta had an external safety that was still engaged. Which everyone in the room was aware of, except Lena. They were just following his lead. It was important for her to make this decision on her own. Once she realized this wasn't the way to go forward, she'd be ready to join them.

Colton continued to work on her emotions. "If you've spent any time with Kulakov, you know his word isn't worth shit. He ordered me shot six times and walked away while I bled out. He has no regard for human life. He will have someone kill you, and then sell your innocent daughter to some pervert without blinking an eye. But if you put the gun down, we can help you get her back. You can trust us."

The gun shook in her trembling hands and tears welled up in her eyes. "I'll think of something," she said, and used her forearm to wipe away the tears before steadying her aim. "I have to save Kenzie."

Chapter Forty-Two

Different scenarios played through Lena's mind at a dizzying speed. Each time she thought of a way to make this work, her conscience presented another roadblock.

She could walk Colton out to the Jeep, but she had no doubt they would take her out before she even started the engine. Colton was huge, he could overpower her easily.

Plus, he had a baby. He was a father.

She couldn't take John's father away. Even if it was to get Kenzie back. How could she look at her daughter and know what she'd done? She'd be just as bad as Viktor.

But Colton was standing right here in front of her. It seemed so easy just to give Viktor what he wanted, so he would give her what they'd agreed on.

She jumped at the feeling of Dane's breath at her ear. He was so close, yet he hadn't made a move to take the gun from her.

"Please don't do this," he murmured gently. "Please trust me. This won't work. You know it won't."

She knew in her heart this wasn't the right thing to do,

but the temptation was overwhelming. The man that could free her daughter was standing right in front of her. It was so simple to take the easy way out, to follow orders. She wasn't strong enough to come up with another way. She just wanted this nightmare to be over.

By the door, baby John made a sound of impatience and gave a short whine.

Lena's heart squeezed painfully.

Oh God.

No. She couldn't do this.

Disgusted with her own weakness, she gave up and held out the gun out to Dane, who tucked it back in his waistband.

She was shocked when it was Colton who pulled her into his arms and held her as she collapsed from despair and the spent emotion. Tears of shame filled her eyes and rolled down her cheeks as the man whose life she'd threatened attempted to soothe her.

"I'm so s-sorry," she sobbed against him, understanding why Dane hadn't allowed her to say those words to him when she'd been the cause of so much pain. Words were useless. But she said them with sincere regret.

"It's okay. I understand. I do." He rubbed her back. "I'm sorry this is happening to you and your little girl. I'm here to help you," he said as he rocked back and forth, and let her cry all over his shirt. "We all are. We're going to work this out so we can all go home with our children. I promise."

Once the gun was away, Colton's wife, Angel, came back and handed him their baby. It was pretty clear by her expression this woman wasn't as forgiving as her husband. But Lena didn't blame her. Not even a little.

Another man stood with a wry look on his face. "It sure would be nice if we could get together once in a while without pulling guns." He stepped closer. "I'm Garrett. This is my wife Samantha." He pointed to the woman who had apparently shot Dane.

At least Lena hadn't actually pulled the trigger.

"It's nice to meet you," she managed to say, though her voice was still weak from stress and crying.

Had she really pointed a gun at another human being? What was she thinking? She could have killed an innocent man. A husband and father.

Dane's arm came around her, and he pointed to two other men who were now also standing. "This is Justin," he said, indicating the man who had glared at her earlier. He was still glaring. "And this is my boss, Supervisory Deputy United States Marshal Josiah Thorne. He's leading the cavalry, and he's going to tell us how to get our kids back."

"Welcome, Lena," the older gentleman said after Justin grunted a grudging hello and sat back down.

It seemed surreal that everyone was able to move right into normal introductions after she'd just threatened one of them at gunpoint. It was as if they'd instantly forgotten how rude she'd been. She never expected their forgiveness, but if they were still willing to help her get her daughter back, she would find a way to make it up to them.

Dane pulled her tighter against him, and she felt slightly encouraged…until she saw the frown on Marshal Thorne's face. At first she thought he was angry over her theatrics, but then she recognized the look.

Pity.

Her heart dropped to her stomach, panic twisting through her veins.

It was obvious. He had bad news.

And honest to God, she didn't think she'd survive it.

Chapter Forty-Three

"What's wrong?" Dane asked, sensing the sudden stillness in the room.

His team knew something. Something bad. Lena tightened her grip on his fingers.

"Nothing's wrong. Exactly," Thorne said as he gestured to two empty seats, silently suggesting they sit.

"You couldn't locate them?" Dane turned to Angel with a look of shock. He'd never known her not to be able to track someone down. She was a computer whiz and ruthless when it came to hunting bad guys.

"Of course I located them." Her tone of offense brought a smile to his face.

"We weren't able to confirm their location, but we are pretty certain we know where they are. The problem is that we are the extent of the team," Colton said while Thorne nodded in confirmation.

"Are you kidding me?" Dane practically shouted. "*Why*?"

It was ridiculous. This was Viktor Fucking Kulakov. There should be an entire branch of the military devoted to taking him down. In the room were only six marshals. And of those six, two were retired and one had given birth a few months ago.

"Why can't we get support from another task force?" he asked.

"I contacted the federal prosecutor and explained the situation. He said after the last blunder when Kulakov got off, he's not willing to move on the case yet. He still doesn't think he has enough to get a conviction. He says if he moves too soon, the best they might get is a plea bargain to a lesser offence, and Viktor would see daylight again in a few years."

"But we can get him on two counts of kidnapping, and attempted murder," Justin complained. "And that's just with the testimony of the people in this room. Surely, there's enough by now to put him away for good. Colton saw a lot of shit going down."

"Again, I explained all of that, but he's still not convinced."

"Is he on the take?" Dane directed the question toward Angel. He was certain she would have already considered checking the man's accounts.

She shrugged and shook her head. "If he is, I can't find anything. Which means he's either clean, or he's tucked it all away somewhere well hidden, and isn't so much as looking to make sure it's still there."

"What if it's in cash?" Lena asked.

Justin sniffed and rolled his eyes. "Yeah. Maybe Viktor likes to show up at the drop like a baller with a briefcase handcuffed to his wrist like in the movies."

Dane fought the urge to lean across the table and hit him for being rude to her. But since she'd just pulled a gun on one of them, he wasn't quite ready to force everyone to make nice.

"Not a briefcase." Lena swallowed and looked up at him nervously. "Plastic totes."

That got his attention. "You've seen plastic totes of cash

being moved around?" he asked her, rubbing circles on her back as he encouraged her to trust his friends.

She nodded and bit her lip.

"Me, too." Colton backed up her story. "I've even moved a few from his boat, myself. When I was on his payroll he dealt mostly with drafts, but after I turned out to be a plant, I bet he's turned to cash transactions since he knows he's being watched."

"You can't get that much cash in a briefcase, anyway, asshat." Angel stuck her tongue out at Justin who stuck his tongue out back at her. Very mature.

"Can we get around the prosecutor?" Dane asked, trying his best to ignore them.

"No. He must have anticipated we would try. He's cut us off. It didn't matter how high I went, the answer was still 'don't touch him.'"

Lena asked the question Dane was thinking. "Then what are we going to do?"

"We save your children and take in Kulakov, so the prosecutor has no choice but to do his job or show his cards." Thorne looked around at the group. "Did you really think we all gathered here so I could tell you to go home?"

Leave it to Thorne to be amused by their concern. Decades in the government had worn him down to the point he often came off as cold or unfeeling, but Dane knew differently. Under that crusty shell was a man who cared about all of them like they were his real children.

Angel rolled her eyes. "If we weren't going to do anything, I could have told Dane when we talked the other day and saved us all the time," she pointed out. "We couldn't talk about a plan over the phone, in case they were somehow listening. If Kulakov has bought himself a prosecutor, who knows who else he's paid for."

"I appreciate your support, but we're only five people."

Dane pointed out. Some of them were worthy of being counted as two, but still they weren't enough for a tactical assault on a madman.

"He didn't count you," Angel said to Colton. "That's so rude." She turned on Dane. "Colton is a great agent. He might not have been on our team, but he's one of us."

Oh. Boy. Dane cringed inwardly. How would he get out of this one?

Colton coughed and looked up at the ceiling.

"What?" She darted a look around the table, then understanding dawned. "*Me?*" Her bright blue eyes fixed on Dane like lasers. He could almost feel the heat. "You didn't count *me*? Why wouldn't you count me? I'm a deadly force, and—"

"Um, Angel." Justin pointed toward his own shirt with a wince. "I think you're leaking."

She glanced down and took in the growing wet spot on her chest and let out a sigh. "Give me the baby," she ordered. "But when I get back from nursing, you had better let me be in on this mission, Dane Ryan. Or else."

"We'll find something for her to do," Colton said when his wife was safely in the other room.

"At least she didn't start crying again. The crying kills me," Justin shook his head.

Dane studied the faces around the table. His friends. These people had become like a family to him when he'd lost his own. He frowned as he mentally calculated the risks. Without reinforcements, they would all be in greater danger. And yet they were all here, ready and willing to take that risk to help save his child.

He knew if the tables were turned, he would be sitting in one of their seats planning a raid to get baby John back without a thought to the danger for himself.

Five years ago, Dane had stepped out of his life and left

his wife and son so they would be safe. He'd thought his life was over. But he'd been wrong. He had his team.

And now he had Lena.

"What's the plan?" he asked, ready to get started.

Chapter Forty-Four

It didn't take long for Lena to realize these people were more than just co-workers. They were a family. They might not share the same genes, but they shared a bond that went deeper than DNA.

She saw the way Colton clasped Dane's shoulder. The unspoken communication between them. One father telling another it was okay, and they knew what the other was going through.

A rush of envy shook her. How much easier it would have been if she'd had someone to talk to, or to pat her on the shoulder and tell her it was okay.

She met Dane's gaze and she realized she now had him. If anyone knew what she was feeling, it was Dane. He was in the same situation, worried for his child, but forced to keep going.

Giving up wasn't an option, and if these people were willing to face Viktor Kulakov outnumbered and against orders, she would gratefully accept their aid. And she'd do whatever she could to help.

Glancing around at the muscles and firepower in the

room made her feel inadequate. Would she be able to help, or would she just be in the way? She'd only ever touched a gun once in her life and it had been that day.

The thought of turning into that cowardly mouse who hid in the corner made tears come to her eyes, but she managed to keep them from falling.

She'd learned from the first night after Kenzie was taken that curling up in a ball and letting the grief and worry claim her, didn't help the situation. Not if she wanted to save her daughter.

Now was her chance to do something. She wasn't a helpless mouse hiding in the corner any longer. She was a vicious warrior, determined to get her child back safe and sound.

Like a choreographed routine, the team members each took a turn sharing intel and offering suggestions. Angel was tapping on her laptop keyboard, giving answers to questions as they were asked. Justin took down notes in a notebook and assigned tasks to the people on the team.

"If you have anything to add, just jump in and say it," Dane whispered to her. "This is fact gathering, and you may have some piece of information we still need."

"I'll help wherever I can," she promised and turned back to the group. She would tell this team everything she could to help their mission. They would not fail because she didn't reveal one of Kulakov's secrets.

Unfortunately, he had never trusted her enough to allow her into his inner circle where she might have learned something that would actually be helpful. She was shocked by how much the team knew already, but then, Colton had lived and worked undercover for Kulakov for almost two years. He had been in deep and knew Viktor well.

Right up until Viktor knew Colton too well, and had him shot and left for dead.

"Your daughter will call you tomorrow?" Justin said, shaking her from her thoughts. "Do you video chat?"

"Yes." And Lena's heart would break into even smaller pieces when her daughter asked if she was coming for her. At least she knew the answer wasn't a lie anymore. She *would* be coming. And it really would be soon.

"Can you record the call so can we can take a look at the background?"

"Of course."

The man, Justin, didn't glare at her this time. He was all business. She appreciated his efficiency. Despite how he might feel about her personally, it was clear he wouldn't allow his emotions to jeopardize the mission.

She looked around the busy table. The marshals were passing around photos, making notes, and pointing out flaws and strengths. The intensity level in the room kept rising as they fed off each other's ideas.

One person threw out a suggestion and the next person took that and improved on it, or pointed out a weakness.

Colton ran a cable from the large television on the wall over to Angel's laptop. She nodded and connected the line.

"Okay. I just hacked into the satellite. I'm moving it now, so we'll have visual in a few minutes on both of the kids' suspected locations."

Lena swallowed. How had this happened? The salon manager from Miami was in a room with soldiers and space pirates.

Chapter Forty-Five

Dane reached out to tug on the end of Lena's ponytail. When she glanced over at him, he winked, hoping to reassure her. She'd turned pale and seemed more than a little overwhelmed.

He knew it wasn't normal for people to share a bag of potato chips while waiting for the feed to come in from the satellite they'd hijacked.

"Are you sure she's not an actual angel? She *is* in control of the heavens," Lena whispered.

"Trust me, she's too devious to be the real deal."

Thorne moved his chair so he could see the big screen, and crossed his arms as the picture came up.

"It's your turn. Enlighten us with your brilliance," Justin said, earning a glare from Angel.

Dane chuckled. No doubt, she assumed Justin was patronizing her, but the truth was, they always relied on her to get them where they needed to go. They might have intel and other people working the tech, but they all looked to Angel to verify it was legit. She could hack into anything.

It was both frightening and impressive.

"We will definitely need two teams if we plan to strike simultaneously." Angel used her pointer to indicate two different targets…with the whole United States in between them. One was in western Canada and the other just north of Florida.

"It's imperative that we hit both locations at the same time. Once Viktor realizes we've double-crossed him, he'll be looking for revenge," Dane said.

He'd figured the operation wouldn't be convenient, since Lena mentioned palm trees and also where Butch was born. Until now, Dane hadn't worried about that. He thought they would have plenty of people to direct a proper coordinated assault.

Now they only had the people in this room.

Angel frowned and stood up. "You're right. But Tobey and Kenzie are about as far apart as they can get and still be in North America."

She rested her hip on the table so she could lean over to circle a place on the paper map with a marker. Vancouver. Then she edged off so she could circle another place closer to her. Savannah, Georgia.

"Viktor always sets up in port towns," Colton said. "I've never been to the Vancouver complex, but I've spent some time at his place in Savannah. I can draw up a map of the inside." He pulled over a tablet and picked up a stylus to start drawing.

"Here's the satellite map of the Vancouver complex," Angel pointed to the screen. The picture was so detailed Dane could see the men patrolling the gate. Unlike with Google Earth, the pictures were live, and the men were moving.

He swallowed. Because the complex was so huge, they would need to stay hidden while they found Tobey, then they would somehow have to get him out undetected, along with any other children that might be with him. Due to the small size of their team, a frontal attack was off the table. Which meant stealth and a quiet extraction. They couldn't risk stirring up the hornet's nest.

"Tobey says they have bunk beds. There are other boys with him," Dane reminded everyone.

Garrett tapped the screen. "My guess is they're being kept here. There are guards posted at the end of this long building. It could be a bunk house."

"Viktor has a bunkhouse at Savannah, too." Colton pointed at the building on the printed satellite map on the table. "He keeps people here until he has enough to ship out in a container."

"From what Lena's described of the place where Kenzie's being held," Justin said, "it's not the bunk house. I'll know more when she calls tomorrow and we can see what's in the background. Hopefully Colton will recognize it."

"It's okay if you don't," Angel said from behind him as she wrapped her arms around his neck. "Don't put so much pressure on yourself." She kissed his temple.

"I spent more time in Philadelphia and Gulfport," Colton explained regretfully. "But I'll do my best."

Even if Colton's knowledge of the Savannah complex was limited, it was more than they knew about the facility where Tobey was being held. Dealing with more boys would also complicate their mission.

Dane hoped they would be able to locate the kids quickly and get them out without alerting anyone. They wouldn't have enough people to engage in a firefight. Not while protecting a group of children.

He looked around the table and wondered how they would be split up. That was Thorne's call. While this wasn't a sanctioned mission, he was still in charge.

Any marshal around this table would be an asset to the mission, so Dane didn't have a preference as to who he was partnered with. He just wanted to get going. He wanted to do something. But he knew they couldn't move until every detail had been worked out.

They couldn't afford to be sloppy or impatient.

Too much was at stake.

Chapter Forty-Six

Lena remained quiet as Task Force Phoenix worked out the particulars of the assault like any other people might plan a birthday party. Justin had gone out to get pizza and beer, and they laughed and told stories while they ate.

They used a lot of acronyms which left her confused, but Lena got the general feel. They had to trust each other with their lives, which had obviously created a bond far deeper than the one she'd had with the stylists at her salon.

No one would end up dead if she cut someone's bangs too short. At least, not every time.

She was actually settling in and feeling like this would all work out until the alarm went off on her phone. Everyone abruptly fell silent and whipped their gazes to her.

"It's time for me to call in to Viktor," she said nervously.

Angel snapped her fingers as if just remembering something. "You need to give him something, some information, so he thinks you're getting somewhere. We're going to need a few more days and we don't want him to get impatient."

"Right." Lena gave a half smile. "We wouldn't want to make Viktor wait when he's so eager to kill people."

Justin laughed at her inappropriate humor. "I think I like her, after all."

Angel handed a paper to Lena and one to Dane. "I've written out scripts, but feel free to improvise if needed."

"You want me to give him this name? Is that safe?" Dane asked, looking surprised.

Thorne nodded. "Yeah. It's a perp who ran off to Mexico before we could grab him up. If we can get Viktor to use his resources to find him, it helps us with another case. And it will keep him chasing his tail for a little while, until we're ready to strike."

Dane's boss was a genius.

Lena took a calming breath, and dialed the number for Viktor. The paper shook in her hand.

"Where are you?" Viktor asked, his voice gruff as if he'd been sleeping. It was almost one o'clock in the morning. But he was the one who'd given her that time to call. She was only doing her job.

She started reading from Angel's script, trying to sound natural.

"We're outside of San Antonio," she told him. "We have a lead."

It was difficult to concentrate with everyone staring at her.

"It's about damn time. Tell me."

"I got him to give me his name." Her voice shook and she swallowed, forcing herself to keep calm so she could play her part.

"Vanderhook's real name?"

She lowered her voice as if trying to hide what she was saying. "The one he's been using in Witness Protection. It's Evan Masters. We went to the construction site where he's been working and showed his photo to his co-workers. They said it's him. He's not scheduled to be there today or tomorrow, but he'll be on site on Thursday. The only address they had for him was a P.O. box, so we'll have wait for—"

Dane suddenly came at her like he meant to strangle her, shouting and getting in her face. "You stupid bitch! What the hell are you doing?"

Chapter Forty-Seven

Dane cringed at the instant look of guilt and terror on Lena's face at his unexpected attack. It brought back memories he'd just as soon forget. Like the way she'd looked for those first few days when he'd treated her so badly.

Hell, he'd just been trying to make it sound realistic. Maybe he'd gone a little overboard.

"Sorry," he mouthed, then picked up the phone she'd dropped in shock, and handed it back to her with a smile. He pointed to the script and tapped a finger to her line, hoping she would realize it was all part of the act.

"Hello? Hello?" Viktor's voice echoed into the room.

"I'm here," she said, cringing as Dane lit into her again.

"You realize he doesn't need us now?" he snapped. "You've just given him the name and place to pick up the guy. I'm expendable, which means my son is expendable, too."

"Give Mr. Ryan the phone," Viktor ordered so loudly they all heard the command.

"Uh, okay." Lena held out the phone and Dane winked at her as he took it.

"What?" he demanded. It wasn't difficult to act belligerent when speaking to Kulakov. Dane really did hate this man, he didn't need to pretend.

"We had an agreement, did we not? You were to bring… Evan Masters *to* me. I will release Tobey to you when you do. There has been no change in plan."

"Bullshit," Dane said angrily. "I bet you have your two giants heading out the door for San Antonio right now. If they get to him first, I'll have nothing to leverage to get my son back."

"I assure you, my men are still standing next to me as I speak. Retrieve Mr. Masters and bring him to Savannah. I'll give you the details when you're en route. Put Lena back on the phone. And Mr. Ryan?"

"What?"

"Let's not forget our manners. Ms. Scott is a valued employee and I'll not have her mistreated."

"Fuck that, and fuck you, too," Dane mumbled under his breath as a final parting shot, to up the realism factor.

Lena gave him a smile of agreement, then flipped the phone the finger before she got back on, her face falling. "I'm here."

"Call me at eleven tomorrow."

"That long?"

"You'll have nothing new to report while you wait for Mr. Masters. Get some rest. I'll want to make sure you're in position for the next day."

"Okay. I'll talk to you then." The call was disconnected on his end before she finished the sentence.

As soon as she looked up, Dane had his arms around her.

"Sorry I startled you," he said against her hair.

"I wish I'd had a moment to prepare for that," she said with a laugh.

Angel shook her head. "He did good. It was better that

you were surprised."

"You're both up for Oscars," Samantha offered with a smile, and yawned. "If it's okay, I'm going to go to bed. I don't have much to bring to the table and I'm exhausted."

"Let's all break for the evening," Thorne said before turning to Lena and Dane. The frown of pity was back. "There's one part of this plan you're not going to like."

Thorne let out a breath as everyone started moving for the door, looking anywhere but at Dane.

It didn't take a genius to know what was coming.

"No." Dane shook his head. "No fucking way."

Chapter Forty-Eight

"What is it?" Lena didn't understand. Dane and Thorne knew each other well enough to communicate without speech, but she was left not knowing what was going on. "What's wrong?"

Dane didn't answer. Instead he released her and took a step toward his boss. A very intimidating step.

Everyone stopped and turned back to them.

"That's bullshit and you know it. I was there when you crossed the line to meet your daughter. I'm damn well going to be on the mission to get my son."

"I waited until it was safe," Thorne defended. This comment brought on a muttered cough from Garrett. Thorne glared at him, then said, "I did not let my emotions get in the way of a mission or put anyone else in danger."

"That's strange, because I distinctly remember being shot in the fucking leg!" Dane gestured to his injury.

Samantha winced. "I'm so sorry about that," she apologized yet again.

"Neither you nor Lena can be trusted to behave as anything but worried parents. And rightfully so. But I can't jeopardize the rest of the team and this mission because you lose your shit when you see Tobey."

"We're not allowed to go?" Lena understood now.

She stood to place herself at Dane's back, both physically and metaphorically. No one could keep her from helping to save Kenzie. Thorne wasn't *her* boss. He couldn't tell her what to do.

"I have a suggestion," Angel said as she patted the bundle in her arms.

"Babe, I don't think—"

"I know, I know. I've been a little emotional since John was born. But a mother will fight for her child with a vengeance no soldier can ever feel. We can use that."

"She'll be a liability," Thorne said firmly.

"She'll be an unstoppable banshee blowing down their door," Angel corrected.

"The Queen of Irrational Mood Swings has a point," Justin said.

Angel stuck out her tongue and he did the same back to her. Lena almost smiled. These two might actually be fun under normal circumstances.

Thorne let out a breath and stood to pace, tapping his index finger against his chin. "Okay. Angel, you're home base, you'll be our eyes and ears. Justin and Garrett will move in for Tobey at the exact time Dane, Lena, and myself move in for Kenzie."

"Uh, you forgot someone," Colton raised his hand.

"You'll watch the baby," Thorne said.

"You're serious? I would be an asset. I know the complex." Colton looked around the group as if they were all crazy.

Lena had to agree. The guy was huge. Why wouldn't they use that?

"You're too big of a temptation," Dane said, shaking his head.

Lena bit her bottom lip as a wave of guilt came over her. She had no plans to turn him over, but she knew from her earlier lack of judgment she couldn't be trusted when push came to shove. She wasn't sure what she might do if her choices were taken away. People were capable of doing anything when under pressure, whether it be pulling the door off a car or pulling a gun on a perfectly decent human being.

This was her daughter. She didn't want Colton too close. Just in case.

"He's right," she said softly, apologizing with her eyes.

He pushed out a breath. "Fine. I'm a temptation. He wants me. What Angel said. I'm a father, too. Use me—that—to your advantage," Colton said.

Thorne glanced at Angel. She was looking down at the baby in her arms, but moved her head ever so slightly from side to side. An imperceptible answer to an unspoken question. No.

She was using Thorne to protect the father of *her* child.

"I'm sorry, but you're staying here." Thorne's tone was quick and decisive. No one said another word.

Lena understood Dane's obvious frustration. He was not on the team going after his own son. Though selfishly, she was relieved he would be staying with her. She didn't know these other people. And pulling a gun on one of them probably hadn't endeared her to them enough to ask them to risk their lives for her. Her child, maybe, but not her.

As everyone finally dispersed, she followed Dane when he stepped closer to his boss. She wouldn't be strong enough to stop Dane if he attacked the older man, but maybe she could slow him down slightly.

"Sir—"

"I know what you're going to say, and I'm sorry, the answer is still no. You're on Kenzie's team. Garrett and Justin will be able to get to Tobey. If you don't want to do that, you can take care of the baby with Colton."

"No, sir." Dane pushed past the man and went outside, leaving Lena there with Thorne.

"Thank you," she whispered.

"I have a daughter, too, and I would do anything to keep her safe." He smiled at Lena. "I'll leave you to calm him down and talk some sense into him." He gave her a nod goodnight.

"Thanks a lot," she said, then sighed before heading out to face her insurmountable task.

Chapter Forty-Nine

Dane walked out into the darkness and breathed in the cool night air. Unfortunately, the tension was still there in his whole body. He was being forced to leave his child's life in the hands of others. People he loved like family, and knew would risk everything—as he would—to get Tobey out safe. It just…wasn't the same thing.

He needed to be there. He needed to know his son was okay.

"I'm sorry," Lena said behind him.

He was happy for her support, but a silly twinge of envy shuddered through him. She was going after her child when he was being denied the same opportunity.

"It's not right," she whispered as she came around and snaked her arms around his waist, and held him tight.

He stubbornly held back, until she kissed his chin. Unable to resist the comfort of her, he gave in with a sigh. "No. It isn't," he grumbled, not ready to give up.

"I know you want to be on Tobey's team," she said, "and I wouldn't stand in your way if you wanted to push it further.

But…I don't know these other marshals. I'm sure they're very good. You trust them, so that would be good enough for me. It's just…I need *you* with me."

Dane went still at her words.

Lena and Kenzie needed him.

But Tobey needed him, too.

Dane needed a moment alone.

The rest of the team had already taken the small cabins closest to the bathhouse. Which left the three empty cabins at the end of the row. He walked Lena to the cabin next to Angel and Colton, kissed her forehead, then walked away without a word.

He wasn't angry at her. It felt good to be needed. But at the moment, he could only think about Tobey. If something went wrong…

Before he realized where he was going, he found himself at the lake. He walked out onto the dock and sat down. The moon reflected off the surface of the water, making pretty silver patterns. But he was in no mood to appreciate the beauty.

"Christ," he said to no one. He was so tense he wanted to hit something. He pulled up a splinter of wood from the dock with clenched fingers, broke it angrily into pieces, and tossed it into the dark depths.

He was so focused on the ripples in the water he didn't hear the sound of footsteps on sun-warped wood until they were right beside him.

He looked up to see Thorne sitting down next to him.

"You know I'm right," his boss said.

Thorne came off as a little harsh, a little rough. It was probably how he had coped with walking away from his wife and child all those years ago.

Dane understood the pain, having done the same thing himself. But that was where they were different. He'd had no choice. His family was being threatened. Dane had known the only way to keep them safe was to take himself—as well as the danger—out of their lives.

It was different for Thorne. As far as any of them knew, he'd willingly accepted a covert, black ops job that would mean walking out on his wife and child for good. He hadn't been forced into it. His family had never been in danger.

Dane couldn't imagine how anyone could do that if they didn't have to.

"I made a decision, and it was the best one for everyone," Thorne repeated with a defiant tilt to his head.

"It sounds like you're trying to convince yourself as much as me," Dane said, tossing another piece of wood into the lake.

"If you fucked something up and it got Tobey killed, you would hate yourself for the rest of your life. I won't set you up for that kind of regret. Trust me, it's unbearable."

Damn it if he wasn't right. He'd known in his head his boss was making the best call. His heart just wasn't ready to accept it yet. He knew Thorne wasn't making this decision to punish him. He was protecting Dane from the possibility of failure.

"You have regrets, boss?" Dane asked.

"Many."

"How did you do it?" Dane asked the question he'd wanted to know for years.

"Do what?" Thorne asked, though Dane was sure his boss knew exactly what he meant. He was just stalling.

"How did you walk away from your wife and Samantha?"

Thorne let out a breath and shook his head. He didn't answer for a long time. The still night stretched out, until finally he spoke again.

"At the time I was offered the position, it wasn't that difficult to walk away from my wife. My previous job had me away a lot, and she was constantly suspicious. Bitter. My work finished off a marriage that was already struggling."

Dane could understand that, but he'd had a child, too. Whatever happened between Thorne and his wife, his daughter had paid the ultimate price.

"As for Samantha," Thorne said, "I figured it would be easier for her if I was completely out of the picture. If I'd stayed in her life, she would have been used to punish me. I wouldn't get to see her. My wife would fight me at every turn, even if we divorced. With my sensitive job, I didn't have time for a battle, or to give Samantha the life she deserved. I thought it was better just to disappear."

Thorne plucked a piece of the dock away and tossed it into the water, hitting one of the rings Dane had created on the surface.

Dane's own marriage had been strained to the point of breaking, as well. He'd felt bad walking away. Who knew? They might have had a chance if he'd been able to stay. Maybe they could have gone to counseling and found a way back to each other again.

But he had been changed by what he'd had to face at work. The decisions he'd been forced to make. Then the ordeal with the FBI, and facing the choice to "die" and go into Witness Protection. He hadn't a clue how to get back to his old self, so how could he expect her to love whoever he became after going through all that?

Walking away from Caroline hadn't been easy, but it didn't break him. However, it *had* been torture to leave his son that morning.

He still remembered promising Tobey they would watch his favorite animated movie when he got home from work that evening. All the while knowing he wouldn't ever be back. He'd had to fight the urge to hug his boy goodbye with more emotion than his normal morning routine.

It had been the last time he'd touched his son. The memory was still something he couldn't summon without his throat getting tight.

The morning he left, he hadn't wanted to alert his wife or make her suspicious, so he'd done no more than a casual peck on the lips and, "Have a great day."

She'd responded with the same words and a frown, knowing his days at work hadn't been great for some time. He wanted her to say something more. To tell him he shouldn't go. That they could move far away, or that she trusted him to do what was best for their family and would stand by him.

Instead, the frown was replaced by a brittle smile. The one she presented to the world to prove that everything in her life was perfect. Even when it was falling to pieces around her.

He'd sat in the driveway for a few minutes, looking up at the fancy home he'd purchased with dirty money. At the time he hadn't known, but that wasn't always an excuse. He should have looked deeper. He should have suspected something wasn't right.

They'd showered him with gifts, promotions, and bonuses. He hadn't realized his soul was being purchased by two men who had no souls of their own. By the time he'd figured it out, he was deeply embroiled in their crimes.

It shamed him to know he hadn't acted right away when he found out what he'd gotten himself into. It had been such a shock, he'd been certain he had it wrong. Three months later he contacted the FBI and learned they were already well into an investigation.

But Thorne hadn't been faced with anything like that. He hadn't been forced into his actions.

"I do regret leaving the way I did," Thorne said. "And I definitely didn't realize what I had missed until I got Samantha back."

That made more sense. Dane knew from experience how unpredictable love for a child could be. He'd thought he was ready when they had Tobey, but those emotions were way more powerful than he'd ever expected. He hadn't understood how he could love that loud, stinky, bundle of wrinkles so damn much.

Thorne had left before Sam was born, so he hadn't felt that overwhelming love before making his decision. He wouldn't have known. Things may have ended differently if he had.

"Your situation is much different than mine," Thorne said. "You did what you had to do to keep your family safe. I looked over your file before I approached you. Your wife wasn't willing to move, even after you explained the danger." He leaned back, resting his palms on the wood behind him. "I'm sure you think it was because she didn't love you enough, or that she was stubborn, but I doubt it was like that."

Dane thought it was.

"Regular people don't respond to the possibility of danger the way you think they should," Thorne said. "They disregard the warnings and deny the inevitability of real danger."

Dane nodded. "Yeah. I've seen the movies where the scientists say everyone should evacuate but no one listens."

They shook their heads together. "It's almost always like that, I'm afraid. It makes our job much more difficult. We're like those scientists."

"But with guns."

Thorne chuckled. "Yeah." After a long silence, he took a breath and moved on to another topic. "Tobey knows you're not dead," he said with a sigh.

Dane grimaced. "It couldn't be helped."

"I know. But it means we'll have to have a chat with him about his safety, and hope he listens better than the people on the news."

"He's a smart kid. I think I can get through to him. If I have the chance."

"You'll have the chance." Thorne smacked Dane on the leg then got to his feet. Fortunately, it was Dane's good leg.

"Since he knows…" Dane swallowed, afraid to ask and have his hope destroyed.

Thorne smiled. "It means he won't be so shocked when you show up again, later in his life."

Dane closed his eyes and pressed his lips together as emotions flooded through him. Those were the words he'd hoped for. Permission to reach out to Tobey someday, when he was old enough to be discreet.

Dane hadn't kept his promise to watch the movie that evening, but hopefully, one day, he could make up for it.

Chapter Fifty

Lena dressed for bed and climbed between the cool sheets with a shiver. There was no heat in the cabin and it was chilly, despite having the windows closed. Even with the extra blanket from the closet she couldn't seem to get warm.

The chill was coming from deep inside her.

She'd actually pulled a gun on someone. She could have killed an innocent man. The father of an adorable little baby. Someone's husband.

Her fingers flexed as she remembered feeling the gun in her hand.

Another shiver racked her body as she heard steps on the tiny front porch of the cabin. Her heart began to race. The door was locked, but it was flimsy, and half the door was glass. It wouldn't keep anyone out if they wanted to get in.

There was a knock, and her heart slowed as she turned on the small lamp next to the bed and crept out from under the covers to answer the door.

It was Dane.

He let out a sigh and shook his head. "I was going to

come up with some reason why I needed to talk to you so you'd let me in, but I don't want any more lies. I'm not in a good place right now. I don't want to be alone. I might do something ridiculous like break down and cry."

She smiled in understanding, and opened the door wider. "Well, we can't have the tough deputy marshal crying, now can we?" she said gently as he walked into the cabin.

"I wasn't cut out for this tough-guy thing. I was a financial officer in my past life. Finance officers can cry if they need to. There aren't a lot of expectations."

She laced her hands uncertainly, not quite sure why he'd come. He hadn't exactly been warm and fuzzy when they parted. "I guess not. How did you get this job?"

"You mean agree to fake my own death?" he asked wryly.

She nibbled on her lip. "That couldn't have been an easy decision."

"I did it for the sake of my family. I'd promised to testify against my bosses in exchange for witness protection, but I was dealing with a lot of guilt about how I'd handled things. I hadn't come forth right away, and found out later that two people had died as a result of my inaction."

"My God. I'm so sorry."

He swallowed and ran his hand through his hair. "One day Thorne showed up and asked if I wanted the chance to redeem myself. It was as if he'd read my mind."

"Wouldn't be surprised. He's a little scary."

Dane laughed. "True. I thought it would give me something meaningful to do while I waited for the case to go to trial. I owed two lives. So, I joined Task Force Phoenix. I figured if I saved two people, I'd have paid my debt."

"Did you?"

He nodded. "But then I didn't just want to be even. I wanted to have Karma credit." He winked at her. "Eventually I stopped counting. It just became me. It's what I do now."

She went to him and wrapped her arms around him. He enveloped her in his warmth.

"Now, I'm hoping Karma kept count," he whispered. "Because I need a big favor."

She wanted to tell him everything was going to work out and be okay, but he'd said he didn't want any more lies between them. She hoped it wasn't a lie, but she just wasn't sure.

Tomorrow they would be preparing for the raid on two of Viktor's holdings to rescue their children. Tonight, they were simply a man and a woman who didn't want to be alone with their thoughts.

She leaned back enough to look up into his face. As she attempted to remember how to make a move on a man, his lips came down on hers.

Chapter Fifty-One

Dane needed Lena. There was no way around that fact. Whatever happened with this mission was out of his hands at the moment. Right now, the only thing he could focus on was that they were two terrified people who needed each other.

This morning, he might have said they just needed the distraction. A moment of pleasure with another warm body, to give them a break from the constant fear and anxiety. But now he realized it wasn't just a distraction that had made him knock on her door.

He wanted *Lena*. No one else would do.

She was the only one who understood what he was feeling. She was the only one who was going through the same thing he was. He'd told her they were in this together. That meant this part, too.

She moaned as he moved his lips down her neck to her collarbone. He slid one hand into her hair and the other under the back waistband of her shorts. He didn't want to go at her like a ravenous beast, but his need was too urgent for him to control. He decided to give in to it, and silently promised to make it up in round two.

He picked her up and stumbled when his leg reminded him it wasn't capable of such things. He cursed and set her back down. This injury frustrated him more each day.

"It's okay. I don't mind walking to the bed. It's just a few feet away." She gave him a naughty smile.

She turned to go, but he stopped her and pulled down her shorts, then slipped off her shirt and nodded. If he was going to watch her walk away from him, he wanted to enjoy it.

"I'll give you a head start," he said.

He stripped his shirt off and stalked toward her. She'd gotten into bed and her naked body was stretched out before him, ready.

He set his Beretta on the nightstand, unbuckled his belt, then sat at the end of the bed to unlace his boots. Her bare foot slid up his spine and back down.

Turning to seize her ankle, he kissed her just below the knee and pulled her closer so he could nibble up her thigh. One more tug had her at the edge of the bed. He kneeled down so he was in the perfect position to taste her.

Her legs draped over his shoulders as he licked her, causing her to moan and buck against him. He smiled and did it again, and again, until she was panting and pulling his hair.

His name came out as breathy pleading, and he locked it away in his memories to recall later.

"Please, Dane," she begged.

He was torn between moving up her body and giving them the quick release they both wanted, or finishing her off first. Unsure if he could get up, he decided to go for the second option.

Inserting two fingers, he picked up the pace with his tongue, making her gasp. Relentlessly, he worked her until she cried out and clenched his fingers in fitful pulses. He didn't stop, only slowed until the tremors softened and her legs fell away.

With her sated for the moment, he had time to get himself off the floor and remove his pants without her noticing his struggle. He might not be able to literally sweep a woman off their feet any longer, but as he looked down on Lena with that contented smile across her face, he knew he was still a man who could satisfy a woman.

His injury hadn't taken that from him, at least.

Chapter Fifty-Two

Lena hadn't bothered to move. She was probably splayed out in some awkward pose, but she couldn't care at the moment. She felt too good. He'd come to her for comfort, and she would do her best to make him feel good.

She felt the shift of the mattress as Dane stood, then the heavenly sound of steel teeth unlocking as his zipper was pulled down. Opening her eyes, she watched as he slid his jeans down his legs and moved for his boxers.

Despite the scars on his leg, she found him incredibly sexy. She also knew those weren't the only scars he carried. There were many more on his heart, and she wished she could soothe those.

She moved first. Rolling onto her stomach, she used the elastic waist to pull him closer, and slid the soft cotton down his narrow hips. His erection sprang out when released, and she nuzzled it momentarily before guiding in into her mouth.

With a curse, he lurched backward, but not far enough to disengage. Braced on one elbow she looked up at him and pulled him closer again. She loved the power she held at the moment. For months she'd been powerless, but Dane had given her some control over her life. And his pleasure.

His hand went to her hair as he made a noise of pleasure, but he didn't dictate her rhythm. He allowed her to set the pace. This simple freedom didn't go unnoticed. Even earlier when she'd made a colossal mistake by pulling that gun, he'd allowed her the space to figure it out and do the right thing.

Once she was sure he wouldn't pull away, she used her hand to roam over his other parts. Cupping and teasing him until he groaned.

She continued exploring him with her hand and mouth… until suddenly he shook his head and pulled away.

"No more," he said, his voice rough, and reached for a condom. Their gazes locked and she saw so much more than just a battered body and flexing muscle. She saw Dane. The man who—despite dealing with his own tragedy—was helping her with hers.

She trusted him completely.

Seconds later, in a flurry of motion she found herself on her back. He pushed inside her with one long stroke.

He lifted her leg to his shoulder so he could get deeper inside her, and she tilted her hips to meet his hurried movements until he tensed and collapsed on top of her. His pulses shattered her, and she joined him in release.

His hot breath touched her hair as a drop of sweat meandered down her chest.

Her earlier chill had been replaced by his warmth. That warmth spread deep into her soul.

Chapter Fifty-Three

Dane woke from a restful sleep with Lena warm and naked in his arms.

Last night he'd been a mess of tangled thoughts and worries, but now he was relaxed and ready to face whatever the day would bring. She'd given him more than just a physical release.

Having her next to him gave him a peace he hadn't felt in so long.

It was still early and he wasn't ready to move. His cock stirred, and he revised his initial plan to get up. He was ready to move, just not to get out of bed.

He reached for another condom, then positioned himself behind her and slid into her welcome warmth. Lying on his side, he was able to rock into her slowly without too much strain on his leg.

She made a happy sound, but didn't open her eyes as she pressed back against him. He kissed her shoulder and moved down to her neck, unable to get to her mouth from this angle.

He wrapped his arm around her, pulling her closer, then

moved down her stomach and between her legs, until he found the spot that woke her fully and had her moaning in response.

Her breath picked up, and a few minutes later she gasped and bucked as her orgasm throbbed around him. He moved his hand to her breasts and held her as he built up the momentum to his own completion.

"Good morning," she whispered a few moments later.

He smiled against her warm skin. "Definitely."

With his hand on her chest, he felt her heart slow to a normal rhythm. She took a deep breath and readied herself to say something that he just knew would bring them slamming back to reality.

"No. Not yet. Give us another minute," he begged.

She patted his arm and slipped away. "You stay here wrapped in denial for a little while longer, while I go take a shower."

"Okay," he answered.

But it was too late. Reality was already encroaching on his delusions. They had things to do.

Important things.

This thing between them was just a way to cope until it was time to set the operation in motion. As soon as they got their kids back, their lives would continue on in different directions. And this…interlude…would simply be a memory of two people helping each other through the worst moment of their lives.

Chapter Fifty-Four

When Lena walked into the lodge together with Dane, everyone instantly fell quiet and looked up. She got the distinct feeling the others had been talking about her.

God. Had she and Dane been too loud last night? Were they all judging her?

Despite the way the morning had started, it didn't take long for the guilt to seep back in. This wasn't the right time to start anything with a man. Especially a man who had his own demons to slay.

She and Dane were both in a horrible place, but that just made them need each other all the more. If nothing else, their pleasure had allowed her to get some sleep, so she felt alert this morning. She was able to think things through with more clarity, now that her mind had been stripped bare and allowed a moment to relax.

There were guns sitting on the dining table where everyone had gathered for breakfast, and she couldn't help but notice Garrett moved his gun closer to his empty plate as she walked over to the table.

They still didn't trust her. Probably for good reason. Her face heated as she remembered her actions from the evening before. Embarrassment made her throat tight.

She took a deep breath and said, "I want to apologize again for what I did yesterday."

Colton wasn't at the table, but he must have heard her through the opening that led to the kitchen where he was making breakfast with Samantha.

"No more apologies," he said, pointing authoritatively at her with a spatula. "I'm fine, and I understand why you might have thought that was your only option."

"I wasn't really worried," Angel said as she burped the baby. "You still had the safety on. If you had pulled the trigger, nothing would have happened."

Lena's jaw dropped in surprise. "Oh." That should have made her feel better, but now she just felt more embarrassed.

"She should learn how to handle a gun," Justin said with a grin. "We have time after breakfast. I'd be happy to show her."

She was glad he wasn't glaring any longer, but that grin looked like trouble.

"Good idea," said Thorne.

Awesome. She barely ate anything. If she'd been nervous before, knowing she was going to be handling a firearm made it even worse.

Her lack of appetite gave her a chance to watch the camaraderie between Dane and the other members of Task Force Phoenix. They really were a family.

She knew blood and DNA didn't dictate who qualified as family. Her in-laws, Denise and Alan Scott, had always felt more like real parents to her than her own. She hated that she had been keeping them out of this nightmare since the beginning. They probably thought she was avoiding them, or was attempting to cut Kenzie from their lives. No doubt, they'd been calling her old number, asking to see her.

But she wasn't getting those calls since Viktor had taken her phone.

She would have been able to call them, but she didn't know what she would say. She didn't know how she would tell them their son had betrayed his child in the worst possible way.

She didn't know how to explain how powerless she was.

Except, she wasn't powerless anymore. The people in this room were ready to help her get Kenzie back. If they were successful, it would be easy to gloss over her lack of communication and beg Denise and Alan to forgive her.

But she had to get her daughter back first. Thankfully, the people here were committed to help with that.

And teaching her to shoot was a step in that direction.

Despite their offer to help, she knew she was still an outsider. And she was more and more certain the looks they threw her way had nothing to do with what had happened the night before, or her inadequacies when it came to firearms. This was something else.

There was a dire warning in their eyes as their gazes flicked between her and Dane.

Don't hurt him, was practically written on their faces.

They could rest easy. Hurting Dane was the last thing she wanted to do. She wouldn't be this close to finding her daughter if it weren't for him.

Originally, she hadn't wanted him to know about Kenzie, afraid he would use her story to punish her. But he hadn't. Instead, he'd offered her compassion and understanding, as well as whatever new connection they'd made in bed together.

She had no idea what would happen next. She was too afraid to plan anything beyond that day. Not until Kenzie was safe. But she knew no matter what happened, she would always be grateful to the man with the warm, brown eyes sitting next to her.

She finished off her coffee and stood to go prepare for her firearms lesson, but before she made it away from the table her phone rang with the familiar happy ring tone.

Kenzie was calling.

Chapter Fifty-Five

Every one of Dane's team members turned to stone, then, as if on cue, burst into action.

"Let it ring two more times," Dane said, coming to stand in front of her so he could offer his support without being seen in the background. Six-year-olds were curious and he didn't want Kenzie to ask questions about him.

Lena glanced behind her. She was up against the pine paneling. She could be anywhere. He nodded and smiled, hoping to relax her.

Angel had handed the baby to Colton and pulled her laptop to the place where Garrett had taken her plate. Her index finger raised in a wait gesture, then she nodded and dropped her hand, meaning she was connected into the tracking software.

The usual strained smile fell into place on Lena's face as she answered.

"Hi, baby," she said as, beside her, Justin pushed the button to record the call so they could all analyze it when it was over.

"Hi, Mama. Will you be coming to see me today?" Kenzie asked, going right for the kill.

Angel winced and Colton leaned down to kiss John on the head. Even as new parents, they must have understood the pain this question caused Lena.

"I'm not sure," Lena said. "We'll have to see."

"Are you busy working?"

"Yeah. Kinda."

"Daddy said you have to work a lot, and that was why you couldn't come stay with us."

Lena cocked her head to side. "Is Daddy there? Can I talk to him?" she asked.

"No. He had to go away a long time ago. He told me to listen to Mr. Viktor."

Lena swallowed and nodded. "Yes. You should do that." No doubt the flatness in her voice was caused by the restraint it took to keep from telling her daughter to do the opposite. To fight and try to get away. But that wouldn't do Kenzie any good right now.

Justin held out a note to Lena, and Dane moved so he could read it, too.

"Is Mr. Viktor there with you today?" she asked.

"No. He wasn't at breffast." Lena smiled at the word, and Dane smiled at her. "I had waffles."

"Were they good?"

"Yep."

"Are you going swimming today?" Lena asked, and Justin started scribbling on the pad.

"Yes. I love to swim."

"I know you do." Lena read the note. "Where is the pool?" she asked, sounding nonchalant.

"Out there." Kenzie's little hand waved around vaguely.

"Can you show me?" That was Lena's own question, to which Angel nodded approvingly.

"I'm not supposed to go alone." Kenzie shrugged.

Justin was writing again, so Dane moved so he could watch what he wrote.

"Ah. Is the pool close to your princess bedroom?" Lena read.

"Nah. My bedroom is waaay over by the fountain." More waving.

Justin pumped his fist in success and backed off to go look at the sat map.

Angel smiled in the way that meant she found something interesting. "She's calling from this building," Angel confirmed quietly.

"Her bedroom is here, by this fountain," he murmured, pointing.

They were homing in on Mackenzie Scott's exact location. It would just be a matter of breaking into the complex and getting her out.

They didn't have nearly as much information on Tobey. And that made Dane nervous.

Chapter Fifty-Six

For the next hour, the team picked over the footage from Lena's phone call with Kenzie. What she'd thought was just an everyday conversation with a few leading questions mixed in was a lot more.

They studied every detail, from the angle the sun was coming in the room at the time, to the person who'd made and disconnected the call—the nanny, who'd only been on screen for a fraction of a second.

By the time they were done, Lena was stunned that they had nailed down which building housed the main residence, and where Kenzie slept, where she swam, and where she ate her "breffast."

"I have an ID on the nanny," Angel said, looking up from her laptop. "There's a missing persons report filed for her."

The team all glanced over the report.

"So, she's also a captive. Damn." Justin banged his fist on the table. "I was hoping we could catch her offsite and use her to get us in. Scrap that, I guess." He ripped a piece of paper from his notebook and, after balling it up, shot it into the trashcan in the corner.

The trashcan was overflowing with ideas that had been passed over.

Lena glanced over at Dane. He was sitting quietly at the end of the table. He hadn't offered anything or made any suggestions in quite some time. He seemed to be somewhere else.

She thought she might know where.

While she'd been caught up in the energy and excitement of tracking the details of her daughter's prison, nothing had been done about Tobey. There were still a lot of blanks on that side of the white board.

Maybe there was something she could do about that.

With a strength she'd thought long gone, she pulled Justin's notebook over in front of her and started working on a series of questions. Justin nodded at it before turning it back around and adding a few more.

Then she wrote out a little skit, similar to the one she and Dane had been given the night before. While she wished she could have practiced, they'd told her it came off sounding more sincere if done without preparation.

At the time, she'd thought it was more about amusing themselves with her discomfort, but she understood better now.

"I'm calling Viktor," she announced, handing Dane a piece of paper.

His eyes widened. "Now? I thought you had until eleven. There's still half an hour."

"Yeah, but you're getting impatient, and I'm worried you're going to blow it today when we pick up Evan Masters. Just run with it," she said with a wink.

Angel threw up her hands. "Give me twenty seconds."

Lena punched in the phone number but waited to hit the call button until Angel gave the thumbs up.

Viktor answered after three rings. "This is not the time

I gave you."

"I know, but everything is going to hell here. I didn't know what else to do."

Justin threw a chair, creating a loud crash. All according to the script.

"What is happening?" Victor demanded.

"Dane is losing it. We were getting ready to meet up with Masters, and he exploded. He's convinced his son is already dead, and that turning over Masters won't get him anywhere. What should I do?" she asked, laying on the desperation in her voice.

Justin tossed another chair.

Victor swore. "Give me ten minutes. I'll have the boy call."

"Fuck this bullshit!" Dane yelled on the other side of the room, and slammed the bathroom door.

"Would you be able to let him see Tobey? Like a video call? It really helps me to know Kenzie is safe when I get to see her."

"I'm not in the habit of helping anyone feel better, Ms. Scott," Victor ground out. "But I'll see what I can do. He needs to calm down. We can't risk this meeting when we're so close to getting our hands on Mr. Masters."

Lena hated how Viktor always used everyone's last name. As if he was so dignified and cultured. He was nothing but a common thug.

"Okay," Lena said, feigning uncertainty. "I'll try to keep him from wrecking the hotel room. I might have to pay for the television."

"Put it on the card." Viktor sighed, as if Dane losing it was an inconvenience, rather than a desperate father breaking down.

She disconnected the call and turned to the marshals. "Tobey will be calling," she announced with a smile, and everyone flew into action once again.

Chapter Fifty-Seven

"I can't believe you did that." Dane took the phone and moved into position by the wall where Lena had called Kenzie. He was pretty damned impressed.

"I had to do something. We don't have enough information on Tobey, and I want to help in some way."

He kissed her hard, so happy to have her on the team. Even if she didn't know how to shoot, she was smart and she cared about him.

He wasn't sure if Lena's performance would earn him a video conference with Tobey, or if it would only be a regular phone call, but the team would be ready for anything.

"Remember," Justin reminded him. "You were really angry and have just calmed down enough to take Tobey's call."

"Right." Dane nodded, dropped to the floor, and did ten fast push-ups, keeping his bum leg in the air. When he stood, he felt flushed and was slightly out of breath. Just as he would have been if he'd lost his shit and trashed a hotel room.

The sound of the phone brought on an immediate silence,

other than his hard breathing.

"Ready?" Lena scanned the group to get a nod from each member.

Angel was last. She rubbed her palms together eagerly. "I'm ready."

Lena answered the phone and immediately frowned into the screen. "Butch," she said, even though no one had spoken yet.

"Can you see me? I don't know how this shit works," the giant complained.

"Yeah, I can see you," Lena said.

"You'd better be taking care of my Jeep."

Dane ground his teeth impatiently.

"I am. Where's Tobey?" Lena asked, reading his expression.

"Right here. Make it quick."

Lena let out a breath and handed the phone to Dane.

For a moment, he had the urge to run away from the phone, as if he were being handed a snake rather than a piece of technology that would allow him to connect with his son.

He was just worried about the possibility of messing things up. Once again, he felt that pain for what Lena went through every morning when Kenzie called.

"Tobey?" he said as his son's face came into view. "Hold the phone out farther. I can't make you out. You're all blurry," he said, more because they wanted to see the room he was in than because he was truly out of focus.

"Is this better?" Tobey asked.

"Much." Dane could see the entire length of the room he was in. "I see you have some friends there."

"Yeah. Guys, wave to my dad," he called back to the others.

Three boys in the room waved, then went back to the board game they were playing. At least they didn't play video games the entire day.

"How are you doing?" Dane asked his son. "Still eating a lot of pizza?"

"Sometimes we have cereal for dinner." Tobey frowned and looked over his shoulder. "That guy"—he pointed to Butch, who was taking his turn in the game—"ate all the crunch berries out of the cereal and left the rest. Who does that?"

Tobey's tone of disgust made Dane smile. If that was the only injustice in the way they were being treated, he would sing Butch's praises for the rest of the man's short life.

Focusing on the script, he put on his worried father expression and asked, "Do you ever get to go outside?"

Tobey shrugged. "Sometimes. We've gone up to the house to watch movies." He gestured in the direction of what Dane assumed was the house he was speaking of.

"Do you have clean clothes? Are you able to take a shower?"

"Yeah. They got me this shirt." Tobey frowned down at his T-shirt with a Canucks logo. It was too big, but it appeared to be clean.

Dane let out a breath. His son was okay. "Are you doing all right?" he asked, just to make sure.

"I miss Mom and Randy. And you." It was clear he'd added that last part for Dane's sake.

He understood Tobey wouldn't miss him. Dane wasn't in his life for his absence to be noticed. Still, it stung a little.

"I'm going to meet a man today," Dane said. "And you will be able to go home." It didn't hurt to reinforce that they were planning to move on Masters today. Even if it was all BS.

"Time's up," Butch yelled. "And it's your turn."

"I gotta go," Tobey said, looking wistful.

"Yeah. Me, too. I'll talk to you soon, okay?"

"Okay. Love you, Dad."

"Love you, too."

In his struggles to turn off the phone, Butch accidentally gave them a 180-degree view of the room they were in. Yes!

When the call was disconnected, everyone took a deep breath and started working.

Dane walked out of the lodge and broke down.

This time for real.

Chapter Fifty-Eight

It was obvious to Lena when Dane rushed out of the lodge that he needed a minute. Whether or not he needed a minute *alone* was unclear.

She wanted to go to him, to offer support or a shoulder, but she wasn't sure if he wanted her there. She looked to his family for the answer to her silent question.

"Go make sure he's okay," Justin offered as Garrett and Angel nodded in agreement.

Not wasting a second, she hurried out and found him heading for the lake at a pace she wouldn't be able to catch. Even with his injury, he was moving like a man looking for a place to implode. He was probably in so much pain over Tobey, he didn't even notice the pain in his leg.

She found him sitting on the dock, his head on his knees and loud sobs racking his body. She'd been there. She knew there was nothing she or anyone could say to make him feel any better.

Instead, she quietly sat next to him and wrapped her arms around him. He allowed himself to fall against her, and she felt his hot tears on her neck as he struggled to get through the agony.

Eventually, he caught his breath and was able to speak. "I don't know why I'm losing it now. I mean he's fine. He has food, a place to sleep, and even a new fucking T-shirt. What is wrong with me?"

"Nothing is wrong with you. You're just seeing the truth between the lies."

He sat up and looked at her.

It was better to rip the bandage off and deal with it. No matter how much it hurt. "It doesn't matter that Butch is playing a game with those kids," she said. "They are not safe. At some point you realize if Viktor gave Butch the order, he would put down his cards and hurt those kids. It's all an illusion."

He looked pained. "I want to leave right now and get him out of there, but I know we have to be smart about this, because we won't get another chance. It's just taking too goddamn long." He rubbed his temples. "How have you survived this for all these months by yourself?"

He reached for her, pulling her against him. Giving instead of taking. His arms around her and the strength he provided felt so good.

"I knew I couldn't give up," she said quietly. "I knew I needed to stay close and do what Viktor wanted until he let down his guard and I was given an opportunity to act. That opportunity is now."

Dane nodded. "Thank God."

"I need to be ready, which means I need to learn how to shoot." She swallowed down her nerves at the thought. "Will you teach me? Because Justin scares me a little bit."

Dane smiled. "Of course." He took her face in his hands and pulled her in for a thorough kiss. Then he leaned back to look at her. "You're the strongest person I've ever known. We're going to get Kenzie back."

"I know we will," she said.

Because there was no other option.

Chapter Fifty-Nine

Dane agreed that Lena needed to learn to shoot. And she wasn't the only one who didn't want Justin to teach her. Though their reasons were a bit different…

Justin was a big flirt. And while Dane understood that whatever was going on between him and Lena wasn't a long-term, official thing, he felt a possessiveness he couldn't ignore.

After cleaning up from lunch, the team split up to take care of things. Thorne was on the phone. Angel had taken over the large table and four laptops. Colton and Garrett were making an ammunitions list.

"Here," Dane said, reaching out to hand the Beretta to Lena. She pulled back with wide eyes. "Take it," he urged.

"Can't you carry it to wherever we're going?"

"No. Put it in the back of your jeans."

"Shouldn't I have a holster or something? It might fall out of my pants."

"Tuck it down in your waistband, and it will stay there. Besides, it's sexier to pull it out of your jeans. Haven't you ever seen an action movie?" He winked at her to let her know he was joking. It might look sexier than a holster, but that position was definitely not as secure. Especially if you had to sit down.

"How do you guys walk around like this? It's cold and bulky." She shifted and bent over.

He reached over to push it a little deeper into her jeans.

Samantha laughed. "This way, when the shit hits the fan, it's easy to get to."

"Even if the shit hitting the fan is an innocent guy just doing what he was told," Dane said with a smile at Sam. He should have let that one pass, but she was just too easy to tease.

As expected, a guilty look crossed Sam's face. "I'm so sorry, Dane."

"Knock that shit off," Garrett called from the living room. "She told you not to move. You moved. It was your own fault you got shot."

"And Thorne told me to take her gun," Dane said good-naturedly. "It was a lose-lose situation, all around."

"I'm sorry," she whispered again so Garrett couldn't hear.

Dane patted her on the back. "It's okay, sweetie. If I'd really been a bad guy, it would have been the right thing to do." He turned to Lena. "You ready?"

She frowned and adjusted the gun again. "I guess so." She walked out of the lodge with more of a limp than he had.

The campground had an actual shooting range, though it was probably used for BB gun practice rather than a 9mm. Still, it would do nicely.

He set up three targets on the rail and came back to stand in front of her. She was still frowning like a wet cat.

He kissed the crease on her forehead and smiled down at her. "You're going to have to take it out of your waistband now."

"I was just starting to get used to it being there," she grumbled.

"You'll have plenty of time to get used to it."

"Do you want me to pull it out slowly while you watch?" Her naughty smile made him twitch.

Maybe they could practice that part later.

Except, they didn't have later. They would be leaving in the morning to head off on their mission. And she needed to be ready. Well, as ready as possible in one day.

"Okay," he said. "When you pulled the gun on Colton, you were holding it all wrong."

She winced, and her cheeks colored. She was still embarrassed about that incident. He decided to address it in the hope she would be able to touch the gun without wincing.

"It's okay. No one is mad at you," he told her.

Her lips thinned. "*I'm* mad at me. I'm mad at me for this whole damn situation. If I had just made sure my ex couldn't get to Kenzie. And if I had done something more when they brought in you and Tobey..."

No one won the blame game. He should know. He'd played it many times over the past five years.

If he hadn't gone to work for Tim Reynolds. If he hadn't been so ambitious and naïve. If he had only forced Caroline to come with him so they could stay together.

"We don't know what happens after that first *if*," he said.

"Meaning?"

"We think if only we'd done one thing differently, then everything else would work out. But we're just looking at that next step—the one we think made everything go to hell. But what if we were destined to fail, anyway? What if you *had* made sure your ex couldn't take Kenzie from the daycare? Maybe instead, he'd have broken into your home and taken her. Maybe you would have fought him and lost."

She made a face. "I don't think I would have lost. Not

when a scrawny-ass drug addict was taking my baby."

He'd give her that. "My point is, we don't know what would have happened next. If I hadn't taken the job with the embezzlers from hell, I might have ended up working for Viktor Kulakov. Who knows? We can't spend all our time looking back and wishing we'd done something different. It's useless."

"You're probably right." She let out a sigh and nodded to the Beretta. "I still wish I hadn't pulled the gun on Colton. If for no other reason than I made an ass of myself."

Dane chuckled, then showed her how to support the gun, and how to aim. When he thought she had a good stance, he told her to pull the trigger.

It didn't even come close to the target. It was way high. The next one hit the dirt about five feet in front of the target. The next one hit the target, but it was the target two rows down rather than the one she was using.

The problem was clear to see.

"It's impossible to hit the target when you have your eyes squeezed shut," he told her.

"I don't," she protested.

"You do when you pull the trigger. You need to keep your eyes on the target."

She grimaced. "I thought I was."

"You're not." He swallowed down the beginnings of panic. If she couldn't shoot, she would be detrimental to the mission. She would just be in the way. She didn't need to be a sharpshooter, but she should not be a danger to herself or Kenzie.

Which meant...he would have to convince her to stay behind.

Chapter Sixty

"You can't shoot the broadside of a barn," Dane said as he held up Lena's untouched target and frowned.

Damn. She'd really thought she'd kept her eyes open that last time. But apparently not.

"I'm sorry," she said. "I've never needed to shoot a gun before."

He wadded up the target and tossed it into the trash can. "Nope. This isn't going to work. We'll find something else for you to do."

She looked at him questioningly. "As in…?"

He pressed his lips together.

Suspicion dawned. Wait. He didn't want her there when they went into Viktor's fortress to retrieve her child? Even though he knew how much it sucked to be told he couldn't be there for Tobey's rescue?

Oh, *hell* no.

"I'm going," she said firmly. "You need every available person to help, and I'm not staying behind just because I'm not up to your standards."

Okay, it was clear by the lack of holes on the target she probably wasn't up to anyone's standards, but still. She squared her shoulders and prepared to fight him on this.

Up until now, she'd gone along with every snotty order and rude comment he'd made, but this was going too far.

"I'm *going*," she repeated, making her voice even flatter.

He seemed to rethink and redirect. "Then you'll have to do better than this, or you'll just get yourself and possibly someone else killed. You flinched every time you pulled the trigger."

"I don't know how not to flinch." She was getting defensive and her voice had risen to the same volume of his. She didn't like the idea of putting anyone at risk because she wasn't ready for this mission, but she needed to be there. "I used to do people's hair! I'm sorry I'm not used to all this tactical crap."

She might have tossed the gun at him, but she knew it was loaded, and that was a gun safety no-no.

Samantha and Angel walked up to the makeshift shooting range.

"Guys! Take a break," Samantha ordered. "Dane, I think Garrett needs you in the kitchen."

Without a look back, Dane stormed off in the direction of the house. Lena was glad to see him go. He was making things worse. How was she supposed to shoot when he was hovering over her shoulder and criticizing her every move?

"I'm sorry. I'm not good at this kind of thing," she confessed to the other women. Though it was pretty obvious.

Sam smiled. "The men are not great at teaching us these kinds of things."

Angel snorted. "I've been teaching Colton how to write code. If I can do that, I can surely teach you how to hit a target." Angel crossed her arms. "Shall we begin?"

Lena nodded with more enthusiasm than she felt.

"Pick it up like you own it instead of the other way around."

"Okay." She didn't know what that meant, but she reached for the gun and picked it up.

"Nope!" Angel yelled, nearly making Lena drop it.

"What did I do?" All she'd done was pick it up. And she'd done it correctly. She'd watched enough movies to know that.

"You flinched when you touched it." Sam frowned. "Here. Let's try this."

Sam took the gun from her, and in a few swift motions she had it broken into a pile of parts. She held up each piece and identified it. Then she handed them over to Lena like a pile of Legos. Soon her hands were full of innocuous pieces of the gun. Then one by one, she put each piece back together to form the original firearm.

"A gun is just a bunch of metal parts." Sam shrugged.

Lena nodded in understanding. It did feel less intimidating that way.

"Fine," Angel said. "Pick up the metal parts and aim it toward the target. You're going to line up the sight on the bullseye. Then let out a breath at the same time you squeeze the trigger. Don't yank or pull the trigger. Squeeze it in a smooth, firm motion."

Bam!

Lena felt herself flinch, though she was pretty sure it had happened *after* the gun went off instead of when she squeezed the trigger.

"Hot damn!" Sam shouted. "You hit it."

"I did?" Lena squinted into the sun and saw a black spot on the paper.

"Barely," Angel said with a sigh. "Try it again, and if you flinch I'm going to give you something to flinch about."

Angel was not very big, maybe five feet tall. She had some killer curves, but was no bodybuilder. Despite the other woman's size, Lena was certain she could back up her threat with no problem.

Lena swallowed and raised the gun again, hoping she wouldn't flinch.

Breathe. Squeeze.

Flinch.

Damn it.

Chapter Sixty-One

An hour after Dane had left Lena, he could still hear the occasional gunshot as Angel and Sam worked with her, teaching her to protect herself. He shouldn't have been such an ass. He shouldn't have walked out on her. But he couldn't make himself go back, either.

Seeing her flinch every time she took a shot made him too aware of what they were facing.

Taking her on this mission was like leading a lamb to the slaughter.

"Believe it or not, she's doing better than my ex-wife." Justin came in through the side door and set down a pair of binoculars. "Jenny wouldn't touch a gun. She wouldn't even try. Even when our handler recommended it."

This was a first. Justin didn't talk much about his past. The rest of the team knew that and didn't push for information. All Dane knew was that his extraction had been messy. He'd taken his family with him, and it hadn't worked out. He and his wife had split up. He'd joined Phoenix and she and their daughter had made the most of their new lives.

"You had a handler?"

"Yeah. Dumb as shit. Nearly got my family killed when we were moving. He talked to someone on an open line. Haley was only a little older than Lena's daughter. Even so, Jen wouldn't learn to shoot to protect them if I was taken out. That put a lot more pressure on me. I was their only defense."

"Knowing Lena's heading into danger is too much. She's not ready."

"Still, she's made a decision to do something outside her comfort zone to protect her child. She'll figure this out, and she'll do what needs to be done. I can tell that about her. You won't have to worry about her when the shit hits the fan."

"Maybe."

Justin smiled in his smartass way. "Though, I can tell you are still going to worry."

"Yes. I will." There was no shame in that.

"At some point, you have to let go. When Jen left with Haley, it nearly killed me not to be able to watch over my kid and have her close. But eventually I realized I'd made a mistake to bring them with me into WITSEC. I should have done what you did and let them live their life out in the real world without me fucking it up for them."

"And let your kid think you're dead?"

"I rarely get to see my daughter. To her, it's like I'm dead, anyway. At least she would have had a normal life."

"Do you really think I did the right thing?" Dane asked, looking for absolution from someone who had lived a life Dane assumed had been better.

"I think you did the only thing you could do, being married to your wife. She wasn't cut out for this life. Maybe if you'd had someone…stronger." Justin nodded out the door he'd come in. "You would have had another option with a different woman. But with Caroline…no. The only safe choice was what you did."

Deep down, Dane knew that. He'd known it from the day he walked out. But hearing it from someone who'd played it differently made him feel better…if only slightly.

"Thanks."

Justin slapped him on the shoulder and went to the kitchen. Dane glanced up when Lena walked into the room with the other women. Everyone else was there, too.

Lena held up her target and shrugged away her success when Justin clapped. There were five shots in the bullseye, and a few others weren't far off. All in all, it was impressive. Especially for someone who'd had no formal training, and had flinched badly every time for him.

He knew this wasn't easy for her, but he was crazy worried that everything go according to plan. There was no room for error.

Error meant someone died.

She didn't understand why he'd acted like a dick. He was pretty sure she wouldn't jump to the conclusion that he'd been rude because he cared so much. Guys normally got over that stupid move by third grade. What would he do next? Pull her hair?

But he'd snapped at her, and he needed to apologize. He needed to make it right. Instead of helping her, he'd just given up and tried to find a way to complete the mission without her.

He should have been encouraging her to do her best. Instead, he'd been standing in her way.

He didn't want to think of the reasons why.

"I get it," Garrett said, coming up to stand behind him.

"Get what?"

"You don't want her to have to shoot a gun. But you don't want her to get hurt. The best thing would be if she wasn't there, at all. You're sabotaging her efforts."

Was that what was going on? Dane knew he hadn't exactly

helped, but actual sabotage was a different level of assiness. Is that why he had decided to cut her out of the mission so quickly? Was he that much of an asshole?

Maybe.

"Unfortunately, she might be put in a position where you can't help her," Garrett continued, "and if that happens, you'll want the person you love to be able to defend herself."

"*Whoa.* No. I don't love her." Dane shook his head to make that very clear. He didn't want to love anyone. Except Tobey. And, okay, pretty much everyone else in this room he loved on some level.

But not Lena. He couldn't love her.

"Oh." Garrett blinked and looked over at where the girls were instructing Lena. "If that's not what this is, then why are you acting like a dick?"

"I'm not," Dane lied. Garrett's raised brow had him adding to his declaration. "Fine. I'm not sure," he amended, and hung his head.

"Is that because you're being forced to help her get her kid, and you can't go after your own?" Colton asked. "If so, I would understand. That was a tough call, but I think Thorne's right. You'll keep on task better going with Lena. You'd be a loose cannon on Tobey's job."

"I know that." Though Dane still hated it. And he didn't mind helping Lena get her daughter back. He would do whatever he could to get Kenzie away from Viktor. But… "I just don't think it's a good plan. I don't want her there, at all."

Colton and Garrett exchanged knowing looks.

"What?" Dane demanded, though he knew what they were going to say before they even opened their mouths.

"You *are* in love."

Chapter Sixty-Two

After all his rules about not wincing, Lena wanted to point out that Dane was doing an awful lot of it as he guided her out of the lodge so he could talk to her.

She wanted to be angry with him and his horrible training skills, but she understood. She wasn't a trained law enforcement officer, and yet he was going to be stuck with her on a mission. He probably thought she was not an asset…and he was right. She didn't have any skills to speak of.

But she would die to save her child, so that made her valuable to this mission.

Swallowing down her urge to start begging, she waited for him to actually tell her she was off the team. Hoping she could convince him with sheer determination and stubbornness.

He couldn't leave her behind.

How would she survive, waiting to hear the outcome of the mission? How could she sit back waiting to find out what happened when Dane and Kenzie were both in danger, and she wasn't there to help?

She couldn't.

"I'm sorry," he said and pressed his lips together. At least he didn't look happy about it. She waited for the next part. The part where he said, "I'm sorry, but you're staying behind."

Except, he didn't say that. And now he was just standing there in front of her…seemingly waiting for something.

She blinked, and kept her mouth shut.

He let out a breath, and finally spoke. "I'm sorry I was a jerk and wasn't patient when I was teaching you to shoot. You obviously just needed the right teacher, or teachers. I apologize for acting like an ass."

Wow.

She couldn't remember Brandon ever apologizing. For anything. Even when it was clear he was in the wrong. Such as the time he'd used their rent money to buy a mountain bike. He'd stood by the decision even when she had to call his parents and ask for a loan.

Dane's apology itself was enough to make her mouth fall open in shock, but it was more a matter of what she *didn't* hear him say that surprised her the most.

"I still get to go with you?" she asked.

"Yeah. I mean, unless you've changed your mind," he added hopefully.

She gave a small smile. "I didn't change my mind. I want to be there." She couldn't help it—she held her hands in front of her with her fingers threaded together. She was officially begging. And she didn't care. "Please."

He looked resigned. "We need everybody we can get. So, yeah, you're in."

"Do you think I'm good enough?"

It wasn't until she'd asked the question that she realized the meaning went deeper than just being able to shoot.

These people had gone through thorough training to be able to handle any possible situation. She'd cut hair. Not exactly life and death. Unless you count the time Macy gave Mrs. Benchoff bangs by accident.

He held up the target and pointed to the cluster of holes in the paper.

"This is better than Justin shoots." He'd kind of whispered, as if he didn't want the other man to hear from inside.

She laughed and he leaned down to kiss her.

"You have a sexy laugh," he said with another kiss. "I hope when this is over and our kids are safe, I'll get to hear it more often."

The smile fell from her lips in a new kind of shock.

He was making plans for what happened after the mission? Plans that involved the two of them together and laughing?

She didn't know how to process that. For the last eight months, her whole life had been consumed with doing whatever needed to be done to get her daughter back. There had been no plans for the future. Even if she'd taken the time to come up with plans, she didn't think they would have included a man. Especially not a sexy deputy marshal.

After her horrible marriage with Brandon, she didn't think she'd ever want another man in her life. But now that the thought had been planted, it was growing.

She'd seen Dane at his worst. Filled with hate and panic while puking at the side of the road. He'd wanted to kill her, and she'd hit him and helped abduct him. After all that, the common problems people lived through seemed like cake.

Lena looked down at the gun in her hand and shuddered. She thought of Sam and Angel, and how well they fit into this life of danger. If Lena was able to save Kenzie, she didn't want that for her daughter.

As much as she liked Dane, she wasn't sure what kind of future they could have.

She must have taken too long to think it through, though, because Dane sighed and said, "Why don't you show me how well you shoot now? I'd like to see you in action."

"Oh. Sure."

She followed him to the range, feeling as though she'd missed the opportunity of a lifetime.

Chapter Sixty-Three

Stupid Garrett. He was to blame for this. He'd mentioned love, and Dane had started thinking about it. While he still didn't think he was in love with Lena, he had to admit, he wouldn't mind seeing her again when this was all said and done.

It would be nice to see how well they fit when they could just be together without all the stress and panic about the safety of their children. When they could just sit back and relax for a little while, when the only stress was the normal day-to-day kind that normal people dealt with.

It was obvious by her reaction she was not on board with that idea.

She'd looked at him as if he'd suggested they run off and get married that second.

Whatever. He'd be too busy, anyway. He was always too busy. He made sure of it. He didn't need time to deal with things like relationships and romance.

He'd had that once, and he'd been forced to walk away. Deep down, he knew why he wouldn't ever try to have that again. He hadn't been enough for Caroline. He'd loved her and thought she'd loved him. But when push came to shove, she'd chosen money and things over him.

They'd gotten married way too young, and for no reason other than he'd wanted her to have his name and to make sure she wouldn't leave him. It had been stupid. But generally speaking, twenty-year-old guys weren't the sharpest tools in the shed. They were just plain tools.

He thought being married meant an unlimited supply of sex, cuddling, and sending each other sexy texts during classes. But it had also meant student loans, disagreements, and resentments. Three years later they'd had Tobey, which had realigned their expectations all over again.

Dane had been busy building his career and she'd been busy making them the perfect family. Or at least making sure they *looked* like the perfect family from the outside.

Inside, it was a lot of snipping at one another. They didn't have a lot of all-out fights. It would have taken more energy than either of them had to work up to that much emotion. It hadn't felt worth it to fight.

There had been a lot of silence. Sometimes he hadn't even remembered why they weren't speaking to one another. He thought maybe she'd lost track, too. They still slept in the same bed, but only because it was so large they never had to touch.

In the end, they had been nothing more than strangers, sharing a home and a baby.

Looking back, maybe it hadn't been love. Maybe it had been two kids trying to pretend they were grownups.

Dane's mother had died when he was ten and his father—the professor—had always been too busy to make them seem like a family. Dane had thought he had it all when he got married and landed a good job. When Tobey came along and they moved into a big house on a cul-de-sac, he'd thought his dreams of being a family had finally come true.

But it had all been pretend. A cardboard cutout of a real life.

He'd thought that was how it was for everyone. But then he'd seen the way Angel and Colton were. Not to mention Garrett and Samantha. They would do anything for their spouse. Even give up their old lives to be with the other person. Being in love wasn't just words. They'd proven it.

Caroline hadn't been willing to give up anything for Dane. Not the big house, not the fancy cars, and not the membership to the country club that they rarely even used. She hadn't even taken a moment to think it over.

It had been a quick and simple no. And just like that, he'd been forced to make the biggest decision of his life.

Alone.

At least Lena hadn't ever pretended. She was always real.

At the moment, she was concentrating on her target so intently her tongue was sticking out a little.

Just as she lined up her first shot, he reached out and clapped his hands right by her ear. She jerked and missed the target.

"Why the hell did you do that? You made me miss!"

She was cute when she was angry. Not that he wanted to push her very far. She did have a gun, and let's face it, his track record with women shooting him was pretty bad.

"When we go into the complex," he said, "it won't be as serene as a shooting range in the trees. It could be loud. There could be distractions. There could be people shooting back at you."

He swallowed down the worry from his last statement. He didn't want to think about that. It wasn't something he ever thought about going into a mission. Everyone knew the dangers. They didn't need to dwell on them.

Unfortunately, she didn't have the luxury of letting things

go unsaid.

"You need to be able to find your focus and keep it no matter what is going on around you," he explained.

"How do I do that?" She appeared to honestly want to know, so he did his best to answer.

He pursed his lips. "It's different for everyone. Justin murmurs to himself. I asked him once what he was saying, and he told me it was the list of things he needed to handle. Like take out this person, cover the other person, move out of the way. That kind of thing."

"How do you do it?" she asked.

He shrugged and glanced away, not really sure how to explain his tactic. But he knew he couldn't hold back even the smallest piece of information if it might help her.

"I put myself in a bubble." That was the best way to describe it.

Her brows came together in confusion.

"It's imaginary, of course. But I'm in my bubble, and nothing can get to me inside it."

"This bubble is bulletproof?" She twisted her mouth as she considered. She didn't laugh or even smirk. She was obviously taking this seriously.

He wanted to lean down and kiss those lips until they relaxed into the softness he'd been missing since they walked into the lodge that morning. But he didn't. He didn't want to distract her. Not in that way, at least.

"Yes," he said. "Metaphorically speaking, the bubble is impenetrable."

"I see." She nodded and raised the gun. "Okay. Try it again."

He spent the next ten minutes making noises and trying to pull her focus away from the target while she ignored him and concentrated.

She hit her mark every time.

"Very good," he praised her with a big smile.

She smiled back. "I was in my bubble."

"Do you think I could come into the bubble for a minute?" He moved closer and bent his head, his lips hovered an inch from hers.

"Yeah, come on in. It's bulletproof, not kiss-proof."

Her arms wound around his neck, and when he moved his hands around her waist to pull her closer, he encountered the gun in the back of her pants.

"God, that is sexy," he said with a groan.

"I don't get it."

"Let's go back to our cabin, and I'll try to explain."

Chapter Sixty-Four

Lena knew what this was. Or what she hoped it still was.

A distraction. Something to keep them from dwelling on the bad things that could happen. A few moments to think about something good instead of all the terrible scenarios and possibilities that played in her mind when she didn't have something else to think about.

Dane was giving her something else to think about.

Once he'd declared her a good shot and fit for duty, he took her hand and led her back to their cabin, where he proceeded to watch as she pulled the gun from the back of her jeans and set it next to his on the side table by the sofa.

Maybe it was some kind of deputy marshal fetish or something, but it was clear that the action turned him on. And okay, when he picked up her gun and checked to make sure it was unloaded, she could maybe see the appeal of watching a shirtless man pull back the slide on a pistol.

When he was satisfied there wouldn't be a misfire, he put the gun down and focused on her. He walked up and pulled her shirt right over her head in one swift motion. Before she could let out a gasp of surprise, he had tugged her bra to the side enough to latch onto one of her nipples.

She moaned and put her hands on his shoulders for support. The sensation had her feeling off balance. He reached for her pants and had them off in no time. He only released her breast to move to the other one.

She fumbled off her shoes and ended up falling onto the bed. He watched her through heavy-lidded eyes as he undid his pants slowly and prowled across the bed toward her.

She almost didn't recognize the nervous giggle that came out of her. She hadn't heard herself do that in a very long time. But there was no other way to respond to his predatory look.

She feigned an escape. A shriek of pleasant surprise was the next sound she made as he grabbed her ankle and pulled her toward him. The truth was, she definitely didn't want to get away.

When he fell over her, he was smiling.

"I caught you. You're mine now."

The words melted into her heart. She wanted to be his. As much as she wanted him to be hers. But for now, they both belonged to two little people who were depending on them.

She smiled up at him. He'd hinted at a future together after the mission. A chance to have him when she was no longer worried sick over her daughter.

She didn't know if it was possible. She wanted a normal, safe life for herself and Kenzie. But this man risked his life daily.

For now, she would enjoy this.

And enjoy it, she did.

Twice.

Chapter Sixty-Five

Dane might not be cut out for love, but whatever this was—this intense chemistry he had with Lena—he'd take as much as he could get. He'd never been with anyone like her. She was a true partner in his bed. Moving with him, matching him with her desire. Each time they were together was a new, unexpected adventure.

He'd needed a distraction from the tension of the mission. He'd wanted a connection with someone. He'd gotten more than he'd bargained for with Lena.

"When was the last time you had sex?" he asked as they caught their breath.

She grinned. "Three minutes ago."

Such a smartass.

"When was the last time you've had sex with someone other than me?" he corrected.

She gave him an unreadable look. "I don't think I ever had sex before you."

He chuckled. She'd given birth, so he knew that wasn't true. "Immaculate conception?"

"Suppressed memories."

"The last time was with your ex?"

Damn. He should have backed off. Her jokes were an obvious attempt to brush off the subject. But Dane wanted to know if this was special, or if she responded this way to every man she'd been with. Why it mattered, he didn't know...and he didn't want to think too hard about an answer.

"Yeah, it was with my ex," she said quietly. "But it wasn't like this. It wasn't even in the same category as this. It was like mowing the grass or doing the dishes compared to this."

God, that made him feel good.

"A simple, 'Dane you're the best I've ever had' would have sufficed," he teased, and she slapped him playfully in the arm.

Her cheeks had turned pink, so he pulled her close so he could look her in the eye.

"It's different for me, too," he said honestly. "I just wanted to make sure you felt the same way."

She nodded but didn't say anything for a long time. He'd almost dozed off when she finally said, "Do you think it's because we both need each other so much? To get through this?" Her voice was quiet, as if she wasn't sure she wanted to be heard.

He thought it over. "Maybe?"

Was that what this was? Normal sex, ramped up by tension and desperation? It was certainly easier to deal with that interpretation than the alternative supplied by Garrett.

Dane grasped onto it, happy to have an explanation that didn't hinge on love. "You might be right. Thank you for helping me get through this."

"You, too. I wouldn't have made it this far without you."

But they still had a long way to go.

Chapter Sixty-Six

Lena could feel the heat in her cheeks as she and Dane walked into the lodge late for dinner. She'd suggested they stay in bed and make a meal of the crackers and a broken-up toaster pastry she'd found in her bag, but Dane said he needed sustenance.

The couples gathered around the table had knowing grins on their faces but were too polite to say anything.

Justin, however, didn't have an issue with being overly polite. "You two look like you've worked up an appetite."

To Justin's left, Garrett knocked him in the back of the head, and to his right, Angel gave him a shove in the arm.

"What? It's pretty obvious they've been at it all afternoon."

Oh God. Lena wanted to be swallowed up by the ground.

"We should have just eaten the Pop Tart," Dane said by her ear with a chuckle. "Your face is so red. It makes me want to drag you back to bed."

"Not helping." She glared at him as she took her seat, but he only grinned wider.

"You're just jealous," Colton said.

"Nah." Justin wrinkled up his nose. "I like the sex part fine. But I don't do the happy part anymore." He waved a finger in their direction as if they were freaks.

"It's good to focus on something other than the mission," Angel said as she scooped up the fussing baby and smiled into his face until he quieted.

Whatever smile Lena may have had on her face fell away, and the familiar mask of fear and guilt took its place. As humiliated as she would have been under normal circumstances, it made it worse to know they probably thought she was a bad parent. What kind of mother spent the afternoon in bed having sex when her child was in danger?

One who needed the man next to her so she wouldn't fall to pieces, she told herself.

She knew Dane was doing the same thing.

Maybe they were using one another...but wasn't that exactly what they would have been doing if their meeting at the bar had been real? They would have shared a night together. Relieved some stress, and gone on their way.

Except, now she didn't know what would happen when it came time for her to go on her way.

She could have her daughter back in a matter of days. This whole mess could be over, and she would be free to continue on with her life.

That thought stopped her short. What life?

She didn't have a home or a job. She had some money in the bank, but it wouldn't last long. She couldn't go back to Miami—Viktor would be looking for her. Unless he was in prison. But even then, he would probably send someone after her to make her pay for her betrayal.

Would she be offered protection in exchange for her testimony? She wasn't sure the prosecutor would need her testimony. She could easily be discredited, since she'd helped

Viktor.

The spaghetti on her plate looked as appetizing as a pile of worms. She swallowed to keep from gagging, and sipped her water.

The rest of the group had moved on, and were talking about more important things than her sex life.

"You okay? You look pale," Dane whispered.

"I'm fine."

No. She wasn't fine. She was terrified.

She tried to erect a bubble of protection to keep the anxiety about the future at bay, but there was no stopping it.

In less than a week, the future would be upon her. One way or another.

She wasn't ready.

Chapter Sixty-Seven

Dane wasn't sure what was wrong with Lena, but he was positive there was something bothering her. Correction—there was something *else* bothering her.

The poor woman had the weight of the world on her shoulders. He wanted to take some of the burden off her, but he was weighed down at the moment, too.

There was only one way he knew to make her more at ease. And they'd spent all afternoon doing it. He decided to focus on finding a different way he could relieve her worries over the mission.

He thought back to the first time he went out on an op. He'd only had one concern. Well, one concern other than possible death.

"Colton?" Dane said, causing the other man to look up from his food while slurping in a noodle. "How many times have you been shot?"

Colton wiped his mouth on his napkin and smiled. "Seven times."

"One of those times was my fault," Angel offered with a

frown. "I froze and didn't react. Colton got shot."

"But he survived. Every time," Dane pointed out. He turned his gaze on Angel. "How about you?"

The group seemed to realize what he was doing, and he could feel their eagerness to share their stories. He loved these people and their willingness to take in anyone. Even a scrawny executive like him, who hadn't even known how to shoot a gun the first day on the job.

He exchanged a glance with Supervisory Deputy United States Marshal Thorne. The boss had a gift for seeing someone's potential and standing back as they got their feet under them. It would have been easy to stick Dane in a small town all alone and hope for the best, but Thorne had seen something in him. Something more. And Dane couldn't have been more grateful for the opportunity.

"I was shot once," Angel answered. "Stabbed once, and cut more times than I can count."

"Forty-three times," Colton said. When Angel looked at him askance, he shrugged. "I counted up your scars once when you were naked and I couldn't sleep."

She rolled her eyes.

"I've been shot four times," Justin jumped in, though it wasn't his turn.

"Four for me, too," Garrett answered when Dane pointed at him.

"I hope you're not counting that cut on your arm," Justin teased.

"It took stitches to stop the bleeding. It counts," Samantha came to her husband's defense. She had been the one to stitch him up. She grimaced. "I'm sorry I didn't do a better job."

"I would have been dead without you," Garrett said with a wink.

Thorne steepled his fingers and shook his head. "I make it a point not to let people shoot me," he said it with an air of superiority.

However, Dane noticed he hadn't really answered the question. Not letting people shoot him didn't mean he hadn't ever been shot.

He let it go and turned to Lena. "I've been shot three times, stabbed twice, stuck on a fence, and bitten by a wicked beast."

"Hey, now," both Angel and Colton protested. The beast had been their German Shepard who had been ordered to attack him.

"The point is, we've all been injured and we've all survived. There's nothing to be nervous about."

Lena pressed her lips together and gave a quick nod. She was quiet for the remainder of the meal.

Hmm. Maybe she hadn't been worried about the danger, after all.

After dinner, they spent a few hours going over every last detail of the plan once more, and mapped out a timeline. Everyone knew what they needed to do, even if they weren't on board with their duties.

"I'm still not sure why I can't go along," Colton complained while everyone stood to leave the lodge. "I spent two years with Viktor Kulakov. I know the son of a bitch better than anyone."

"Which is why he's gone to such extreme measures to get you back. We can't have you stroll in there and not expect him to do something desperate," Thorne replied while Angel kept her eyes on the baby in her arms.

It was clear she was struggling with what she knew as a marshal, versus what she felt as a wife and mother. She wanted to keep her husband out of harm's way.

"We can handle it," Dane said. "You and Angel will feed us information and keep us coordinated."

Dane took Lena's hand as they walked to their cabin. "Are you okay?" he asked when the silence grew and they'd reached the tiny porch of their temporary home.

"I wasn't worried about getting hurt," she confirmed his earlier thoughts.

"Then, what's wrong?" He opened the door for her and followed her inside the cozy cabin.

"For months, I've wanted to do something to get Kenzie out of Viktor's grasp. At the time, I had no idea how to do it. I just wanted to get her away from him. But now that the time has come to make a move, I'm worried about the risk. I mean, she's fed and healthy, and she gets to do crafts. If this doesn't go right…"

"I get it. There's some comfort in inaction, since the kids are not in immediate danger. But that won't last forever. This is our chance to get them back. Kenzie might be okay right now, and I'm glad, but she's not happy. She misses her mother. We have to do this."

"You're right. I know that. Just tell me this is all going to be okay." She rested her forehead on his chest, and he wrapped his arms around her back, feeling the tension in her shoulders.

"It's going to be okay. My team is the best. You can trust us."

She let out a breath and nodded. "I do trust you," she whispered. "Completely."

Chapter Sixty-Eight

When Lena looked up at Dane, it was obvious her words had touched him.

The air between them seemed to sizzle, but with something more than sexual desire. It was a slower, warmer kind of feeling.

His palm held her cheek as he gazed at her without moving. Something was happening between them. When he kissed her, she felt her world was righting itself.

She thought he might push for more, especially when he pulled off his shirt. But when he helped her out of her clothes, he handed her the T-shirt he'd been wearing, still warm from his body.

They'd showered after their earlier activities, so after getting ready, he slid right into bed and held out his arms. "Let me hold you tonight."

"Are you afraid I might fall apart if you don't hold me together?"

"I'm worried *I* might fall apart if I don't have you to hold onto."

Tears came to her eyes as she snuggled against his chest. His warmth soaked into her bones as well as her heart.

Whatever happened next, she knew she would be facing it with Dane standing next to her. She was as ready as she could be, and the plan was solid.

It was time to take the risk.

It was time to change from the mouse hiding in the corner into the fury pounding down Viktor's door.

He would pay.

She would make sure of it.

Chapter Sixty-Nine

Dane and Lena didn't speak, but that didn't mean they didn't communicate. They'd found another way to offer each other strength and assurances. As if he had lain with her every night for a hundred years, Dane could tell she wasn't sleeping. He could feel the stress in her body and knew she was playing out every dark fear in her mind.

He rubbed her back and kissed her hair.

"Don't," he whispered.

It might have been easy to keep kissing her and lull her into a sex-induced oblivion. But they were too close for sex. The moment too intimate to use lust to distract them from their worries.

"Tell me there's nothing to worry about and I'll stop," she challenged.

He could have lied. He could have told her everything would go according to plan, and it would be easy...but if it wasn't...

"Worrying won't do anything but wear you out and make you sluggish tomorrow," he said.

"I know. But every time I close my eyes I think of something that could happen that I'm not prepared for. Tell me a story, so I'll fall asleep."

He laughed and tucked her a little closer to his chest.

"What kind of story? Like with princesses and dragons?"

"No. Something boring. So I'll doze off."

"It's too bad my father isn't here. He could put a rock to sleep."

"He's a professor?"

"Was. He died about two years after I…died."

"I'm sorry."

"It's sad, really. He was the only person I wasn't worried about leaving. He wasn't a bad father. He didn't beat me or yell at me. But he forgot I was even there, and in some ways, that might be worse."

"Was he always like that, or just after your mother died?"

"My mother forced him to be present. But I never could. I couldn't make him be something he wasn't. He never got it. He didn't realize that people mattered more than books and papers and someone's ideas and strategies for a war that happened years ago. He missed out on knowing me. And he never learned from that."

"You mean Tobey?"

"Yeah. For some reason, I expected Dad to take an interest in Tobey. Probably because I was so interested in him. Every moment he did something new and amazing, I couldn't imagine missing any of it."

Until he'd been forced to miss all of it.

"I don't think it was unreasonable to think he might like being a grandfather," she said. "Many people who didn't appreciate parenthood relish the idea of being a grandparent."

He went on to tell her how his father had forgotten Christmas. Twice. And how Dane had gone overboard with everything, trying to be a better father than his own.

His strategy worked. At some point he said something funny, and she didn't laugh. When he leaned over to look at her, she was asleep.

He wasn't far behind.

But unfortunately, he didn't get to stay asleep for very long. He was awakened by a gut-wrenching sound from his past.

Chapter Seventy

It took a good minute for Lena to realize the child screaming didn't need her. It wasn't her child, but maternal instincts were difficult to suppress.

Poor John was having a rough night, which meant his parents were also having a rough night.

"I remember cringing at that sound," she said into the darkness as baby John gave his lungs a workout in the next cabin. "Because it meant I had to get up, and I was always so damn tired."

Dane chuckled softly. "I remember pretending to sleep through it so my wife would have to go take care of him. She eventually figured it out. Who would be able to sleep through that?"

They laughed together.

"Now I feel ungrateful," she said. "What if losing Kenzie was payback for all the times I complained or didn't get up right away? I should have cherished every single second."

Another wave of guilt crashed over her, nearly drowning her with the intensity of her failures.

"There are some things about parenthood that would be impossible to cherish. Like when they come into your bedroom in the middle of the night because their stomach hurts, and proceed to throw up all over you."

She groaned.

He continued. "How about when you just want to run into the grocery store for one quick thing and your kid asks for something. And when you say no they start screaming and throw themselves on the floor in some kind of alligator death roll."

"What about when someone gives them a gift and they scrunch up their nose and throw it." She shook her head and made a face.

"Oh, yes. I wanted to shake the little shit," he said without real conviction.

"You don't have a girl, so you probably haven't had to deal with six changes of clothes in one day. Or all the laundry."

"No, but I did have to deal with ripped knees and grass stain on *every* pair of pants."

She squeezed her eyes shut. "I'd take all of it and then some, just to have her back again." Lena's chest felt tight and her throat burned.

"I would, too," he said with a roughness to his voice.

"It's worse for you. Even if everything goes according to plan, you won't get Tobey back," she said sadly.

"True. But it's okay. I gave him up before for his safety. I can do it again. Especially now that I was able to tell him I still love him."

She didn't possess the kind of strength it must take to be able to walk away from your child, knowing they were better off without you. She hoped she never needed to find out.

And as hard as it was for Dane, it would be all that more difficult for Tobey. Because even if he now had an inkling of the danger, he surely wouldn't understand the reason Dane had walked away. He would always know Dane was out there somewhere, but wasn't able to be with him.

"Tobey won't want to give you up," she said.

He looked conflicted. "Maybe not."

"What will you do?"

"I'm not sure. It won't be easy. I guess I'll have to ask him to keep it a secret."

She felt for him. What a thing to ask of a child. "Don't you marshals have something to wipe out a person's memories?" she joked.

"I wish. If we did, I'd use it on you."

She glanced at him in surprise. "On me? Why?"

He grimaced. "I'd wipe out your memories from our first few days together. When I was such an ass. I'm sorry I didn't give you a chance to explain."

Her pulse came back to normal. "I didn't deserve it. I hurt you and Tobey. I should have done someth—"

He cut her off. "No. If you had made a move against Viktor, he would have had you killed."

There was little doubt about that. "And yet, I'm getting ready to make a move on him tomorrow."

"Right, but you're prepared now. It's different."

God, she hoped so.

Chapter Seventy-One

Everyone was in their zone during breakfast the next morning. Most of the team had a routine they followed when mentally preparing for a mission. Some paced, some meditated. Justin cracked jokes, while Angel went on the internet and looked up photos of cake disasters. Garrett checked and rechecked his weapons and ammo.

Dane tended to pace and think. But of all of them, his routine was the one that seemed to drive the rest of the team batty.

As soon as he'd made his first lap, Angel groaned and got to her feet. "I can't watch this. It makes my blood pressure go up."

Fortunately, they weren't made to wait long. Thorne came in and told them everything was a go, and they immediately grabbed their gear and went out to the vehicles.

Lena had gone off alone to make her call to Viktor, who still thought they were in San Antonio having difficulty with Masters. She'd told him one of Masters' co-workers had tipped him off, but they'd pressured the co-worker into calling him and telling him the coast was clear.

When the last of the stuff was in the Jeep, Justin pulled Dane aside. "You okay?"

Dane took a calming breath. "Yeah. How about you?"

Justin would be working with Garrett to get Tobey and the other boys out of the bunkhouse in Vancouver.

Justin nodded. "I'm ready. I just want you to know that Tobey is in good hands."

"I know. I wouldn't be heading to Savannah right now if I didn't trust you to get my son to safety." He hadn't even questioned it.

It had never been a matter of doubting his team. It was more that he felt he needed to be there. But that wasn't the plan, and he was determined to do whatever he could to help not only Tobey, but Makenzie Scott, as well.

His friend squeezed his shoulder. "You're holding it together really well. If someone had taken my daughter, I would have lost my shit," Justin confessed.

Dane gave a humorless laugh. "I did lose it. You missed me puking by the side of the road," Dane admitted while rolling his eyes at his weakness.

Justin thumped Dane's shoulder gently with his fist. "I'm just saying I understand how much your son means to you, and because of that, how much he means to me. I'll do everything you would do if you'd been allowed to come on this mission."

"I appreciate that." Dane gave him a fist bump. "Thank you. I know you'll take care of him. Be safe."

"You, too. I'll see you in a few days."

"See you then." They gave each other a manly slap on the back and headed in opposite directions.

Dane hopped up in the passenger side of the Jeep as Lena was buckling in the driver's side.

"We're ready?" she asked nervously.

"Yep. Let's go save Kenzie."

Chapter Seventy-Two

"The waiting is driving me crazy," Lena complained. "I want to move in."

Only two days ago she had been reluctant to plunge into danger, but here she was, antsy and pacing. She wanted to get it over with.

She wanted her daughter back.

But part of her also wanted more time with Dane. She didn't know what would happen with them when the mission was over.

He would go on to save other people, and she would…

She had no clue. Hell, she didn't even know where she was going to live.

"What's the first thing you are going to do when you get Kenzie back?" Dane asked.

She was surprised how close the question was to what she'd been thinking. As if he could read her mind. Though, that would be nearly impossible considering how quickly her thoughts were jumping from thing to thing.

"I'm not sure," she admitted. "I don't have any plans past

getting her back. Maybe I'll take her for ice cream and let her tell me every detail I've missed over the past eight months."

"You can't go back to Miami," he said. It wasn't an order, more of an observation.

She nodded. "I figured. But I wouldn't want to, anyway. It's not like I can stroll into the salon and pretend I still have a job. I'll have to start over somewhere else." She shrugged. "I'll figure it out afterward."

After this next step was over. Because God knew what was going to happen.

Someone knocked on the door to their hotel room, and her heart stopped. Thorne had told him he would come tell them when it was time.

When Thorne walked in with his normal serious expression, she expected him to tell them the other team was in position and it was time to go. As much as she'd wanted to get moving a few minutes ago, her feet were now frozen in place.

But instead of telling them to get their stuff, he frowned and shook his head.

"We've got a big problem."

Chapter Seventy-Three

"What do you want to do?" Dane's boss asked after dropping a bomb.

Both Thorne and Lena were looking at Dane, and he wasn't sure how to answer.

He'd always turned to Thorne for instruction. Hell, the guy's title was supervisor. Why wasn't he supervising them?

"If you want to wait until I get back," Thorne said, "I can tell the rest of the team to hold off. But if they get assigned other cases, it might be a while until we can all get back together."

"We don't have *a while*," Dane complained. "Viktor isn't going to believe Lena when we keep coming up with excuses for not locating this fictitious Masters person. He's going to get suspicious, and that will put the whole mission in danger."

"Then you want to proceed with just the two of you?" Thorne asked.

It sucked that Thorne was being summoned back to Washington, D.C. at the worst possible time. But for him to refuse would mean he'd have to explain. And if he told the truth, their mission would be over before it began.

He had to report to his boss to keep everyone from noticing all of them were hunting down an off-limits Viktor Kulakov.

"Can you give us a moment?" Dane asked Thorne as he put his hand on Lena's elbow and led her out onto their balcony.

"What are we going to do?" she asked as soon as they were alone.

He eased out a long breath. "We have two choices. We can either hold off until Thorne comes back, and risk having someone else called away, or we can try to extract her with just the two of us."

It wasn't fair to put the burden on Lena, but this was her child. And if he made the decision and it went badly—which there was every possibility of happening—he didn't want to be the one to have made the call.

Lena had the most to lose. It had to be her choice.

"I can't take much more of this," she said, her voice strained. "I just want to get on with it."

He smiled at her strength. Or maybe it was impatience. Regardless, he felt the same way and agreed with her decision.

He nodded. "Okay. Then let's go."

Chapter Seventy-Four

Thorne left at the same time Lena and Dane headed out for Viktor's complex. Thorne wished them luck and told Dane not to fuck things up.

Right.

Lena knew he was just trying to make her feel less nervous. Of the two of them, she was the one with the potential to fuck things up the worst. She may have already ensured their failure with her hasty decision to go on the mission without Thorne.

As they parked down the street from the gated entrance of the compound, she was having serious doubts. She was not cut out for this kind of thing. Yes, she could shoot at a piece of paper. But she'd never shot a person before. And the paper hadn't shot back.

Still, she needed to do whatever she could for her daughter. And that meant walking into danger with a gun and sheer determination.

The sun had gone down on the humid day, and she felt the chill of the night envelop her as she stepped out of the

Jeep.

While she focused on her breathing, Dane communicated with Angel via their earbuds, so they could synchronize the attack with the other team.

She and Dane were outside the mansion in Savannah, Georgia, while the others were waiting outside a complex in Vancouver. They were working in tandem. One attack on two fronts. Angel and Colton were keeping everyone informed and on track.

Lena pulled the gun from her holster as if she'd been doing it every day of her life.

"Are you ready?" Dane asked.

"Yes." She hoped it wasn't a lie.

He nodded and grabbed a small backpack of emergency gear and slipped it on before pulling on a gas mask. She fumbled with her own, and adjusted the strap in the back.

She didn't like the idea of gassing her own daughter, but it was the safest way. It meant everyone inside would be rendered unconscious, and they could simply go in and get Kenzie without the need for violence or the possibility of being outnumbered.

Dane hopped up on the high fence and hung there on his stomach as he reached down to pull her up. She was impressed by his strength. She wasn't a frail girl, and he handled her as if she weighed nothing.

As planned, she instantly got in position so he could lower her down on the other side. He hung suspended by his fingers for a second before dropping into a crouch next to her.

"We're inside." She heard his words beside her as well as in her com.

Before they even stood to take a step, they encountered the first obstacle.

Of the canine variety.

"Shit. I really don't want to get bit again," he muttered

as he pulled a canister from his belt and tugged the pin out. Smoke poured out of the device, and he tossed it on the ground in front of them as the Dobermans bore down.

The smoke hindered her visibility, but the dogs did not pass through the thick cloud. Dane leaned down and trussed up the dogs like a cattle wrangler did to a steer.

"Clear. Come on." He held out his hand and she took it.

It felt the same as when they had walked to the cabin the night before they left. Casual, like a date instead of the dangerous extraction of a hostage.

Unfortunately the person handling the dogs was not far behind. Dane let go of her hand and slid into the shadow by the corner of the house.

Leaving her out in the open.

As the man approached, Dane leaped out behind him. She didn't see exactly what he did, but the man dropped to his knees and fell over. Before she could look, Dane had gripped her arm and was pulling her along behind him.

Her whole body shook with tension, anticipation, and fear as they passed the fountain and made it to the door of the smaller house behind the main mansion. She'd been worried she might freeze up and not be able to move. Now she was worried about not being able shoot because she was moving too much.

He tried the door and it opened. He tossed a canister inside and checked his watch. She imagined her daughter inside being knocked out by the choking smoke.

"Moving inside the East Building," he said after a full minute had passed, his voice cool and professional.

"Copy," Angel answered over the com.

He gave the signal that he wanted Lena to follow close behind. The small cottage was dark except for a light coming from the bathroom. Kenzie always made her leave the light on in the bathroom so she could find her way in the middle of the night.

Lena's chest squeezed. Her daughter was close. She was going to be able to hold her. Any minute now.

Dane's headlamp came on, and he moved through the small living room Lena recognized from some of the calls with her daughter. The living room was open, and she could see the island counter that surrounded the kitchen area.

The lamp's beam moved to the first door on the left. They weren't sure where the bedrooms were, or which one could be Kenzie's.

When Dane pushed the door open, she hoped to see her daughter lying in the bed. But it was a queen-size bed, and it was made, the cover pulled tight in a professional manner.

Sweeping the room with the light and finding nothing, he pulled the door shut and stopped at the next one. It was the bathroom, and it was clear no one was inside.

The next door was a child's room. There were toys—dollhouses, chalkboards, and a kitchen set—along the wall by the window. The small bed in the corner was covered with a turtle blanket. But there was no one inside.

The next door was the entry that led out the back. They moved through the kitchen toward the two doors on the other side of the cottage.

Her breath caught at the sight of Kenzie's drawing hanging on the refrigerator. She could tell it was her daughter's by the way the horse had giant square legs and her name was written at the bottom. She would probably not become an artist.

At the next door, Lena heard a noise from inside. Her heart raced, eager to open it and greet her child.

The door opened and two little girls—groggy and coughing from the gas—stumbled out toward them. Dim light from a princess lamp inside the room lit up the small area.

Lena gathered them in her arms with an involuntary

sound of joy, looking at each one for some familiarity. But there was none. Neither of the girls was her Kenzie.

One of them fell heavily against her, and Lena carefully laid her on the floor.

"Do you know Kenzie?" Lena asked the bigger girl, whose eyes were big as plates looking at their gas masks.

The girl nodded nervously.

"Where is she?"

The girl shrugged and her eyes drifted shut.

Lena tried a different tactic. "Which room is Kenzie's?" she asked with a gentle shake to keep her awake.

The girl pointed to the room she had just come from. Lena laid her down, then hurried inside, checking every corner, but came up empty.

There was no one else inside.

Just four small beds and two dressers.

The other girl had curled up next to the smaller one and passed out.

Dane moved to the next door—the last room they hadn't checked.

But he came out shaking his head worriedly.

Kenzie wasn't there, either.

Chapter Seventy-Five

Dane's heart fell as he watched Lena check the bedroom for the third time. He'd done a thorough sweep. In the closet, under the bed. Nothing. A six-year-old was fairly small, but he knew she just wasn't there.

"Two children found," Dane said into the com. "Neither is Kenzie. She's not in any of the rooms. We're moving to the West Building."

"I'm only getting one thermal in the West Building," Angel answered. "Northwest corner."

Dane picked up and handed the smaller girl to Lena, then carried the older one out of the house, and they laid them both out in the fresh air. Hopefully, they would wake up soon and he would be able to get some information from them.

He slipped his mask off, and Lena did the same.

Taking her hand, he led her into the bigger house through the sliding rear door. He kept the Beretta up and ready, and headed toward the thermal Angel had seen.

The northwest corner of the house was a bedroom. He swept the room and found the heat source. A small boy was huddled in the corner. He was mumbling, but Dane picked up a few words in Mandarin.

Damn.

He picked up the boy, who whimpered but didn't struggle, and carried him out to the girls.

"Angel? You have anything else other than a group by the entrance of the East Building?"

"I have heat by the fence where you came in. That's it."

Just the dogs.

"Shit," he muttered.

Lena's daughter wasn't here, at all.

From the pain in her multi-colored eyes, it was obvious Lena understood the situation.

"I'm sorry," he whispered, knowing it wasn't good enough.

The sound of sirens broke through the quiet tension.

"Police en route," Angel said. "I'll make sure they know the situation before they arrive."

No doubt, Thorne had a favor ready to be called in, if needed.

The older girl began to stir, and Lena went to calm her.

"What's going on with the Vancouver raid?" he asked, his heart in his throat. He was almost afraid to ask.

"I'm still waiting for confirmation."

Still waiting? What was taking so long?

Two police officers walked up to the gate, and Dane stepped into the small booth to open it so they could enter.

"U. S. Deputy Marshal Dane Ryan," he identified himself, and shook the officer's hands.

He introduced Lena, and told them they didn't know the children's names or who they belonged to. Just as the older girl was telling them her name was Molly, he heard Angel in his ear.

"We have him."

"You have Tobey?" he confirmed, joy leaping through his whole body.

"Yeah. He's safe. We have an ambulance and police on the scene. Someone's been hurt."

"Who?"

"We're not sure. We lost contact with the team. I spoke to the police, and they verified Tobey and the other boys are safe. They couldn't tell me what happened, or who was hurt."

"Keep me posted. Let me know as soon as you hear anything," he said.

Lena's head snapped up, concern in her eyes. "What happened?"

He swiped a hand through his hair. "Tobey's okay. But someone else was hurt. I'm not sure if it was Garrett or Justin." He felt as though he'd been slugged in the chest. Someone in his family had been hurt, and could be dying.

She gazed at him for a moment, then said, "You need to go."

He pressed his lips together. The urge to go to his son was strong, as well as to be by the side of whoever was wounded. But he couldn't leave Lena here by herself. She had no ID. He should have had Angel make her one, but now there wasn't time.

"No. I can't leave you alone," he said. "What about Kenzie?"

She swallowed and looked away. "We can't do anything, anyway. Not until we figure out where he's taken her." Lena nodded to the little girl clinging to her. "I'll stay with the girls until their parents come to get them. Maybe they can give us a clue. You need to be with Tobey. Go. I'll be fine."

"Are you sure?" he asked, everything in him pulling toward Vancouver…but not wanting to abandon Lena.

"Yes. Go."

He leaned down and kissed her forehead. "We're not giving up," he assured her. "We're *going* to find your daughter. Don't worry." He knew that wasn't going to work, of course she would worry. But it was the best he could do at the moment.

He pulled the emergency credit card from the backpack and handed it to her. She moved to push it away but he forced it into her hand, along with his Beretta since he couldn't take it on the plane last minute, and the keys to the Jeep. "I'll be back for you as soon as I can. Until then get a hotel room, and try to remain calm. I'll call you when I land. Phone?"

"Yep." She dug it out of her pocket and showed it to him.

"Good. And you still have the com, right?"

"Yeah," she said, touching her ear.

"Use it if you need to. I'll have Angel monitor the channel on the hour."

He kissed her, using his lips to convince her this wasn't the end.

He turned toward one the police officers. "Can one of you give me a lift to the airport?"

The next flight out was only forty minutes from now, but he booked it from his phone, and prayed he wouldn't have to wait until the next morning. He was dropped off at the terminal, and asked the cop to take care of Lena until he got back.

"Sure," the man agreed, and shook his hand.

Dane raced through security and made his flight with only a few minutes to spare. Once in the air, he took a deep breath and closed his eyes, waiting for the peace of knowing his child was safe to settle over him. But it didn't.

He was too worried about Lena. And especially Kenzie.

She was in grave danger. By now, Viktor would know Lena had betrayed him. What would he do to the little girl to get his revenge? If Dane was worked up, Lena must be a total mess.

He'd hated having to leave her behind. But he'd be back, and they would work together to find her daughter. He wouldn't rest until Kenzie was safe and Lena could smile that real smile he'd only seen a few times.

Chapter Seventy-Six

Lena's stomach had dropped when Dane had driven away. He'd promised her he'd be back and that they would keep going until they found her daughter...but she wasn't so sure.

What if he didn't come back? What if his team abandoned her? What would she do?

Molly tugged on her hand, and Lena quickly pulled her lips up into a reassuring smile. They'd been driven to the police station and were now ensconced in a comfortable interview room with Officer Lucas, the cop who'd brought them. Molly's little sister, Hannah, had been hanging onto Lena like a baby monkey ever since she'd woken up from the gas.

Molly had finally been able to tell them their last name.

"We haven't found any missing persons reports on Molly or Hannah Myers," the officer said with his brows pulled together. "Why wouldn't they have reported their kids missing?"

Lena swallowed and said, "The man who kidnapped them would have threatened their lives if the parents went to the authorities." She turned to Molly. "Sweetie, do you remember your phone number yet?"

They'd asked the little girl twice already, and she'd just started crying. Lena decided to try a different approach when it appeared the same thing was going to happen again.

"I have an idea," Lena said while using her free hand to make a drawing motion. The officer handed over a piece of paper and a jumbo crayon. It was brown and broken, but holding it seemed to calm Molly slightly.

"Let's play a game," Lena said to her. "Can you write your name for me?"

Molly nodded enthusiastically and took up most of the paper to draw her name, both "Ls" were backward, but Lena smiled and praised the little girl.

"Can you draw me a picture of your house?" she pressed, having to change to another piece of paper when she asked her to draw her school.

"I ride the bus to school. Hannah still goes to baby school."

Lena grinned conspiratorially. "What is the name of your big-girl school?"

Without hesitation, the little girl spouted out, "Waldo Pafford Elementary."

Officer Lucas let out a quick breath and started typing on a laptop computer. All Lena could think was how glad she was the girl didn't go to a school with common name.

"Hinesville, Georgia," the officer said.

"Do you girls live in Hinesville?" Lena asked excitedly. They both nodded. "Officer Lucas, can you give us a hint on that phone number?"

The younger officer looked up at her for a second, then nodded. "Let's see. I'm going to guess your phone number starts with…" He made a show out of pretending to think really hard. "Nine-one-two?" He waited with his face scrunched up until Molly laughed and nodded.

"Good job, Officer Lucas. Can you guess the next three?"

"Hmm. Maybe…eight-seven-seven?"

Molly clapped her hands. "Yes!"

Myers was a pretty popular last name. Lena would gladly help to call every one of them in the phone book. They could wait until the next morning to contact the school and follow up that way, but it would be quicker and easier if Molly could just tell them her number. "Molly, your turn. What are the last four numbers?"

Using her fingers, she held up each number as she said them.

The officer gave her a thumbs-up and turned away with the phone.

Not being familiar with Georgia, Lena wasn't sure how far Hinesville was from Savannah. It turned out it wasn't far, at all.

Less than an hour later, their parents came rushing into the station. The girls screamed with excitement and ran into their open arms.

Lena hated the twinge of envy that washed over her a second before she allowed herself to be happy for the family and hopeful that she would soon be reunited with her own daughter.

"Good job," Officer Lucas said, patting her on the shoulder.

At the parents' request, Lena sat with them while they were questioned about what had happened. Mr. Myers explained that he had worked for Viktor only long enough to figure out what was going on. He'd contacted the local police, but they'd brushed it off as a disgruntled employee making trouble for his employer. Viktor had grabbed up his kids to make sure he didn't push any harder to be heard.

"I tried to do the right thing," the father said, "but if I had contacted the police, he would have killed them."

Or worse, Lena thought, as fear stabbed through her chest.

What would Viktor do to Kenzie when he found out Lena had betrayed him?

At that exact moment, her phone rang.

She was about to find out the answer to her question.

Chapter Seventy-Seven

Seeing Viktor's name pop up on the display produced an exponentially higher level of terror than normal. Glancing at the police officer, she excused herself and ducked out of the room so she could answer without alerting the others to her own horror.

"Hello?" she said, trying her best to sound normal.

"My, my. Haven't we been busy?" Viktor sounded almost amused. As if this were simply entertainment to him. It was clear he knew what she'd done.

Time for some damage control.

"It's not what you think," she rushed to say. "Ryan got away from me right after I called you last time. I had no idea what he was planning."

"Spare me the poor acting," Viktor drawled. "I sent Butch to meet up with you in San Antonio at the hotel where you said you were staying. You weren't there."

"No, I was." She wasn't about to give up.

"You were in San Antonio this morning, but somehow you drove to Savannah in eleven hours?"

That would be impossible. She should have made sure she had a backup plan.

"Viktor, please don't hurt Kenzie. This isn't her fault. He threatened me. Told me to do what he said or he'd have me arrested."

"So you chose to deal with me rather than the police? Certainly, you misjudged the greater threat with that decision."

"Viktor, please. I'll do anything you want."

"You seem to like hanging out with the police. I wonder how they'd feel if some evidence turned up proving you'd murdered your ex-husband?"

Lena choked. She'd long assumed Brandon was dead, but she hadn't had anything to do with it.

"They always suspect the spouse," Viktor said with a chuckle.

"*Please*, Viktor," she pleaded knowing her begging only amused someone as callous as Viktor.

"You've proven to be unreliable. I'll get Vanderhook myself and make a nice profit on your daughter."

Before Lena could say anything else, the phone went dead. Only a few minutes later, the phone was deactivated.

Oh God. She had messed up. She'd trusted Dane to help her get Mackenzie back. But now her daughter was in more danger than ever. And Lena had no leverage to work out a deal with Viktor.

Dane had caused her to lose her daughter, probably to a horrific fate.

It didn't matter if he came back. It was too late for Kenzie.

Lena wondered if Dane had ever hated her even a fraction as much as she hated him at this moment.

She didn't think it was possible.

Chapter Seventy-Eight

Dane arrived in Vancouver and was whisked off to the hospital by a waiting car. His heart beat frantically with worry. Toby was safe, but someone on his team was hurt. It happened occasionally, but it never got any easier.

The team had all rushed to his side every time he'd been injured. They might joke and tease one another, but when it came down to it they were there for each other without question. Just like family.

"What's happened?" he asked the driver who looked familiar, but wasn't on their team.

"I'm not sure. Thorne just told me to pick you up."

"Thorne's here?"

"Yeah. He just got in an hour ago."

Garrett stood as soon as Dane stepped into the emergency room. Seeing him answered the question Dane had been about to ask. If Garrett was in the waiting room, it meant Justin was in the emergency room.

"How is he?" Dane asked, quickly glancing around to see if Tobey was there, too. He wasn't.

Garrett shook his head as Thorne came to stand next to him.

"It doesn't look good," Thorne answered in a tone that might have sounded cold to someone who didn't know him better.

"What happened?" Dane asked.

"We thought we were clear. We had Tobey and the other boys between us. Tobey was the last one, and Justin was pulling up the rear. Someone from the roof fired into the group. Justin grabbed Tobey and pulled him down under him. Justin was hit before I could take out the shooter."

It was plain to see Garrett blamed himself for not reacting faster. It was normal to feel like you should have acted faster, or anticipated an attack. The problem was, they were humans, not superheroes.

Later, when Garrett was thinking straight, he would see he couldn't have done anything differently. Rather than tell him it wasn't his fault, Dane remained silent. Eventually, Garrett would understand.

"Dad?" Tobey was speeding down the hall in a wheelchair.

Seeing him took Dane's breath away. Thank God! "Are you okay?" he asked, eyeing the wheelchair.

"Yeah. I hurt my knee, and they didn't want me to walk on it." Tobey rolled his eyes.

Dane smiled. It seemed like such a grown-up reaction. Dane kept thinking of Tobey as that five-year-old he'd left at home that morning so long ago. But he was growing up.

"I'm so glad you're okay."

"The other man…?" Tobey looked concerned.

"They're taking care of him right now. I'm sure he'll be fine."

Over Tobey's head, Dane saw a doctor step into the waiting room looking grim. Garrett and Thorne went over to him, and there was a brief exchange.

Seconds later, Garrett bent over at the waist and let out a strangled sound.

Oh God. Justin hadn't made it.

Dane swallowed down his grief for the moment so as not to upset his son. He'd deal with it later. Or try to.

"I'm so glad you're okay," he said again, and gave Tobey a big hug.

His son hugged him back, then looked up. "I'm glad you're okay, too. I thought maybe I had been dreaming you were there when I got kidnapped. But you really were there."

"Yeah. I'm real." Dane ruffled his boy's hair and frowned. "But I have to be a complete secret. Just you and me, buddy. No one else can know I'm really alive. Okay?"

"Why not? I bet Mom would tell Randy to leave so you could move back in."

Dane gave him a weak smile. As if it would be that easy.

"No. That's not how it works. Besides, I left because some bad guys were trying to keep me from telling on them. If they knew I was still alive, they might try to use you and your mom to get to me." Dane figured it was best to tell Tobey the truth. As much as possible anyway.

"Oh." Tobey frowned. "So, I have to pretend I didn't see you?"

Dane crouched down to be at his son's eye level. "Do you think you can do that?"

Somehow, it seemed unrealistic. Dane remembered being this age when his mother died. If he had seen her alive again, he would have told the whole world.

"I guess so." Tobey bit his lip and his cheeks flushed.

"What is it?"

"Mom already knows I talk to you."

Chapter Seventy-Nine

Dane froze, wondering how Tobey would already have had a chance to tell Caroline he was alive. Had the cops called her immediately?

Damn. And Dane had gone to all this trouble to keep them safe. Now what would he do?

Then Tobey looked away, his cheeks still slightly pink as he shrugged.

Ah.

Dane understood. His son had conversations with him. Even though he wasn't there to offer any help or advice.

He didn't think he could hurt any more than he already did, but his heart fractured into microscopic pieces.

"What kind of things do we talk about?" he asked with an encouraging smile.

"Well, I told you I liked Lucy Arnold even though she has a boyfriend."

Dane hiked a brow. "Lucy Arnold sounds like trouble if she has a boyfriend."

Tobey made a face. "I don't like her anymore."

That was good. Ten was a bit too young to have The Talk. Not that it was Dane's responsibility. Caroline would freak out if Tobey learned the facts of life from his invisible dead dad.

"What else?" he asked with a smile.

Tobey let his head fall to the side as if weighing whether or not to tell him this next thing.

"I asked you if it was okay for me to call Randy my dad. He told me it was okay, and he said you wouldn't mind. But I wasn't sure, so I went to our special place and I asked you."

"Our special— You mean the fort?" Dane asked.

"Yeah."

"It's still standing?"

The two of them had built the fort in the woods behind the house. It was nothing fancy. Just particle board and an old pallet. Tobey had wanted a treehouse, but both Dane and Caroline were worried he'd fall out of it and break something. They settled on a fort instead.

Tobey grinned proudly. "Yes. I fixed it myself when the one side fell down."

"Good job." Dane ruffled his son's hair, just as proud.

"So, should I?" Tobey asked.

Dane pretended to have gotten lost in the conversation. "Should you what?"

"Should I call Randy dad?"

Dane's first reaction was *hell* no. That guy wasn't Tobey's father.

But then the more sensible part of Dane's brain kicked in. The part that knew Randy was a stand-up guy. And it would probably mean a lot to Randy to have the official title, since he was filling the role. If Dane really were dead, he wouldn't be here to complain. And even now, he felt a sense of gratitude to the man who was taking care of his family so well, when he wasn't able to do it himself.

"I think he would like that. What do you think? He is a dad to you, right?"

"Yeah. I guess." Tobey pressed his lips together.

Dane knew what he was going to say next. "I'm still your dad," he told his son. "And I always will be. Okay?"

Tobey nodded.

"But if someone else is being your dad, too, and you want to call him dad, it's okay with me. Don't feel pressured, either way. Do whatever makes you feel comfortable."

Tobey nodded again with a little more enthusiasm. "Will I see you again?"

Dane swallowed down the "Yes" he so much wanted to say.

"I'm going to be around sometimes. It's still super dangerous, but I might check in with you from time to time, now that you know the truth. Because I love you so much. As long as it stays a complete secret. Okay?"

"Okay."

"But this is the *only* secret I want you to keep from your mom," he said firmly, making sure he did the right thing.

"It's kind of a big secret." Tobey smiled at that, and Dane agreed.

"I'm sorry you have to keep such an important secret. It's not fair to you."

Tobey straightened, looking much older than his ten years. "I don't mind. As long as you're not really dead, I'm okay with it."

Dane winked and gave him a hug. "Good. Now we'd better get you back to your mom. She's so worried about you. Are you ready to call her and tell her you're okay?"

Tobey's eyes lit up and he nodded.

Dane cocked his head at Thorne, asking him to come over.

"We're ready to call Caroline. Is it okay if I stay with

him?"

"Sure. He knows how important it is that no one knows you're alive, right?" Thorne looked down at Tobey. "If someone found out your dad is still alive, they might try to hurt you and your mother."

"I made it clear," Dane assured the other man, wishing he hadn't brought it up again. Thorne was a little scary to adults. To a child, he must be even more frightening.

Tobey's eyes went wide. "I won't tell anyone," he promised.

Thorne held out his phone, and Tobey dialed his mother's number.

"Mom?"

"*Tobey*?" Her voice was so frantic, Dane could hear it from a few feet away.

It made him think of Lena and what she was going through right now. She must be terrified. He planned to call her as soon as he had Tobey squared away.

"I'm okay. I'm in…" Tobey turned to them, and Dane almost supplied the answer but realized he couldn't speak. He was dead.

"Vancouver," Thorne offered. "We'll be bringing you home."

"Deputy Marshal Thorne says he's going to bring me home. He has a badge and everything."

After a few more words, Tobey handed the phone over to Thorne so he could assure Caroline that Tobey was okay and homeward bound.

After they hung up, Tobey asked, "What about the other kids that were with me?"

Dane almost melted with pride that his son's first thought was for his fellow captives. "I'm sure they are on their way home to see their parents, too," Dane assured him.

Thorne gave him a single nod. "You ready to go home?"

Thorne asked Tobey with a smile that didn't make him any less terrifying.

"Yeah." Tobey turned to Dane, tears suddenly filling his eyes. "I'm glad you're not really dead, Dad."

"Me, too, Son." Dane bent down for one last hug. "I love you so much. I'll see you sometime. And if you ever need me, come to the fort and talk to me. I just might hear you."

Tobey wiped his tears with a sleeve. "Okay. Tell Garrett and Justin I said thank you for saving me."

"I'll let them know." Dane swallowed down the burn of his own tears for his friend, who'd given his life to keep Tobey safe. A debt Dane could never repay in a million years.

He walked Tobey out to the car waiting for Thorne, his arm around his son's shoulders.

"I'll make sure he gets home safely," his boss said.

Dane took a steadying breath and one last, lingering look at his son as he climbed into the car. "Thank you. For everything."

When the car was out of sight, he went back inside to help Garrett make arrangements for their fallen hero.

• • •

Several hours later, Dane checked his phone for the hundredth time that day. Still nothing from Lena. He'd called her right after Tobey left, only to find out the number had been disconnected.

Damn it! He should have thought to give her the burner phone from the backpack. But neither of them had been thinking straight.

She should have contacted him by now. He'd given her the credit card, at least. She could have used the phone in her hotel.

Giving up for the moment, he called someone else.

"Yeah?" Angel's voice sounded thick with tears.

"I know you've got other things on your mind," Dane said softly, "but I need a favor."

"Anything. I just don't want to think about what I could have done to stop this."

He understood. He was piling the guilt pretty high on his own shoulders.

"Lena's phone's been disconnected. Can you track it to a hotel so I can call her? She's also going to need an ID so she can fly. I'll need to go get her—"

"You stay there and help get things settled with Justin," Angel said. "I'll trace her phone and go pick her up myself. We'll all be there soon."

Chapter Eighty

Lena was losing her mind.

It had been three days since her last phone call with Viktor. She was still in Savannah. She spent most of her time camped out in front of Viktor's abandoned complex, hoping he would come back with Kenzie.

Two handguns sat next to her on the console of the Jeep. She didn't think they would be enough to take down Viktor and his entourage, but from watching the *Wizard of Oz*, she fantasized that if she melted Viktor, all his followers would be grateful and swear their allegiance to her. Maybe they would even break into song. In one daydream, she imagined Butch telling her to keep his Jeep in thanks for saving all their asses.

Right.

She took a break from her delusions to wonder where Dane might be. Was he okay? Was Tobey okay? She knew he'd needed to go. She had sent him off even though he'd offered to stay.

But this whole situation reminded her painfully of the strict promise she'd made to herself.

The one she'd broken for Dane.

She knew she shouldn't—*couldn't*—rely on anyone but herself to get through life. Her marriage with Brandon had sent that message home in a big way. It had been nice to allow Dane to take some of the burden and worry off her shoulders, but in the end, this no-win situation was all on her.

It wasn't Dane's fault. He'd tried his best to help her, and she knew there were no guarantees. He hadn't sugar-coated the possible outcomes. There'd been no way to know Mackenzie wouldn't be there when they arrived at the compound. Lena knew if her daughter had been where they'd expected her to be, Dane would have done whatever necessary to get her out safely.

But now Lena was alone. She hadn't called him yet. She liked to think it was because she spent all her time sitting in the Jeep and didn't have a working phone, but she knew there was a different reason.

She was afraid.

What if he still harbored anger for her part in Tobey's kidnapping and didn't care what happened to her or Kenzie? She didn't think that was the case. She'd experienced his kindness. But she didn't know what she would do if he told her they were at the end of the trail, nothing to do, her daughter was gone and so was he.

It was easier to sit here, waiting for Viktor to come back so she could end this.

One way or another.

She only slightly wondered if she was losing it.

The tapping on the glass next to her made her jump and hit her head. She rolled down the window to see Angel standing there. Her expression grim.

"Let's go," Angel said, and nodded to the console. "Bring those."

Lena shook herself out of her surprise, scooped up her

weapons, and jumped out of the Jeep. She stopped at the back to grab her bag, and tucked the guns inside.

"Where are we going?" she asked as she hurried after the woman, who walked really fast for having shorter legs. "Where's everyone else?"

Everyone meaning Dane.

"We're going to a funeral."

Lena stopped walking. Fear gripped her heart, and the guilt she'd felt earlier shattered into worry for the man she'd come to care for. He'd said someone on his team had been injured. It appeared it was worse than that.

"Justin," Angel answered before Lena had the chance to ask.

"Oh God. I'm so sorry." She'd come to care about all the people on the team. It was obvious they all loved one another like family. And they'd taken her in and accepted her, even though she didn't belong.

"Dane is making the funeral arrangements. That's why he didn't come get you himself. He called, but your phone was disconnected. Luckily, I could still track it."

Of course she could. The woman was scary.

"I don't have anything to wear to a funeral," Lena said, feeling embarrassment heat her cheeks.

"We'll stop somewhere before we fly out."

"I can't get on a plane. I don't have ID."

Angel smiled. "It's a private plane."

They sent a private plane to pick her up? She appreciated everything they were doing, but there was one thing that was more important right now. "What about my daughter?"

"We're still working on the plan," Angel said. "We'll finalize after the funeral."

"Of course." Lena didn't want to be rude or disrespectful. She just wanted her daughter back. When they got to a black SUV in the parking lot, she hesitated.

Her daughter had been in Savannah. That was the last place Lena had seen her…even if it was by phone. True, Kenzie could be anywhere by this point, but what if they brought her back here and Lena wasn't there?

"Are you coming?" Angel asked, popping back up from the driver's door.

Her daughter's life was at stake.

Could she really trust these people to get her back?

Chapter Eighty-One

Dane's heart hurt. He'd said goodbye to his son, and now he was being forced to say goodbye to his friend and teammate. Except, this goodbye was forever.

Team Phoenix had gathered and were consoling one another while making the arrangements. But it wasn't until he saw Lena that he finally broke down. She'd been given a key to his hotel room, and when he stepped into the room, she rushed toward him.

He pulled her into his arms, holding her too tight as he cried into her hair.

"I'm so sorry," she said holding him just as tightly.

He was glad for her strength, because at the moment he worried he might fly apart into a billion pieces.

"Justin saved Tobey," he choked out. "He protected him with his own body."

"That is what you are all trained to do," she whispered. "Justin did his job well. He was a hero."

"He's gone because he offered to help me."

"Don't do this," she said, stepping back to grip his upper

arms. "You were telling me just a few days ago how it doesn't work like that. We don't get to look back and wish we'd done things differently. And it wouldn't work, anyway. You would never have been able to tell Justin he couldn't go. He wouldn't have stayed behind."

True, but it still hurt to know it was this particular job that had cost his friend his life.

"I have no doubt you would have done the same thing if you had been there," she reminded him.

He nodded. He would have stepped between Tobey and a bullet and been happy to do it, if it meant Tobey—or any other child, for that matter—was able to live a full life.

He nodded and looked down at her. She was wearing a dark gray dress and make-up.

"We need to leave soon," she said. "You should get changed."

He leaned down and kissed her, glad she was keeping him going so he couldn't fall over.

The funeral was well attended. Justin's ex-wife and his daughter, Haley, were standing in front by the casket. Dane gave the young girl a hug and told her how sorry he was, hoping she didn't pick up on the guilt that colored his words. She no longer had a dad because her father had made the ultimate sacrifice to save Dane's son.

"If you ever need anything, please call me okay?" he said. "I was good friends with your dad, so even if you just want to talk about him or if you have questions. I'm in WITSEC, too. You can reach me through your handler. Remember, I'm here, okay? Anything you need."

But he knew it wasn't enough. Not nearly.

"Okay. Thanks." Haley looked a little overwhelmed from all the attention, but not heartbroken like the rest of the team.

He backed off with one last apology. He remembered what Justin had said before leaving on the mission. That his daughter already saw her dad as dead. They'd been completely out of touch, Justin's penance for forcing them into this life of hiding. Obviously, the girl didn't feel a deep connection with her father.

Dane could have been in this very same situation.

Lena squeezed his hand, as if reading his mind.

"Everyone deals with things differently," she murmured. "Haley will miss him, even if she doesn't realize it yet." Lena linked her arm through his and led him to the area where the rest of his group waited.

When the service was over, Thorne gathered the team at a nearby restaurant. They sat in the back room at a table for eight.

The empty seat made the air catch in his lungs. Justin was gone.

Lena rested a sympathetic hand on his thigh.

"Justin wouldn't want us to be sitting here like lumps," Angel said as she wiped tears from her cheek. "If it had been one of us, he'd have told an embarrassing story about the person to make everyone laugh."

"I have an embarrassing story," Garrett said with a sigh. He turned to his wife. "This was before I met you."

The disclaimer meant it was no doubt a story involving women and drinking. Dane wondered if he had been there, too.

"Thorne sent Justin and me on a job to get intel from some corporate jackass. We show up as consultants who'd been hired to make their network more secure."

"Why wasn't I sent on this job?" Angel asked, being the computer whiz.

"Because we needed to get the information from the woman who was sleeping with the guy."

"Oh."

"The day we start, we walk in when they're having a little retirement shindig for one of their co-workers. There's a cake that says Best Wishes, and everything. We're trying to play it cool and act like we belong, so Justin snags a piece of cake."

"Of course. He couldn't pass up food," Dane said with a smile.

"Right. Well, I passed on the cake and moved to the other side of the group so I could mingle and see who the players were. I'm into a conversation that seems to be leading somewhere when I look up and see Justin has already contacted the woman. Even after we agreed it would be me, because…"

He paused awkwardly while looking at his wife.

"Because you hadn't seen any action in months," Dane offered, having heard this story before.

"Yes. Okay." Garrett's cheeks turned pink as he continued, "I can only see him from the back, and the woman's expression looks disgusted. I mean, she is really not into him, at all, and I think that's great because I'll get a turn. But then, I'm also concerned because if Justin couldn't interest her oozing his famous charm, what chance do I have?"

"You're charming, too," Sam said, rubbing his shoulder.

"I lost visual on him for a minute as I maneuvered my way back to that side of the room. He ended up walking up to me when the woman practically ran away. I asked him what went wrong, and he said he had no clue."

Dane was already laughing.

"But I figured it out pretty quickly," Garrett said.

"What was it?" Angel asked.

"The icing on the cake was blue…and so were Justin's teeth, tongue, and lips. He looked like he'd snacked down on a Smurf."

Everyone laughed, but eventually the silence drifted in again.

Dane glanced over at Lena, who hadn't said anything, but from the look on her face, he knew it was time to ask the team to do the unthinkable.

They'd just lost one of their own, and now he had to ask them to risk their lives again. For an outsider.

Chapter Eighty-Two

Lena understood the stories and banter Dane's team exchanged were all part of their healing process. Under normal conditions, she would have been eager to help them deal with their grief. But it wasn't easy to sit there doing nothing when every second counted for her daughter.

Up until everything went to hell, she'd known Kenzie was relatively safe. She'd spoken to her little girl every morning, and seen with her own eyes that she was being taken care of, despite the imminent threat.

Now that security was gone. Her daughter could be anywhere. And anything could be happening to her. That thought made Lena tense with fear.

Dane must have noticed because he slipped his hand in hers and gave it a little squeeze.

Angel cleared her throat. "Justin wouldn't want us dicking around talking about him when we have a job to do," she said, her voice trembling a little. "He was always anxious to get going. Let's focus on the next attempt to get Mackenzie."

Lena looked at Dane, who seemed as surprised as she was.

"I wasn't sure how to ask," he said. "But we definitely need all your help."

Tears came to Lena's eyes, brought on by the emotions she was feeling because of these generous people. And especially for the man holding her hand. He hadn't given up on her child. She felt ashamed to have even thought it was possible.

She also felt something else. The overwhelming affection she knew was love.

Unable to stop herself, she reached for him. He pulled her into his arms and let her cry.

"I'm sorry," she managed to say. "I thought maybe you'd given up on us."

"No. Of course not. We're going to get her." He rubbed her back and kissed her hair. "I won't stop until she's safe, Lena. I promised you, and I plan to keep that promise."

She choked out another sob and hugged him tighter. Unable to speak, she hoped her squeezing him breathless conveyed her gratitude.

When she'd gotten herself together, she moved back to her own seat. Thorne took control of the meeting, asking for updates.

Ten minutes later, it was clear they didn't have a confirmed location for Viktor or for Kenzie. Lena wanted to cry again.

"I thought we were tracking his phone." She tried to keep her impatience in check.

"I can only track it if it's on," Angel said. "He's got it turned off. Or…it's been destroyed."

"What about one of the other numbers? Butch has called me twice to make sure I was taking care of his Jeep."

Angel nodded. "Do you still have the phone so I can get the number?"

"Yeah. It's in my room." Lena had been keeping it charged up in case Viktor reactivated it to get in touch with her. Plus, there was still a video of her daughter recorded on that phone. She'd watched it more times than was healthy.

Thorne nodded. "Good. Lena, give Angel the number, and let's all get some rest. We'll reconvene in the morning," he announced.

Rest? Lena didn't want to rest. She wanted to find her daughter.

Now.

"Dane?" Thorne called as they were heading for the door.

Dane paused and waited. Lena hung back, too.

"Did you tell her about the other thing we found in Vancouver?" Thorne asked.

Dane grimaced. "No. Not yet. I guess I'll do that now."

He led her out of the room and gestured toward the elevator.

"What is it?" she asked. "What did you find?"

He frowned and pressed the button for their floor before pinning his dark gaze on her. "Your husband."

Chapter Eighty-Three

"Brandon? Brandon was in Vancouver?" Lena's face went white.

Dane didn't know how much more Lena could handle. He was used to being around Angel, who had been through hell but could deal with anything far better than he ever could.

At the other end of the spectrum was Caroline, who didn't handle things very well, at all. Even when she'd come out to meet the officers when they dropped Tobey off, she'd collapsed. Dane had been watching from inside a van that had followed the police cruiser. Just in case.

Lena seemed much stronger than Caroline, but he didn't want this to be the straw that broke her.

"Yeah, but—" he said, leading her into her hotel room.

"You're sure it was him?" she interrupted, and started to pace the length of the space, her expression going from shock to anger.

Dane had seen her angry before. He was glad not to be the cause of it this time.

"In a manner of speaking. They found his body."

"Oh." She dropped heavily onto the edge of the bed and stared at the floor. "I suppose I knew he was dead. I guess I figured he would have been disposed of at sea, or in the Everglades."

"I can see why that would make sense, but he wasn't. He was buried behind one of the buildings at the Vancouver complex. Once the compound was secured, they put dogs out, and they alerted at the grave."

She took a deep breath and looked up. "How do you know it's him?"

"The wallet in his back pocket had his Florida driver's license. They'll use dental records to verify it, but that's our guess right now."

Her face went pale again, and he saw her fingers were shaking.

Damn it. He should have done this better. The guy had been the worst kind of father when he'd put their child in harm's way, but at some point Lena must have loved the bastard.

"I'm sorry," Dane said, because it was the thing you said when someone died and you didn't have anything better to say.

He'd felt bad for Justin's wife and daughter having to stand there as lines of people said they were sorry. Those words meant nothing, but there wasn't anything else to be said.

"It wasn't like I didn't expect it, you know?" She was staring at her fingers. "I mean, I figured he'd either get himself into trouble or overdose." She shook her head and let out a breath. "At least I know for sure now."

"Yeah," Dane murmured.

She swallowed and took another deep breath before she looked up at him. "I thought you'd left me."

They hadn't had a chance to speak before the funeral. He'd been wrapping things up with Thorne.

"I'm sorry. The federal prosecutor wasn't pleased that we made a move against Kulakov on our own. And since he's still not ready to make an arrest, even with all the kidnapping charges, we've gotten the order to stand down."

Her eyes widened. "We aren't going after Kenzie?"

He held up a hand. "Of course we are. It's becoming more and more obvious the prosecutor is working for Viktor, even if we can't prove it yet. We're not waiting. We'll make our move as soon as we know where we're going."

She closed her eyes briefly, then asked, "How is Tobey?"

Dane pressed his lips together to rein in the emotion. The little time he'd had with his son just made him want more.

"He'd hurt his knee," he said, "but he'll be fine. He promised to keep my secret. We'll see what happens. He's ten. It might be hard to keep something like that bottled up. But we didn't really have any other choice. He saw me, and I didn't want to lie to him anymore."

She gave him a sympathetic look. "Now that he knows the truth, will you be able to see him?"

"We know how dangerous that can be," he said, reminding them both of how Tobey wouldn't have been in danger if someone hadn't been following Dane and seen him watching Tobey at the soccer field. "Maybe later when he's older. Or if my former employer, Tim Reynolds, is ever put in jail."

"Is there any chance of that happening?"

Dane shook his head. "Doubtful. When his partner killed himself, all the blame for their indiscretions went with him, and all the assets of the company went to Reynolds. Reynolds was left the innocent, oblivious partner. I'm the only person who knows how involved Reynolds was. He's rich, and rich men can afford to cover up a lot of sins."

She placed her hand on Dane's. "I'm sorry."

Maybe there was something in those words that did help. If just a little bit.

She leaned against him, and he wrapped his arm around her.

"Will you stay with me?" she asked quietly.

He had his own room down the hall, but he didn't want to leave her. He didn't want to be alone. He nodded and kissed her hair.

After helping her out of her gray sheath dress, he undressed down to his boxers and waited on his turn for the bathroom. It felt comforting to share space with another person. It had been one of the things he'd enjoyed about being married. He was never alone. Not like he'd been as a child after his mother died. At home, his father was always closeted in his office, and later, he hadn't come home from the university for days.

It was easy to see, now, why his relationship with Caroline hadn't been strong enough to survive. He'd latched onto the first person who had treated him like he mattered. He'd been so desperate for human contact, he'd held onto Caroline for no other reason than that she kept him from feeling alone.

He'd loved her for that, but he hadn't been in love with her. He'd often heard people say that, but he hadn't really understood the distinction until now.

Lena came out of the bathroom in one of the T-shirts he'd left behind. He got ready and came out to find her in bed already asleep. He slid under the covers next to her, and she snuggled up against his side.

Whatever this was between them, it felt like more than just someone to fill the void, or a distraction. It was much more than that.

She was still in his arms the next morning when they were wakened by his phone. It was early, so he cursed as he reached for the device.

"Yeah?"

"Angel's found something. Come down to the lounge in ten," Colton said, sounding like he'd just been ripped from sleep, himself.

"See you there."

...

Lena's hair was still dripping as they got off the elevator and made their way to the hotel restaurant. All things considered, she felt pretty good. Dane had joined her in the shower, so her usual two-minute wash had come with a nice view and someone to scrub her back.

She felt well rested for once, thanks to being held in his arms all night. He'd seemed to know exactly what she needed. And what she'd needed was someone to hold her and tell her everything was going to be okay.

He hadn't pressed for more. He hadn't tried to distract her with sex. He probably knew it wouldn't have happened. Things were different now that she didn't know where her daughter was, or if she was okay. No way could Lena indulge in pleasure when her daughter could be in pain.

They glanced around the cozy restaurant. Samantha and Garrett were walking in from the other entrance. Thorne was on the phone in a corner booth. Angel was seated at a table feeding John a bottle while Colton watched with a peaceful smile.

It must be nice to have that feeling of safety, and a husband who was truly a partner.

Brandon had said he wanted children, but it turned out he'd only wanted to do the fun things. He wasn't interested in the nighttime feedings and diapers, or really any of it, other than the few minutes a day when the baby was clean and happy.

As Mackenzie got older, Brandon had started using drugs, and Lena kept him away from Kenzie as much as possible.

Angel handed the baby to Colton, who happily took over the feeding.

Lena pushed down a twinge of envy so she could focus on Angel's news.

"Our ship has come in," Angel said. "Or it's on its way, at least."

Thorne ended his call and came to join the group. "Go on."

Angel continued, "Kulakov is meeting a shipment at Long Beach Port in California. He keeps a home and a yacht nearby. When he goes to the meet the freighter at the port, he'll take most of his entourage with him, and we can move into the house to get Mackenzie."

"How do you know she's there?" Lena asked.

Angel glanced over at her and frowned. "We don't."

The thought of rushing into another empty compound made Lena's stomach heave. She swallowed as Dane rubbed the back of her neck.

"I've been to his place in Long Beach," Colton said. "Like Angel said, he keeps a yacht at a nearby marina. *Glorious Morning* is a big yacht. My guess is after meeting the shipment, he's planning to leave the country. If he's paying the prosecutor but was still targeted by a police raid, it might be enough to make him run. This could be our only chance to grab him."

"Oh God," Lena whispered and covered her face. Was he planning to take Kenzie with him out of the country?

"Is there any chance we can get more people on this job?" Garrett asked, looking at Thorne with a frown.

Thorne nodded. "I've reached out to another team and secured three more marshals."

"I'm going," Colton said calmly.

"It's not necessary for you—" Thorne started, but was cut off.

"I'm *going*," Colton repeated, looking at Angel. "I know the last time you had me grounded was because you thought it was too much of a risk. But I can't sit here when I could be helping to save someone's child. You can't ask it of me. What if it was John? Wouldn't you want as many people as possible helping to bring him home?"

Angel let out a shaky breath. "Of course."

"Okay, then. Grandpa Thorne can watch John while we go take care of this together," Colton said with a glance at his boss.

Thorne nodded in agreement. Lena knew he wasn't the baby's real grandfather. But as the father figure for Task Force Phoenix, he had taken on the role.

"Thank you all so much." Tears streamed down Lena's face as Dane pulled her close and kissed her hair. She didn't know what she would do if Viktor took Kenzie out of the country. Anything could happen to her out there. Horrible, awful things, things that she couldn't think about.

They had to get her back.

Thankfully, she now knew the team would do everything in their power to make that happen.

She owed these people more than she would ever be able to repay.

Chapter Eighty-Four

With a plan in place, they all headed out en masse. Dane was proud to be part of Phoenix, which truly treated each other like family.

Angel had secured a new ID for Lena so she was able to fly. They all took the next flight to LAX. Once there, they rented a house and obtained a shit-ton of weapons and ammunition.

Thorne was in constant contact with everyone…when he wasn't taking care of John.

The furnished house had three bedrooms. Angel immediately turned the dining room into a command center, and started showing Samantha how to operate the satellite feeds and the domestic communications.

They didn't have much time—the freighter was due to arrive the next evening. Once it was loaded with Viktor's cargo, they expected him to jump on his yacht and flee.

What they didn't know was if Kenzie would be part of the cargo on the freighter, or if she would be travelling on his personal vessel. Or maybe she wasn't there, at all. Maybe she'd already been sold or shipped off elsewhere.

Dane looked over at Lena, who stood back from the hustle and bustle of the team. "It's going to be okay," he told her. "If she's there, we'll get her back."

Lena's eyes filled. "And if she isn't there?"

"I promise we won't stop looking for her." He wrapped his arms around her and pulled her close.

"I really wish I hadn't hit you over the head with a bottle," she murmured into his chest, making him laugh.

"When this is all over, I'll use that guilt whenever I want to get my way."

Her smile was strained, but at least he'd gotten a smile from her. She was so tense, he worried she would snap at any minute.

"Come on," he said gently. "We've done everything we can. Everything is in place, we can't do anything more until tomorrow evening. Let's go up to bed."

She nodded and placed her hand in his when he offered it to her.

They'd taken the room at the end of the hall, which was the smallest. The other two rooms had queen-size beds, while this one was only a full.

He didn't mind sharing a small bed with her. They slept close together, anyway.

She sat on the bed and flopped back with a deep breath.

He bent to take off her shoes, then pulled her back up to a sitting position so he could take off her shirt. She helped get her pants off, and he handed her one of his T-shirts. Before her body was covered with the clean cotton, his own body reacted to the sight.

Stripped down to his boxers, he pressed her back onto the bed and kissed her. When his cock lurched against her, she gasped.

"Just ignore him," Dane instructed with a wry smile. "He

has misinterpreted the situation. Usually when I get in bed with a beautiful woman, it's his turn."

She laughed and shook her head. "Can you tell him I'm sorry for the confusion?"

"He understands. Roll over. I'll give you a back rub."

She did as he asked and sighed as his hands moved over her. "I don't deserve this," she murmured.

"It's just a back rub."

"No. I mean I don't deserve to have your team put themselves in danger—for you to be in danger—because of me."

He gave her a sincere look. "We do this all the time for people we don't even know. Sometimes for people who are complete assholes. There's nothing worse than protecting someone who should be going to prison, but is in WITSEC because they can put away a bigger fish. But with Mackenzie? It's a no-brainer. We want to help."

He paid special attention to massaging her butt muscles when he worked his way down there, then moved back up.

"Tell me about your daughter," he said, so she could stop worrying for just a little while.

Lena thought for a moment, letting out an emotional sigh. "She's small for her age. She looks a lot like I did when I was little."

He smiled. "So, beautiful, then?"

She laughed and went on. "She swims like a fish, and once you get her into the pool it's hard to get her out without a fuss. Usually she's well behaved, but a few months before she was taken, she'd picked up a smart mouth from a kid at daycare. She told me she hated me, but when I cried, she apologized right away. I remember thinking at the time it was the worst thing that could happen—to have my daughter tell me she hated me. But it's not."

"No. I'm sure it won't be the last time she says that, I'm

sorry to say. I hear teenagers tend to use the sharpest weapons at their disposal."

She let out a long breath. "I hope I get the chance to have to deal with my daughter telling me she hates me. How ridiculous it sounds to say that."

"I understand."

"I'm so sorry you can't be with Tobey."

"For some reason, it's a lot better now that he knows I'm alive. I feel like he's less likely to forget me that way."

"That makes sense." She was quiet for a spell, and when she spoke again, her voice was soft and slow with exhaustion.

"Kenzie is kind. She always worries about people. Once we saw a homeless person on the way into the grocery store, and she wanted to get her something to eat. She picked out a meal and gave it to the woman when we were leaving. In the car, she asked if we could go back the next day to take her a sandwich."

"Did you go?"

"I thought she'd forget, but she didn't. But the woman had moved on when we got there…"

Lena's story drifted off, and her breathing slowed. She was asleep. He softened his touch and covered her with the blanket and turned off the light before pulling on his jeans and going out to the living room where the team was gathered.

"Is she sleeping?" Samantha asked with a compassionate frown.

"Yeah."

Angel shook her head. "I can't imagine what she must be going through. If someone took my son and threatened his life, there would be hell to pay," she said fiercely.

Dane didn't doubt that for one second.

"What happens on Tuesday?" Garrett casually asked.

"Tuesday?" Puzzled, Dane looked around at the others. Today was Sunday. They would be raiding Viktor's home tomorrow evening. Tuesday was…nothing. Tuesday it would all be over.

"Oh." He understood now. They wanted to know what he was planning to do when this was over. "You mean me and Lena."

Everyone nodded.

"I'm not sure," he admitted. "We haven't talked about it yet. It's always seemed premature to bring it up, you know?"

They backed off and turned to another equally difficult subject. Tobey.

"Are you planning to see him again?" Garrett asked.

"Yeah. I am. I mean, I don't know exactly when, but I'll reach out to him. Check in. Now that he knows I'm alive, I think it would be upsetting for me to just drop out of his life completely. Again. He might think I don't care about him. I know I can't get involved, and no one else can know the truth, but occasionally I'd like to make sure he's okay."

"I don't blame you," Colton said. "I'd do the same thing if it was John. I wouldn't be able to stay away."

"You'll have to be careful," Garrett warned.

Dane nodded. "Yeah. I will."

"You probably thought you were being careful before, but someone was watching you," Garrett pointed out.

"I know." Dane had been reckless. He shouldn't have showed up in public. He would do better the next time. "I'll be a lot more careful."

"Justin always wished he'd gone into WITSEC alone," Garrett said. "He always felt guilty because he made his wife and child give up their old lives. Thorne told him to bring his family."

Everyone looked up. They'd not heard this.

"Really?" Sam said.

Garrett continued. "Yeah. Justin told me once when we were on a stakeout."

"What exactly did he say?" Angel asked in disbelief.

"I think it hit Thorne a little too close to home—Justin deciding whether or not to walk out on his daughter." Garrett looked over at Samantha, the daughter Thorne had walked out on, himself. "Thorne couldn't make Justin do it. He told him to bring his family along. Justin always regretted doing it. Especially after the marriage fell apart and they split up."

"Thorne told me he regretted it, too—that advice," Dane said, recalling a conversation he'd had a few years ago with their leader.

"Thorne's getting soft in his old age," Angel joked.

"He doesn't seem all that soft to me," Garrett said with a grimace.

"You're his son-in-law, he's supposed to hate you. You touch his daughter," Colton said.

They all laughed, and Dane wondered how much longer they might have this easy camaraderie. How long before everyone drifted apart and moved on with their new families?

Garrett only did the odd job here and there for Phoenix. Donovan was out of the country most of the time—as he'd been for this mission. Angel and Colton were only here because Dane needed them. And now Justin was gone.

Why wasn't Thorne recruiting anyone new for the task force?

Suddenly, Dane wondered. Was he about to lose this family, too?

Chapter Eighty-Five

The next day, Lena woke knowing this day was going to be the most important one in her life. Today she would either get her daughter back or lose her forever.

While no one had said anything specific, she knew the importance of apprehending Viktor before he left the country. Because once he was gone, her chances of finding Kenzie were slim. If they couldn't hold him, they had no leverage to make him give her up.

If he was leaving the country, it could also mean he was going to meet one of his customers. The evil kind who brokered in little girls. With Lena's betrayal, he no longer had any reason to keep her daughter around. The fact was, Kenzie could already be lost to that terrifying underworld.

Lena felt sick and the room spun as if she'd had too much to drink, despite having gone to bed sober.

Dane nuzzled closer and wrapped his arm around her waist. He was warm and smelled like soap and clean sheets. He was also aroused in the way men were in the morning.

How nice it would be if this was her real life. If the only

thing she had to worry about was being quiet so they didn't wake Kenzie. If she could snuggle in bed with this man, knowing her daughter was safe in her own bed, right down the hall.

The joy of that thought brought tears to Lena's eyes, but she blinked them away.

Dane's job was saving people. Right now it was Kenzie, but it wouldn't stop with her. He would go on other missions and jobs that would put him in danger. And that danger could possibly follow him home. The situation with Tobey had made that likelihood crystal clear.

She couldn't risk being part of that. Couldn't put herself in that kind of danger. If she got Kenzie back, she would do whatever she had to do to keep her safe. Not just the normal things like stranger-danger and taking smaller bites, but the long-term things, like who was allowed in her daughter's life.

She had responsibilities, and she hadn't taken them seriously enough before.

She'd never make that mistake again.

Dane stirred and made a small groan of happiness. She wasn't sure if it was because he'd slept well or because his erection was nestled up against her hip.

"Good morning," he said in a voice deep and scratchy with sleep.

"Good morning." Her voice, by contrast, sounded high and flinty. It was impossible to disguise her worry.

"Today's the day we get your daughter back."

He sounded so confident she wanted to believe him. But they'd been in this place before. She'd woken up a little over a week ago with the same hope in her heart.

Hopefully, today would be different.

The outcome *must* be different.

Chapter Eighty-Six

It felt like Christmas morning when Dane walked out into the living room. Not the Christmas mornings he'd had after his mother died, but the fun kind with a tree and presents and a big breakfast.

While there was no tree, there were plenty of presents. At least, of the weapons and ammunition variety. And Colton was in the kitchen fixing the big breakfast.

The thing that really made it feel like a holiday was the spirit and excitement of everyone in the house.

With one exception.

He'd heard Lena crying in the bathroom on his way down the hall. He'd wanted to knock and go in to soothe her. But the only thing that would make her feel better was a guarantee he couldn't give.

They had even less intel than they'd had with the first raid. And like the first time, their resources would be split between the house and the yacht.

Garrett and the two borrowed marshals were taking the house. It wasn't a sprawling estate like in Savannah, so it wouldn't take much to check it. And with Viktor being offsite, the place wouldn't be heavily guarded. That would leave Colton, Angel, Lena, and Dane to check *Glorious Morning* and keep Kulakov from getting away.

Facing Kulakov meant facing all his bodyguards.

Lena had been given the option of staying with Garrett to check the house, but she had chosen to stay with Dane. He hadn't said anything, had let it be her decision, but he was pleased with her choice. It meant he would be right there with her if she needed him.

When she came out to join the rest of the team, she took a tiny portion of eggs and sat off to the side.

Dane filled his plate and went to sit next to her. "Are you going to be able to do this?" he asked gently.

She nodded immediately. "I'll be ready. I just don't know how everyone else can be so casual about this. I'm scared. Aren't they scared?"

"Of course. We just handle it differently. We can't let fear take over, or we would be useless. We have to put it on the back burner and deal with it when the mission's over."

"I don't know how you do this constantly. I'm not just scared for me. I'm worried about you. And what if Viktor gets to Colton? Angel is so small. I know she could kick my ass, but compared to Weller or Butch..." She finished the sentence with a shudder.

"We're all trained for this. It's our job."

"But Justin—"

"Bad things happen to good people every day. Let me tell you, I was in more danger in my corporate office with the great view than I am today."

She shook her head. "That's different."

"You need to find a way to push it out away from you so it can't mess you up. If you freeze up inside, that's when it gets dangerous."

"I think I need a minute." She dumped her uneaten eggs in the trash and went out the back door.

An hour later, she still hadn't come back in. He went to the back door, and when he didn't see her, he stepped out on the small deck.

"Lena?" he called, but got no response.

Holy crap.

She was gone.

Chapter Eighty-Seven

Lena should have let someone know where she was going, but when she walked out of the yard, she hadn't known where she was going.

Of course she would return. She wouldn't miss something as important as her daughter's rescue. But she didn't want all those people put in danger, either.

She pushed her sunglasses back up on her nose and secured the bun on the top of her head. As disguises went, this one was pretty broke-ass, but it was what she had.

Pretending to focus her attention on the cell phone that didn't work while walking and spying proved to be more than she could do on a single pass. Waiting ten minutes, she walked back down the street on the sidewalk closest to Viktor's Long Beach home.

Was Kenzie in there? Could she be looking out the window? Would she recognize Lena if she saw her?

It took every bit of strength she had to make sure she kept to the sidewalk and didn't divert through the gate. She kept walking a mile and half to the marina where *Glorious*

Morning was docked.

The yacht was as pretentious as its name, and Lena wanted to light it on fire for what it represented. It wasn't bad enough that Viktor had gobs of money, multiple homes, and a warehouse complex. He also owned ships and had enough people to protect him from people like her. Regular people whom he'd threatened.

On board, she saw a few men readying the boat—none she recognized. A maid, burdened down with three large shopping bags, boarded with no help from the guard on duty.

Surely, they wouldn't bother to get the yacht ready unless Viktor was planning to leave on it.

Noticing a car with the trunk still open, she stepped closer to take a look. The trunk was filled with more grocery bags. The maid was already on her way back for another load. This was a lot of food for a weekend excursion. This was enough to stock a galley for a number of weeks. Long enough to get to another country.

Lena took a deep, calming breath and plastered a smile on her face. She had an idea.

"Hi, I'm Jenny. Are you new?" she lied when the maid returned.

"Kind of." The other woman winced as if embarrassed it was that obvious. "I'm Rose."

"I know it's a pain, Rose, but you should lock the trunk between trips," Lena said, trying to look concerned. "In case someone came by and tampered with something Mr. Kulakov might eat."

Wow. Where was all this coming from? She'd opened her mouth and the lies just flew out.

"Oh. Yes. I'm sorry."

"It's okay. I won't say anything. Did you need a hand carrying this onboard?"

God. What was she doing? She couldn't just stroll onto

Viktor's yacht. What if he was onboard already? What if Weller or Butch were here, checking things over?

But…what if Kenzie was onboard and Lena had a chance to sneak her off the boat without anyone getting hurt?

"I wouldn't want to bother you," Rose said.

"It's no problem. I'm going up to check the media equipment for the trip. No sense going empty-handed. Besides, we don't want this food sitting out here in the heat, right?"

"Thank you. That would be great." At mention of the food going bad, the maid hurried along.

It wasn't until Lena's arms were weighed down with food and she was heading for the *Glorious Morning* gangplank that she realized this was a terrible idea that could easily go horribly, dreadfully wrong.

Chapter Eighty-Eight

Lena's hands trembled as she reached the guard standing at the gangway. He was probably going to ask her what business she had on the boat. Or her name, at least.

What name had she given Rose? She was so nervous she couldn't even remember.

She needed to act like she belonged.

"Rose?" she called to the woman a few feet in front of her.

"Yes?"

She made sure to wait until she was almost to the guard, then asked, "Did you remember the orange juice for his cocktails?"

"Oh, yes. Three gallons."

"Good. I didn't see them in my bags."

"No. They're already inside."

Their conversation kept the guard from stopping her. In fact, he didn't look remotely interested. She wondered how much the guy was being paid. Too much for the lax job he was doing. Not that she was complaining.

It took a moment for her eyes to adjust from the bright

sun on deck to the dim lighting in the galley. She set her bags next to Rose's and turned toward the staterooms.

"Let me know if you need any help. I'm just checking the televisions, then I'll be heading out."

"Thanks for your help. I appreciate it."

Lena continued on her way, wondering what the hell she should do now. She was on the vessel Viktor would be using to flee the country. Surely, there was something she could do to ensure it wouldn't be able to leave.

Unfortunately, this was only the second time she'd ever been on a boat. And the first time was more of a canoe than a seafaring luxury yacht.

All the important gauges and buttons were up on the bridge, above the deck where the other men were working. Even if she could get past them, she wouldn't know what to do.

On instinct, she pulled her phone from her pocket as if to call someone to help. But it was still useless. She'd kept it charged just in case Viktor reactivated it and called her about Kenzie, but for now it was nothing but a fancy way to tell time.

She froze in the act of putting it back in her pocket and looked at it again.

It wasn't just telling time. It was also capable of being tracked by a certain little spitfire computer whiz.

Oh, yeah.

She smiled broadly, and turned her focus to finding a place to hide the phone so no one would find it and toss it overboard.

Chapter Eighty-Nine

"I think your girl ran off," Garrett said with a frown as Colton handed out the gear.

Dane pressed his lips to a thin line. "Lena didn't run off. She wouldn't just walk away when we're about to rescue her daughter."

He didn't bother to mention that Lena wasn't his girl, either…mostly because they hadn't yet gotten around to classifying the relationship.

A relationship that wouldn't matter if she had, indeed, run off.

Where the hell *was* she?

He was picking up his car keys to hit the streets and look for her when the front door opened and she rushed in.

"Am I late?" she asked, as if she hadn't been gone the entire day.

He tamped down his irritation. "No. But I was about to go search for you."

"I'm here now." She looked…guilty or something. Guilt with a side of pride, maybe?

"What's going on?" he asked.

"In ten words or less," said Garrett, "we need to leave in about twenty minutes."

Lena straightened. "I was on Viktor's yacht."

"*What?*" the whole team said at once.

Startled, she took a step backward. "It just sort of... happened. I went for a walk and I knew where he lived because I'd seen the address on your maps. I just wanted to see if maybe Kenz was in the backyard playing or something."

"Was she?" Dane asked, hopeful.

Lena shook her head. "No. So, I walked past the house and ended up at the marina. It's obvious his staff is getting *Glorious Morning* ready to go on a long journey."

"What if he had seen you there?" Garrett snapped.

"He wasn't on board. I know because I was. I walked on with the maid who was stocking the refrigerator and pantry. I tried to think of a way to keep the boat from being able to leave, but I couldn't come up with anything. So, instead, I hid my cell phone in one of the cabinets on deck. Angel should be able to track it if he gets away, right?"

They all looked at her, then at one another in surprise. Dane was sure he had the same baffled expression on his face.

Good God. She'd managed to get on board and plant a tracking device on Viktor Kulakov's yacht? Dane was vaguely surprised she hadn't stayed to cut and color his hair, too.

Wordlessly, Angel whirled and headed for the dining room where their makeshift control center was set up.

"Good job, Lena." Samantha was the first person to break the stunned silence. Probably because she wasn't as shocked as the rest of them, having been a normal person who'd had to live through an extraordinary situation.

Dane knew Garrett had once underestimated her, but when it counted, Sam had stepped up and saved his life. Dane also knew while Garrett was glad to be alive, he hadn't been too happy she didn't listen to his orders but had put herself in danger.

Dane could relate, big time.

"I'm proud of you for thinking of it," he told Lena when she tentatively stepped closer to him. "But I'm also mad as hell you risked yourself like that."

She shrugged. "It wasn't much of a risk. I just helped the maid carry some groceries. Once I was onboard, no one seemed to care."

"Holy shit, it's working," Angel called out from the dining room.

"I figured if he gets away, we'll have another shot at him," Lena reasoned.

Dane felt the pride surge again.

His girl had done one damn fine job.

Chapter Ninety

After the rush of adrenaline from her earlier adventure, Lena felt exhausted and ravenous. Unfortunately, she hadn't gotten back in time for lunch, and there was no time for a nap.

Instead, she was whisked off to sit in the parking lot at the marina where she'd been just an hour earlier.

Her part of the plan was simple. She was supposed to stay close to Dane, and if—*when*—they saw Kenzie, Lena was supposed to have her daughter come to her. She would make sure she got Kenzie out of harm's way as quickly as possible, in case bullets started flying.

That part was more of an instinct that an actual plan. Getting her daughter to safety was imprinted in her genes. It didn't take any thought or planning.

Still, they'd gone over it all four times.

She'd been caught up in all the preparations, but it was clear she wasn't cut out for this. As much as she might have wanted Dane in her life, she wouldn't be able to stand this constant tension. She didn't have the strength to live her life on the edge like these people did. Planning for every possible outcome.

For now, she would do her part. But more than that? She didn't think it possible.

Colton and Angel would be moving on the guards while Dane focused on Viktor.

Initially, Colton had wanted to take point on Viktor, but it was decided he might not be able to stop himself from taking the man down if Viktor actually surrendered. Viktor had cost Colton a lot, and no one would blame him for getting emotional and going over the edge.

Certainly not Lena. She could understand better than anyone else what Viktor was capable of. He had to be stopped. She was fine with whatever happened to the monster.

"I have a visual on Viktor leaving the main gate at the port. His cargo has been loaded on the freighter and he left the pier four minutes ago," Samantha reported. "I just made an anonymous call to the port authority telling them I believe there may be something illegal inside the container. They are en route to investigate."

"Excellent. Garrett do you have anything?" Angel asked from the back seat where she was sitting with Colton.

Garrett's voice came over the com. "First floor secure, moving to the second."

Lena realized she was squeezing Dane's hand too hard when he adjusted his fingers.

"Sorry," she whispered.

"It's going to be okay. We'll find her," Dane promised, two seconds before Garrett came back on the radio.

"No one inside the house. It's been cleared out. We're going to redirect to the marina. Be there in twenty."

This was it, then.

Lena prayed Kenzie was here. Because it could very well be their last chance to save her child.

Chapter Ninety-One

Dane expected Garrett's news to have sent Lena into a panic, but instead, it seemed as though the opposite had happened. He'd felt the tension leave her body in one soft sigh.

Her manic grip released, and she closed her eyes as if she'd found peace.

Had she given up? Would she be able to move when the time came? *If* the time came?

There was no guarantee that Kenzie was still with Kulakov. Had he put her in the container with a bunch of other captives at the port? It was a worry, but Dane didn't think that was what had happened.

Kulakov had threatened Lena with an especially grim fate for her daughter if she betrayed him. Including a personal delivery to a special buyer. That would play in their favor.

Unless he'd been bluffing. Viktor Kulakov did have a flair for the dramatic.

Before Dane could ask Lena if she was okay, a black town car pulled up in front of the dock. Weller jumped out of the passenger seat and moved to the back door on the same side.

He opened it while his gaze darted around the parking lot.

Dane had purposely parked under the light so the glass would reflect like a mirror.

The door opened, and Viktor slid out of the car wearing a white suit and a straw fedora. He looked like the poster boy for Drug Smugglers R Us. What a cliché.

Dane heard Colton's sharp intake of breath at seeing the people who had tried their best to kill him.

Viktor studied the parking lot nervously, then nodded to Butch who climbed out from the other side of the car.

The dock was dark except for a few scattered street lights, but the yacht was all lit up like a Christmas tree.

"Where is she?" Lena whispered. "She has to be here."

Up on deck, two more men came to stand at the rail by the gangplank.

"We've got four guards visible," Colton said from the back seat, slipping into deputy marshal mode and keeping everyone on the com informed. "Angel?"

"I can get the two on deck from here," she said next to him. She raised a high-power rifle and twisted her neck to the side. "You get the two with Viktor."

"I've got Viktor," Dane said, keeping his voice even. Too bad he couldn't shoot to kill. They would need him to tell them what he'd done with Kenzie.

Viktor moved around to the side of the town car. The side away from them that was wreathed in darkness. He looked down for a moment, then turned toward the brightly lit yacht.

"Are we doing this?" Angel asked.

They were supposed to recover Kenzie, but she wasn't here. However, there was a good chance the authorities would want to speak with Kulakov regarding the contents of the container. Whether it was full of drugs or people.

If the team stopped him, he might be willing to bargain his freedom for Kenzie.

"Let's move," said Dane.

Angel was the first one out. She propped the rifle on the car next to them, and two pops later the guards on deck were down.

Viktor looked behind him briefly, then ducked and rushed toward the gangplank as the boat's engines roared to life.

Lena was right next to Dane as he ran across the parking lot. Colton moved to the side and took out Weller, while Butch tucked in behind Kulakov.

Dane raised the Beretta to shoot Butch but saw something else. Two tiny legs between Viktor and Butch.

Legs clad in pink leggings with purple hearts on them.

A little girl.

"It's her," Lena whispered, her voice choking with emotion as they sprinted down the dark marina dock.

Once Kulakov got the girl on board, they would be much harder to hunt down. The team had to stop him now.

"Yell for her," Dane ordered, hoping hearing Lena would make Viktor stop or slow down.

"Kenzie!" Lena shouted, her voice cracking badly.

"Mama!" Kenzie called, then did exactly what Dane wanted her to. She flailed and slipped out of her captor's grip and turned back toward Dane and her mother.

As Dane and Lena rushed onto the dock, Butch spun around to shoot, but Colton shot first, knocking him to his knees.

"Baby!" Lena yelled.

Viktor snatched the girl by her shoulder and pulled her back into his grip.

Butch aimed his gun from his position on the ground and shot at them.

"Get down!" Dane yelled at Lena, just as a bullet burned into his leg.

Falling to the ground, the only thing that went through his mind was *Fuck! Not again.*

Chapter Ninety-Two

Lena heard Dane's order to take cover, but her brain couldn't process it. Her daughter was right there. Only twenty feet away. But she couldn't get to her because Butch was shooting at her, and Viktor was pulling Kenzie in the opposite direction.

Colton fired again and Butch fell back, the gun dropping from his hand. But now another man had rushed to the rail and was firing at them from the deck above. For some reason, Dane wasn't returning fire.

During target training with Angel and Samantha, Lena hadn't been sure she'd be able to shoot an actual person. Now there was no doubt.

She raised her gun and aimed it at the guard. She pulled the trigger. When he went down, she refocused her sights on Kulakov.

Stepping onto the gangplank, Viktor stopped to hoist Kenzie up in his arms, either to use her as a human shield or to get her to move faster. She was much too close to him for comfort, but Lena had to take a chance. She wouldn't get another one.

She definitely didn't want to shoot Kenzie by accident. Instead of aiming for his back where she might miss a vital organ but hit her daughter if the bullet went through and through, she aimed higher. She let out an even breath and squeezed the trigger with a slow, solid pressure.

The gun went off.

Kenzie screamed.

As a mother, Lena knew every one of her daughter's cries.

This one was pain.

Chapter Ninety-Three

Tucking her gun in her waistband, Lena ran to help her daughter. Kenzie was pinned under Viktor Kulakov's body. He'd been hit in the back of the head.

She pulled Kenzie out from under the heap and turned her so she wouldn't see either of the men who were now dead, lying in pools of blood.

"Mama," her daughter sobbed and held onto her neck with all the strength in her little body.

Lena didn't mind, even if it did make it difficult to breathe.

She carried her daughter back to where Dane was sitting on the dock looking like a storm cloud.

"Are you okay?" she asked with a frown.

"I was shot in the same leg," he growled. "Can you believe it?"

She gasped in surprise. He hadn't so much as moaned in pain. She hadn't even realized he'd been shot.

Sure enough, his thigh was covered in blood. She could see now in the light from the end of the dock.

There was a lot of blood, but she could tell it wasn't gushing as one would expect if the bullet had hit an artery. The fact he was shot in the same place might be a good thing…since he had survived being shot there before. Her reasoning wasn't medically sound, but it kept her from freaking out.

The wound looked as though it hurt like a bitch. Yet, he was smiling at her daughter, who was clinging to Lena like a baby monkey.

"Hi, Kenzie. I'm so glad you're okay," he said. But his words slurred, his head leaned to the side, and his eyelids drooped shut.

Chapter Ninety-Four

"Kulakov's dead?" Dane asked as he was loaded in the ambulance. He'd started to pass out a few minutes ago, but Angel had smacked him in the face a few times to get him back. He was considering demoting her from best friend status.

Angel and Colton jumped into the ambulance with him. Mostly because Angel was applying pressure to his wound, and Colton went wherever Angel went. Lena was being pulled away by another emergency worker.

"Oh, yeah. Real dead," Colton assured him. He even cringed, indicating it must have been especially gruesome.

"Good." Dane smiled despite his spinning head. Viktor deserved an ugly kind of death.

"Who made the shot?" Angel asked.

"Lena," Colton said.

"It was a clean shoot," Dane said. "There was no other option but to take out Kulakov with deadly force."

Angel raised her brows. "Um… But he wasn't armed, and he was shot in the back of the head."

Dane ground his teeth. "I said it was a good shoot."

Angel held up her hands. "Look, I'm not sorry the guy is dead. And I don't really care how he got that way. He put my husband and family at risk just by breathing. All I'm saying is, questions will be asked. Make sure you have the right answers."

"Kulakov was dragging Kenzie away. Taking her to another country. A mother has a right to protect her child. No parent on the planet would fault her for stopping him any way she could."

"Okay," Angel nodded once. "That's good."

Whether Angel believed that was what really happened or if she thought he'd simply come up with a good cover story, he wasn't sure. It didn't matter.

Colton slid down to the floor of the ambulance, squeezed his eyes shut, and rested his head on his knees.

"Hey. I can't take care of both of you," Angel said. "Why are *you* falling apart?"

Colton shook his head slowly and looked up. "Everyone I love is finally safe," he whispered, his eyes glistening with unshed tears.

Dane reached out with his bloody hand and gripped Colton's shoulder. "Thank God for that."

Dane realized how right Colton was. Colton's entire family, including baby John, were now safe. His friend could go home and let his brothers and mother know he was still alive.

Even better, Tobey, Lena, and Kenzie were also safe now. Viktor couldn't hurt them anymore.

With that single bullet, Lena had saved almost everyone.

Everyone but Dane.

Chapter Ninety-Five

Lena and Kenzie were being pulled toward a different ambulance than the one Dane, Angel, and Colton were in. The paramedics wanted to take Kenzie in to be checked over, and Lena wanted that, too.

Her daughter wouldn't leave her side and was clinging to her arm in a way that made Lena wonder if they would be spending every minute of their lives together from now on. At the moment, that prospect sounded pretty damn good to her.

"Are you okay, sweetheart?" she asked for probably the hundredth time in the last forty-five minutes.

Kenzie nodded against Lena's side but didn't speak.

"I'm so sorry I couldn't get to you sooner. That I couldn't get you away from the mean man until now."

"He wasn't mean, Mama," Kenzie said in a small voice. "He was nice. He always had candy."

Lena decided not to argue with the candy litmus test for the time being. For now, she would just be happy that Viktor hadn't mistreated her child. Despite his horrific plans for her future.

"Does anything hurt?" Lena asked while taking in the large bump on Kenzie's forehead from the fall.

"It hurts here," Kenzie said pointing to the wrist where Viktor had gripped and dragged her.

Lena lifted it tenderly and gave it a kiss. "Okay. When we get to the hospital, the doctors will take a look. They'll make it all better."

"I missed you, Mama."

If Kenzie had wanted to say the one thing that would make Lena's heart break the most, she'd chosen her words well. She'd thought having Kenzie ask when she was coming to get her was difficult. This was unbearable.

"Oh, baby, I've missed you so much." She didn't want to squeeze Kenzie too tightly. Not until she'd been seen by a doctor and Lena was sure everything on the inside was fine. But she couldn't resist giving her a long hug.

"Daddy said he was taking me away for a fun trip, but when I asked if you were coming, he said you didn't want to because you were mad at me."

Lena had to school her face not to give away her explosive feelings over that lie. "Of course I'm not mad at you. Not at all."

The subject had come up numerous times during their video chats. It had been difficult to convince Kenzie she wasn't angry when she also hadn't shown up to take her home. Lena understood why she might still be worried about it.

At the hospital, it took forever for Kenzie to be seen and released with a clean bill of health. Thankfully, her wrist wasn't broken or sprained, just bruised.

"Can we go home now?" Kenzie asked.

Lena wanted to cry. She didn't have the heart to tell her daughter that they no longer had a home. Or that she only had four hundred dollars in the bank. Thanks to Viktor, her entire life had been put on hold.

She shuddered as she thought of the man. She'd actually killed him. She'd done it to protect her daughter, and she knew if faced with the same situation, she wouldn't hesitate to do it again. But still, she had taken someone's life.

"We'll leave in a minute, but first I want to check in on the friend who helped me find you." She hoisted her daughter up on her hip even though, at six, she was way too old to be carried. Surely, some spoiling would make them both feel better.

Kenzie's leg pushed at the gun tucked in her jeans. Lena adjusted her little body and kissed Kenzie's hair. It was so nice to have her close. She never wanted to let her go.

They went to information and waited while a surly-looking receptionist made a number of adjustments to the contents of her desk before looking at Lena with her brow raised. "Yes?"

"Hi. I'm looking for Dane Ryan."

The woman studied her monitor for a few seconds and looked at her. "Are you family?"

"No. But I—"

"I'm sorry. I can't tell you if he's a patient unless you're family."

"I already know he's a patient here. He came in with a gunshot wound. I just need to know where he's been moved."

"I can't tell you that."

"Fine. I'll just wait over here." She pointed in the direction of the waiting room.

"Mama, I want to go home," Kenzie said against her neck.

"I know, baby, but I can't get into the house where we're visiting since I don't have a key. And my friend is hurt, so we're just going to sit here until he comes out. You can sleep if you want."

"I'm not tired." Of course Kenzie would never admit to being tired, even as her eyelids sagged. Lena knew it would be no more than ten minutes before she was out like a light.

As her daughter snuggled in her lap, Lena watched for any sign of Angel, Colton, or Garrett. They were probably with Dane.

She prayed he was okay. He'd been talking as he was loaded into the ambulance, but what if something had happened afterward?

"Excuse me, ma'am. Did you say you were waiting for a patient named Dane Ryan?"

Lena looked up into the eyes of the biggest police officer she'd ever seen. "Uh. Yes?" The last word came out sounding like a question.

"Were you involved in the shooting at the marina?" he asked.

Lena swallowed, not sure what to say. What were they telling the police? Was it still a secret? She'd waited too long. The officer frowned and moved on to another question.

"Can I see some ID?" he asked.

"Uh. I'm sorry, I don't have it." Her real ID had been taken, along with her personal phone and credit cards by Viktor. Her new ID was back at the house, which she didn't have access to at the moment.

"I wanna go home," Kenzie complained, and when she shifted her foot, she dislodged the gun that had been tucked into Lena's waistband. The nine-millimeter fell between the gap in the seats and clattered to the floor.

The officer's eyes widened slightly and he let out a sigh. "Ma'am, I think you'd better come with me."

Chapter Ninety-Six

Dane woke to the telltale smell of a hospital. He remembered being brought in with a gunshot wound to his thigh. The same thigh that had been shot before, and bitten by a dog. And then shot again. He recalled the trip in the ambulance, but things kind of faded out from there.

His leg should be hurting, but the pain was numbed by whatever was dripping into the IV attached to his arm.

"Hello there," a smiling nurse greeted him as she stepped into the room. She took care of business first—checking the bag and the monitors he was hooked up to. "How's the pain?"

"Bearable."

"The doctor will be in shortly. Do you know what happened?"

"Not after I got to the hospital."

"Your femoral artery was nicked. You were losing a lot of blood. You had to have an operation to repair it."

He winced, and not just from the bright sun filtering through the windows. "How bad is it?"

"The doctor will be in to discuss it with you."

Dane sure didn't like the frown on her lips when she turned toward the door. But the sound of grumbling from the hallway distracted him. He would recognize Angel's bossy voice anywhere, since it was the usual tone she used with him.

"We *are* his family, and we want to see him. We heard he was awake. You said we only had to wait until he woke up."

"Please let them in before her head explodes," Dane whispered to the nurse by his bed. She nodded and went out to intervene.

One by one, Garrett, Sam, Angel, and Colton piled into the small room. His gaze remained on the door, waiting for the missing member of their team. But she didn't come into the room.

"Where's Lena?" he asked.

"I told you he was going to notice," Angel said with an eye roll as she smacked Garrett in the arm.

Lena wasn't there?

Where the hell was she?

Chapter Ninety-Seven

Lena decided to answer the detective's questions as honestly as possible. Which included telling him she was the one who shot Viktor Kulakov.

After an initial screaming fit, Kenzie had been allowed to stay with her. Fortunately, she was sleeping by the time they got to the bad parts where her mother admitted to shooting someone in the back of the head.

Lena didn't feel guilty, exactly. It was just the kind of experience that stuck with a person.

When she'd asked for a phone call, the officer who'd brought her in politely explained that she hadn't been arrested, but was just being held for questioning. She persisted until they brought her a phone.

The problem was, she didn't know anyone's number. They had been stored in her own phone—the one she'd left behind on *Glorious Morning* in case the team needed to track Viktor. A lot of good it was doing there now.

"Do you have the phone number for the United States Marshal's office?" she asked, hoping the two cops wouldn't laugh.

The detective pursed his lips. "I can find one, I'm sure. Who do you need to call?"

"Supervisory Deputy United States Marshal Josiah Thorne." She half expected to see them tremble from just his title and name, but they gave another simple nod.

After some redirections that still counted as one call, she got a voicemail and left a quick message explaining things. She asked him to call the Long Beach Police Department and get her out of this place.

The detective's questions continued, some of them repeated so many times she worried he was too tired to do his job correctly. She knew *she* was too exhausted to answer the same question four damn times.

"I'm telling you, it wasn't a robbery," she gritted out. "He was taking my child onto his yacht, illegally, and against her will and mine. He'd threatened to sell her, as in human trafficking. I was protecting my daughter. Tell me you wouldn't have done the same thing in my situation."

Eventually the two cops left, and she must have fallen asleep in her chair with her daughter sleeping in her lap. When she awoke, it was light out, and the detective came in the room wearing a clean shirt and a smile.

"You're free to go."

"I am?" She'd been there so long, she worried this was some new technique designed to break her.

"SD Thorne called and explained everything."

Lena wanted to point out that *she* had explained things multiple times and they hadn't believed her, but she decided to keep her mouth shut and get out of there.

She was so relieved, she might have jumped out of her chair if her leg wasn't asleep from the weight of her waking child.

And then it struck her.

She was free to go.

But where?

Chapter Ninety-Eight

The doctor had come in to talk to Dane about his leg and the discussion hadn't gone well. He should have expected the bad news. How many times could a person be injured in the same place before the damage couldn't be repaired anymore?

For now, he still had his leg, but it was a wait and see kind of thing. The doctors were optimistic.

Dane planned to do whatever he had to do to walk away from this intact.

He wasn't allowed to leave the hospital in case his artery decided to blow up again or his leg fell off. He also wasn't able to get up and walk around. That, paired with not knowing what happened with Lena, had him restless and irritable. He refused to believe she would have bailed on him without so much as a goodbye.

Which meant something must have happened to her. Something bad.

It would be just her luck to be kidnapped by some other drug-smuggling asshole immediately after escaping Kulakov.

Angel and Colton had left to go relieve Thorne and get

back to the baby. Garrett and Sam had gone back to the house to wait for Lena, but last time he checked, she hadn't shown up.

Thankfully, Thorne arrived that afternoon and shed some light on the mystery. He explained how she'd been detained by the police, and how he'd called the precinct and forced them to release her.

"When I was done reading Viktor's rap sheet, the detective sounded as if he wanted to hold a parade in her honor for protecting the community from that monster."

Which explained where she'd been.

But where was she now?

An hour later, Lena arrived at the hospital with Kenzie in tow. When Lena smiled at Dane, he felt as if everything was going to work out just fine.

Then she glanced down questioningly at his leg, and he remembered the situation he was in. He was facing months of rehab and physical therapy. He wasn't going anywhere anytime soon.

He couldn't ask her to stay with him through all that. She had her own life to go back to, to rebuild. She had her daughter. She could live a normal life now.

Dane had left his own family behind so they wouldn't have to live in hiding. He couldn't ask anyone else to sign up for that.

Thorne gave Dane's good leg a hard pat and rose from the guest chair. "I need to make some calls. I'll be back." He squeezed Lena's shoulder and whispered something to her that made her smile before he ruffled Kenzie's hair and left the room.

Dane reached out for Lena's hand as she took the seat Thorne had vacated.

"I would have been here sooner, but this place has some intimidating security. No one would tell me what room you were in. So, I went back to the rental house. Garrett and Sam gave me your room number."

He made a mental note to get her a working cell phone as soon as possible.

"I heard you were detained by the police," he said, taking her hand.

"Yeah. It turns out the cops didn't think it was cool that I was carrying a gun in a public place."

"Sorry about that." Dane grinned, not as sorry as he should be since he was envisioning it. "Hi, Kenzie. How are you doing?"

The little girl was tucked up against her mother. He wasn't sure if she was normally a shy child, or if she was still traumatized from her ordeal. From the things Lena had said, and being in the room during a couple of their video calls, Kenzie had seemed like a precocious and charming child. But sometimes kids were different with other adults.

Today, all she did was nod and keep her head down.

"This is the nice man I was telling you about," Lena told her. "He's the one who helped me find you."

The girl glanced up and studied him for a moment. She stood straighter and held out a paper to him. It was a small piece of chain hotel stationary. Probably the hotel where Lena stayed last night after leaving the police department.

There was a drawing of what he guessed was her and her mother. They were smiling, and there was something in Lena's very large hand that looked like a gun. In uneven scrawl that tapered off the page were the words, "Thank you, Dane."

Dane's heart squeezed. "You're very welcome, sweetie. I'm glad you're back with your mommy, and that you're safe."

"Did Mama shoot you, too?" she asked timidly.

Obviously, there was some interest in her mother shooting a gun. Dane smiled and deferred to Lena on the question.

"No, baby," Lena said. "Remember? I only shoot bad people. And only when they are trying to take you away from me. Dane is a good guy."

Kenzie nodded, pacified by the answer for now, though Dane guessed it would come up again.

"Can I draw another picture?" Kenzie asked.

"Sure." Lena pulled the pad of paper from a small pink backpack and handed over a pack of crayons. Kenzie took them over to the deep windowsill and set up her art studio.

"How is she?" he asked Lena.

"She's fine. Completely fine. Thanks to you and Task Force Phoenix."

He grimaced. "I'm not the one who took out Viktor. You did the right thing, Lena. I'm not sure if you're having trouble dealing with…everything. It's not easy, no matter how much the person deserves it."

She nodded. "It's strange. I know I did the only thing I could do. I know it was justified. But then I'll have a random thought, like, maybe he would have been reformed in prison and would have used all his power for good."

Dane shook his head. "Kulakov would never have ended up in prison. Angel found where the prosecutor was holding his dirty money. Viktor would have walked away scot free. He would have caused other people the same pain he caused you. The way it went down was best, all around. Trust me on that."

"I'm sure it will get easier to deal with."

"With time," he said.

"How about you? How are you feeling?" she asked.

"Good, but I'm stuck here for a few more days." He was staying positive.

"I thought it was common policy for a hospital to push you out the door as soon as you opened your eyes. You must have some great insurance."

He shrugged. "My artery was nicked, so the doctor doesn't want me moving around until he's sure it will hold."

Her face paled, and the smile dropped from her face. "I didn't realize it was so serious. You were talking and joking when they loaded you in the ambulance. I'm so sorry. I should have stayed with you."

And this was why he couldn't tell her he wasn't out of the woods yet. Because she would stay. Then what?

"From what I saw, you didn't have much choice in the matter," he said.

He had given up his chance at having a family when he was forced to leave Caroline and Tobey. Besides, Lena had other things to take care of. Like the little girl who was smiling at him.

"Besides," he added, "it wouldn't have been good for Kenzie to see all that. The blood and everything." Such as when they cut off all his bloody clothing and he'd been buck naked for the ride to the hospital.

"I suppose."

Her fingers clenched his, and he pulled them from her grip so he could stroke the back of her hand to calm her.

"I'm okay. Really. A month or two of physical therapy, and I'll be good as new."

She seemed to relax a little at that.

They sat there for a minute or two watching Kenzie draw by the window. The sight reminded him of Tobey. He had been about her size when Dane left. Tobey had liked drawing and creating things, too. Each day a new exhibit had been added to their growing art gallery of Tobey's works.

The silence, though comforting, grew…until he decided he needed to broach a difficult topic, the elephant that had sneaked into the room.

"What are your plans now?" he asked.

There. It was out in the open. He'd been the one to ask.

She swallowed and glanced over at her daughter. "When I left Miami to go find Kenzie, I didn't realize how long I would be. I gave one of my friends a key to my apartment so they could take care of the mail."

"And you never came back."

"Right. I called her today at the salon. Before the landlord evicted me, she managed to get some of my stuff. She has a few boxes of pictures and files she's kept at her place. She didn't have anywhere to store the furniture, so I guess it's all gone."

Lena shrugged as if it wasn't important. Having your child's life threatened put material things into perspective.

"I'm sorry," he said. "That sucks."

"Yeah. Garrett helped me rent a car. I'm going to Miami, then I'll see what's next."

"Do you still have the credit card I gave you?"

She dug in her purse and pulled it out. "Yes. Here."

He pushed it back in her hand. "No. You keep it. In case of an emergency." He pointed at her when it looked like she was going to protest.

She let out a breath and bit her lip. "I'm never going to be able to thank you enough for everything you did for Kenzie and me. I wouldn't have blamed you if you'd left after you got Tobey back."

"*I* would have blamed me," he said. He picked up his phone and handed it to her. "Can I have your number?"

"You're trolling for women's digits at the hospital?" she joked.

He winked. "Desperate times, and all that."

She hadn't said a word about…them. So, he knew he should just let her go. No strings. No guilt. But he wanted to be able to check in and make sure she was okay. Even if he couldn't offer her anything else, it didn't mean he didn't care about her. A lot.

She tapped the number into his phone. As he watched her fingers play over the screen, he thought of how good it felt to have those fingers touching him.

"Make sure you take my number, too. In case you need anything," he said wanting at least that small tie to each other.

She gave him a warm smile. "Are you going to jump out of bed and come running to save the damsel in distress again?"

"Of course." He sat up a little straighter and winced at the pain. "Or, you know, I could send in the troops."

She chuckled at that, but then turned serious. "Thank you seems like a pathetic attempt to tell you how grateful I am for what you did."

He waved it off, when all he wanted to do was take her in his arms and cover her with kisses. "All in a day's work."

After a glance at her daughter, she bent over to kiss him. It was a soft kiss on the mouth, a casual brush of lips that wouldn't have meant anything except for the way she lingered just a little too long for it to be casual.

Her eyes opened and gazed into his for a second, then she pulled away. Was that reluctance he detected?

"Kenzie, we need to go. Can you say thank you to Dane?"

Kenzie came running over with her newest drawing. This one was of the three of them. He knew one of the figures was him because he was lying in a square box and his leg was bandaged. He also had a line from his arm to a pole beside the bed.

In the picture, Kenzie and Lena were standing next to him. He and Kenzie had big smiles on their faces. It was an apt representation—Lena wasn't smiling in the picture.

"Thank you for this," he told Kenzie. "I'll hang it on my refrigerator door when I get home so I can think of you every day."

Lena pressed her lips together and gathered up the crayons, then ushered Kenzie toward the door.

It took all Dane's strength not to ask her—no, beg her—to stay with him. But he couldn't do that to her. She had a life and other responsibilities.

"Take care of yourself, Dane. Don't push it."

"You do the same," he said.

With that, Lena stepped out of the room.

And out of his life.

Chapter Ninety-Nine

Tears were running down Lena's face by the time she hit the exit of the hospital. She didn't want to cry in front of her daughter, but it was impossible to hold them in any longer.

She didn't know what she'd expected. Maybe for him to ask her to stay? No. Why would he want her hanging around when he had his important job to get back to? She was just being ridiculous.

Besides, hadn't she told herself a dozen times or more she couldn't get involved with him because doing so could potentially put herself and her daughter in danger again? No way could she live through these last eight months again. And what if the relationship didn't work out? Look what had happened with Justin's family after living that kind of life. It wasn't as though she and Dane knew each other well enough to be making such life-altering decisions.

She thought she'd prepared herself for this breakup. She'd known since the first time they kissed it was a temporary thing. Two people scared and desperate to feel something other than guilt and terror. They'd needed each other to get through the worst thing a parent could live through, and now that danger was past. Now they'd go back to being two normal people.

Well, a normal person and a U.S. Deputy Marshal on a covert task force.

So, why was this so much harder than when she and Brandon had split?

Swallowing down the lump in her throat, she took a deep breath, ready to face whatever came next. She had been through so much and come out intact.

She could do this, too.

"Mama, what's wrong?"

She took her daughter's hand. "Nothing, baby. I'm just sad I won't get to see my friend anymore."

"I'm sad I won't get to see Molly and Hannah anymore, too."

Lena frowned, then remembered the two little girls that had been taken from the house in Savannah. "I'll bet. But it makes you feel better knowing they're back with their mommy and daddy, right?"

Kenzie brightened. "Uh-huh."

Then it should follow that Lena should feel better that Dane was going back to his family, of sorts, too, right?

They would take care of him.

She got Kenzie settled in the back seat and slid into the driver's side as she fought the urge to stay in Long Beach so *she* could take care of him. It was more than just the urge to pay back a debt she felt she owed him.

Smiling at her phone, she tucked it in the console of the rental. She had his number, and he had hers. Maybe he would call.

She brushed away the tears and turned the car east.

Chapter One Hundred

"Goddamn! Son of a bitch! Motherfucker!" Dane shouted as he put weight on his leg for the first time at his nurse's orders. It was amazing a human could forget how painful something was until they experienced it again.

The last time he'd been shot in the leg, the bullet had hit muscle and flesh. It had still hurt like a bitch. This time, the bullet had hit bone. A piece of that bone had nicked his artery. Steel plates had been screwed into his femur to offer support as it healed. That hadn't been pleasant. But he'd take whatever pain he faced now if it meant he got to keep his leg.

He was officially out of the woods. But if he was being honest, the physical pain from therapy wasn't the worst of it.

His heart was in bad shape, too.

In the two weeks since Lena walked out of his room, he'd been released from the hospital. Garrett and Sam had flown him back to his home in D.C. where he'd hired Nurse Sadistic to help him get back on his feet. Mrs. Fletcher had no bedside manners to speak of, but she had gotten him up and walking in record time.

"Stop being such a baby," Angel said as she stepped into the room.

To add to his pain, Angel had come to visit for a few days to make sure he was going to survive. This, despite assuring her every night when she called that he would live.

"Don't you have a baby to take care of at home?" he grumbled.

"I do. But his father is handling that baby so I could come take care of this one." She flashed him a devilish grin. The one she used when she thought she was funnier than she was.

"I want a new best friend," he muttered.

"We'll fill out the appropriate paperwork and see what we can do about that." She winked and came to stand by him as if he was supposed to lean his weight on her.

He'd seen evidence of her strength many times, but he wouldn't lean on her for fear her tiny body would snap and Colton would snap him.

"I've got this," he mumbled. "Go sit over there and watch the show."

"The cursing and stumbling, you mean?"

"I find your lack of pity and sympathy disturbing," he said with an eye roll, grateful his injury hadn't been cause for pity. If she'd lost the sarcasm, he'd know he was really in trouble.

"Have you called her?" Angel asked, crossing her arms over her chest.

He silently wished she'd go back to pestering him about his recovery. He knew exactly who Angel meant by *her.*

"Let it go," he warned.

"Come on, Dane. You two were good for each other."

"She has a life. A normal one with her daughter. A life I don't fit into."

Clearly, since Lena hadn't called him. Not once. Not even a text.

"Ten more steps, Mr. Ryan," the nurse snapped when

he'd stood still too long. He knew for a fact he didn't owe ten more steps. She'd said twenty, and, surely, he'd already done fifteen. She was punishing him for stalling.

"I have work to do here," he said to Angel. "Can we talk about this later?"

"Sure. Later. I hope you call her and have something else to talk about, other than the fact you're a big—"

"Yes. Thank you," he cut her off before she called him more names. "Thank you for coming and offering your kind support." He couldn't hide the mocking tone in his voice.

She frowned at his sarcasm as he took another excruciating step toward recovery. "I'm just saying," she said with a poke to his arm, "you need to call the woman."

Chapter One Hundred One

Lena rang the bell at her former in-laws, Denise and Alan Scott's home, and stepped back. She and Kenzie didn't have to wait long before Denise opened the door and gasped in surprise.

"Nana!" Kenzie cried, obviously not noticing the immediate tension as she leaped into her grandmother's arms.

"Kenzie! Oh, I'm so glad you're okay. Come in, dear," she said to Lena over Kenzie's head.

She hadn't even closed the door behind her before Alan rushed into the living room.

"Are you both okay?" Denise asked as Kenzie ran to her grandpa.

Lena had called them after Brandon took Kenzie, hoping he had gone to his parent's home in Charleston, South Carolina. When that hadn't been the case, she told them not to contact the police, that she would take care of it.

All these months later, she finally had.

"We're fine now. I'm sorry I didn't call sooner. We were

dealing with…some things, and I wanted to come speak to you in person."

Lena had wanted to make sure the body found in Vancouver was, indeed, their son before she faced them with the news. She'd just gotten verification last week that his identity had been confirmed. The death certificate had been overnighted to her, and was in her purse.

"I'm afraid I have some bad news about Brandon." There was really no good way to say this.

Alan was holding Kenzie. He looked at her, his face going pale. "Sweetie, why don't you run downstairs to the playroom? I'll be down in a second," he said.

Kenzie clapped. "Can we play restaurant?"

"Sure we can," her grandfather promised. "Go on. I'll be right there."

When Kenzie was out of earshot, they all sat at the dining table.

"Can I get you something to drink, dear?" Denise asked. The Scotts had always treated her like a daughter. Even after the divorce. Not having parents of her own, it was important to Lena that Kenzie got to visit them whenever possible.

"No, thank you," she said, gearing up to tell them.

"He's gone?" Alan asked, though it came out as more of a statement.

"Yes. I'm sorry."

"He was killed?"

"Yes. About four months ago, the coroner said."

"Was it drugs?" Denise rubbed her temples. "I knew something was terribly wrong when he came here asking us for money. We offered to help, but when he said he needed a hundred thousand dollars, we realized it was more than just a few late bills."

"If I thought it would help, I might have given it to him," Alan said with a sigh. "But I could tell from his behavior it would only be the first time. He'd be back, asking for more and more."

"I'm so sorry," Lena offered helplessly. "Maybe if I hadn't—"

"This is not your fault," Denise was quick to say. "He gave you no choice but to file for divorce when he started fooling around with other women and not coming home. No one expected you to put up with that."

Lena leaned over to hug the woman who had been like a mother to her. In the years since the divorce, Lena had backed away from the Scotts because there was no legal tie anymore. They came to Miami to visit Kenzie once, and last summer they'd bought Kenzie and Lena tickets to come to Charleston, but Lena had assumed they'd only been interested in seeing their grandchild, not her.

She realized now she'd misunderstood the situation.

"I had Brandon cremated after they were done with the autopsy, but we could have a service here," Lena suggested.

"That would be nice." Denise sniffed and pulled a tissue from a box on the side table. "We'll keep it small," she said.

Lena swallowed, unsure if now was the time to ask for a favor. But she didn't really have a choice if she wanted a place to sleep tonight.

"I had something else I wanted to speak with you about." She swallowed down a wash of guilt over not being able to provide a home for her daughter. She hated Viktor Kulakov for putting her in this position.

"What is it?" Alan asked.

She took a steadying breath. "Because I've been searching for Kenzie all this time, I've been out of work for eight months, and I lost the apartment in Miami. Kenzie and I are basically starting over."

"We can give you some money," Alan offered easily.

Lena's tight muscles relaxed just a little. "I appreciate

that. But what I was going to ask was, can Kenzie and I stay with you for a few weeks? Just until we've found a place to stay and get settled. Since we're starting over, I'd like to live here in Charleston, so she's closer to you. Once I find a job, I was wondering if you might be able to watch her some of the days I'm at work?"

The two retirees looked shocked.

Oh God. Maybe she was asking too much. They probably didn't want to be strapped down by a child when they could go play tennis at the country club, or travel the world.

Lena plunged on. "It's just that, after what happened, I'm kind of leery about sending her to daycare." Leery was not the right word. Terrified was more accurate. She knew it hadn't been the daycare's fault. Brandon was Kenzie's father, and they hadn't had any reason to stop him from taking her. If the person in charge hadn't been new, or if Lena had been there, or had thought to leave instructions to prevent him from taking Kenzie, it never would have happened. If they'd even called her to ask first, Brandon might have been stopped.

"Of course, dear," Denise said quickly, and gave her a wide smile. "We'd be delighted. You can stay as long as you like. Between the three of us, we'll make sure Kenzie has someone with her at all times."

Denise seemed genuinely excited to be able to help, and Lena felt the stab of guilt again for thinking they only liked her when they were legally obligated to. Her own mother hadn't been very interested.

"Thank you. I'm sorry to impose, but I just need a little help getting back on my feet."

"It's not imposing, Lena. You're family," Alan said with a watery smile.

Denise met her gaze. "We're just a little shocked, because right after you got married we asked Brandon if you would move to Charleston, and he said he wanted to, but you refused."

A familiar surge of irritation went through Lena. Brandon had always been a liar, manipulating people so he wouldn't be the bad guy. Even with his own parents, apparently.

"He never asked me," she said.

She bit back the urge to defend herself by showcasing Brandon's many flaws. They knew their son as well as she did. They knew how he was.

Denise nodded and patted Lena's leg. "The important thing is you're here now. I guess I'll get started on Brandon's service. Let me go find the number for the funeral home."

Lena was surprised they were taking all of this so well. Their son was dead, but they were handling it like troopers.

Denise left the room, and Lena looked over at Alan.

"We lost our son many months ago," he said with a shaky voice. "We knew where he was headed and expected someday we'd get a knock on the door telling us he was gone. It hurts like a son of bitch, but it's also a relief in many ways. We don't have to wait any longer."

Lena stood and went to hug him. He allowed a brief squeeze, but then he pasted a smile on his face and pulled away. "I'm fine. Really. And I promised a certain little girl I'd go downstairs and pretend to eat plastic food. If you'll excuse me?"

Lena smiled and nodded. "I hope you have a taste for it. You're going to be eating a lot of it."

"Thank you, for giving us Kenzie."

She swallowed down the emotion and smiled back. "Thank you, for giving us a home."

Alan blinked a few times, then looked away, as if her words had reminded him of something. Instead of going downstairs, he turned and went the other direction, toward his study.

Denise returned to the living room, talking to someone on the phone. She covered the phone to speak to Lena.

"Would you come with us this afternoon to help set things up? I know you two weren't married anymore—"

"Yes. I'll go with you." Brandon hadn't been her husband for three years, but he'd still been Kenzie's father. And she wanted her little girl to be able to say goodbye properly.

Alan had come back to the room carrying a piece of paper. He twisted it into a cone and let it uncoil. Denise said goodbye and disconnected her call.

"What is it?" Denise prompted when her husband hadn't spoken.

He shook his head and looked up at Lena with an unreadable expression. Whatever he was going to say, it was big.

"When Kenzie was born, I told Brandon he needed to make sure his family was taken care of, in case something happened to him. At the time, he was working on the docks, and it was a dangerous job. I helped him get a life insurance policy."

Lena recalled paying the annual premium while they had been married. "I remember."

"When he moved out of your home after the divorce, he had his mail sent here since he didn't have a permanent address. When the bills came, I paid them myself, because I knew whatever he was doing was far more dangerous than working on the docks."

Surprise shot through Lena. "That's… I had no idea."

He unfolded the document and handed it over to her. "He never changed his beneficiary after your divorce."

Wait. What?

She stared down at the paper, seeing her name at the bottom. She scanned back up to the top and saw the policy amount. Good lord.

Five hundred thousand dollars.

The rest of the words became unreadable as tears filled her eyes, and the paper shook in her trembling hands.

"My God. I'll be able to buy a home for Kenzie. I won't have to struggle to make a good life for her." Her voice came out as a strangled whisper.

"Honey, we never would have let you struggle, anyway, but now you don't have to worry about a thing," he said.

There were now two men in her life she would never be able to thank enough.

Which brought her thoughts straight to Dane.

She hadn't reached out to him, partly because she knew he would want to help her, and she already owed him too much.

And then there was the issue of his dangerous job. She'd had her fill of danger, more than enough for a lifetime, regardless of how much she loved him.

So, why was the first thing she wanted to do was to call and tell him about her good fortune?

And, yes, how desperately she missed him…

Chapter One Hundred Two

Dane knew this was a bad idea.

After how bad his last bad idea had turned out, he should have learned his lesson. But here he was, sitting in Tobey's fort, hoping the boy came out this afternoon.

It was hot, and the fort had not been made to fit his body. It had been designed for a four-year-old Tobey. As evident by the two-foot plastic sliding board used to exit the fort. Tobey wouldn't even fit on that now. Dane should have built it for him to grow into. He hadn't thought ahead.

Before he could berate himself even more, he heard the shuffling sound of feet hitting earth. And a few seconds later, Tobey stepped into the fort.

His eyes widened. "Dad!" He gasped and quickly looked around.

"Hey, bud, is anyone with you?" Dane tried to see through the cracks in the wood.

"No. Mom and Randy are watching TV." Tobey made a disgusted face. "They don't let me go anywhere alone anymore, but I kind of snuck out of the house."

Dane could imagine Caroline's fear after Tobey's abduction. Honestly, he didn't think it was out of line. If he had still been around, he would be keeping his son close, as well.

"Since I'm your dad, I also have to say you shouldn't ever sneak out of the house. But at the moment, I'm really glad you did this one time, since it will give us time alone to talk."

Tobey sat at the opening of the tiny enclosure with a smug smile on his face. "Cool."

"So, how are you doing?" Dane asked.

"Good, except Mom keeps kissing me a lot. I hope she gets over it before I have to go back to school. What if she kisses me when she drops me off at school?"

Dane chuckled. "There could be worse things. It builds character."

"How are you?" Tobey motioned to the bandage on Dane's leg. His shorts had pulled up when he'd contorted himself into the tight space.

"I'm fine. I got shot in the leg. No biggie."

"You got shot?" Tobey's eyes lit more with awe than sympathy.

"Yeah." Dane shrugged and gave himself over to the moment that his son thought he was cool.

"Can I see the hole?" Tobey asked eagerly, leaning closer.

"Sorry, there isn't a hole anymore. They stitched it up."

Tobey deflated. "Oh. Okay."

"Anyway, I wanted to let you know all the other boys who were with you got home to their families, too."

Tobey lit up. "That's good. I kind of miss hanging out with them. I mean, I was scared a little because the guards had guns, but it was also kind of fun to be able to play video games all day."

Dane grinned. "And eat pizza."

"I hate pizza now."

They laughed together, and Dane hoped it was the only side effect of his ordeal.

"I think you should probably get back," he said regretfully. "I just wanted to check in and make sure you were doing okay."

Tobey's face fell. "When will I get to see you again?"

"I'm not sure," Dane said sadly. The fact was, he shouldn't even be there now. He wanted to be part of his son's life, but he couldn't. It just wasn't safe. "It probably won't be for a while. But I want you to know that I'm thinking about you and I love you. Always."

His son's lip trembled. "I love you, too, Dad."

"Tobey?" Caroline's voice penetrated the stillness of the trees around them.

"Shit," Dane said, then corrected to "Shoot."

"Yeah?" Tobey called loudly. He was still sitting at the entrance to the fort, like he was protecting Dane from being seen.

"Who are you talking to?" Caroline asked from the edge of the yard.

She hadn't come any closer, and Dane recalled her incredible fear of snakes, spiders, mice, insects, Bigfoot, and anything else that might lurk in the woods behind their home.

"Uh..." Tobey paused for a few seconds, then gave up with a frown. "Dad."

As a father, he was very glad his son wouldn't lie to his mother, but given the circumstances, it was quite inconvenient.

"You feel closer to him out here, huh?" Caroline said without a trace of alarm in her voice. "Do you remember when the two of you built your fort together?"

"Yeah." Tobey nodded. "It was fun."

Caroline obviously thought Tobey was talking to Dane in spirit form, rather than in real life. That did make more sense. He relaxed.

"I understand you miss him," she said gently. "But you can't run off like that. I was scared witless when you weren't in your room."

Tobey sighed. "Mom, the bad guys are all dead. They won't come get me again. I promise."

Dane hoped that was true of all bad guys in general.

"Come on," she called brightly. "We're going to order pizza for dinner."

Tobey let his head fall back and groaned. "Great. I'm coming."

Before he hopped down, he reached out and bumped fists with Dane's in a very manly gesture. Dane would have preferred a good hug, but this brief contact would have to do for now.

"Bye," Tobey whispered and ran off.

Dane listened to his son's footsteps tromp through the bracken, then turn silent as he stepped into the grass-covered yard.

"Are you coming?" Tobey asked.

"Go on in. I'll be there in a second," Caroline said.

Dane shifted silently so he could look through a small gap in the wall of the fort. He winced at his shoddy craftsmanship, but the narrow break let him see Caroline, who was still standing at the edge of the woods. He could also make out Tobey's form as he ran to the house and went inside.

"Thank you," Caroline whispered so softly Dane barely heard it.

Dane tensed. Oh, shit.

Fortunately, she spoke up a little as she continued. "Thank you for watching over our boy and bringing him home."

Relief buzzed through him when he realized she was speaking to him as if standing at his grave, rather than because she suspected he was sitting cramped up in their son's fort.

And he was, indeed, cramping up. The muscle in his injured leg was twitching painfully. He needed to stretch it out, but to move would give her yet another thing to be afraid of in the woods.

The ghost of her former husband.

"I also want to say I'm sorry," she murmured.

Dane pushed the pain away so he could listen more carefully.

"I'm sorry I didn't listen to you when you said there would be danger. I wish I hadn't been so selfish..."

He heard tears in her voice and instinctively wanted to comfort her. But not only was it physically impossible at the moment with his leg locked up the way it was, but it was no longer his place. She had a new husband who loved her more than Dane ever could have.

He realized now more than ever, they wouldn't have made it as a couple. If she'd come with him into hiding, she would have resented him for having to give up all the things she'd grown accustomed to. Their marriage hadn't been strong enough to survive the added resentment.

Checking the gap again, he saw her walking across the lawn toward the house. He waited until she was inside before moving. When he did, the action caused a groan.

"Goddamn, fuck me sideways. That hurts." He moaned in pain as he stretched out his leg and stumbled out of the fort. He managed to make his way through the trees to the car he'd parked on the next street and got in.

Behind the steering wheel, he caught his breath and pulled out his phone to take it off silent.

He had a text.

From Lena.

Chapter One Hundred Three

Lena went to the bedroom she was sharing with her daughter to get her phone, only to find Kenzie speaking carefully into the phone, using the voice feature to send a text. It was almost scary the way kids picked up on technology.

It was even more scary that Kenzie was texting someone. Before Viktor, Lena had always allowed Kenzie to text her grandparents…using the voice commands since she was too young to spell most words. But at the moment, those grandparents were in the next room, so there was no reason to text them.

"Who are you texting?" Lena asked as she came closer.

"Dane. I wanted to know if he liked the pictures I sent him."

Holy hell.

Lena hadn't sent Dane any pictures…even though Kenzie drew him one nearly every day to say thank you. Apparently,

Lena wasn't the only one who felt like they owed him the world.

The reason she hadn't sent them wasn't a very good one, either.

She'd wanted to wait until she was set up in their new house. Once they were settled, she was planning to invite him to visit. She wanted him to see she wasn't a mess anymore. That she was capable and successful.

"Can I have that?" She swiped the phone from Kenzie and nodded toward the door. "Why don't you go see if Nana wants help putting the groceries away?"

Thankfully, Kenzie jumped up. "Okay. But tell him I'm going to draw him a picture of a dragon today."

Lena gave her daughter a smile. "I'm sure he will love it."

Kenzie paused by the door and tilted her head to the side. "Does he like dragons?"

"Doesn't everyone?"

Kenzie seemed to be in agreement, and left the room.

Lena dropped onto the bed and brought up the text thread on the phone.

Sure enough, it had started with Kenzie.

LENA: IS YOU LEG ALL BETTER?

Only autocorrect had kept it down to one typo, Lena was sure.

A long time had passed before Dane answered. Had he not been sure whether he wanted to get involved with her again, or was he stumped by her poor grammar?

DANE: IT'S GETTING BETTER. PHYSICAL THERAPY IS A BITCH.

She frowned but gave him a free pass on the cursing since it was logical to assume he was texting her, not a six-year-old.

LENA: WHAT IS PRETZEL TROPHY?

Lena winced at the screen. What the heck was— Oh. Physical therapy.

Dane hadn't answered that one.

LENA: DID YOU LIKE THE PITCHER I MADE WITH THE RAN LOW.

This was like playing an impossible game of charades. Pitcher was obviously picture. But ran low?

Fortunately, the next icon was an emoji of a rainbow. Got it.

DANE: IS THIS KENZIE?

Lena let out a breath of relief that he'd finally understood.

LENA: YES.

DANE: HOW ARE YOU?

LENA: GOOD. MOMMY AND ME ARE LIVING WITH MANAGED AND POPPYSEED.

It seemed Nana and Poppy were not in the dictionary.

LENA: I GET TO SWIM. DO YOU LIKE TO SWIM?

DANE: I DO. I GET TO SWIM IN PRETZEL TROPHY.

Lena smiled. Smartass.

LENA: CAN YOU COME SWIM WITH ME? I HAVE A DO FUN.

Lena was pretty sure that was supposed to be dolphin, in reference to the large inflatable dolphin Kenz loved to ride on.

DANE: WHERE'S YOUR MOMMY? WE'D HAVE TO ASK HER.

LENA: **I GET**

That was where Kenzie's conversation had stopped.

Lena stared at the phone in her hands, wondering what to do next. What could she type that wouldn't make him want to swoop in to save the day?

LENA: THIS IS REALLY LENA. SORRY ABOUT THAT. I HOPE YOU'RE DOING WELL.

DANE: HI. I'M GOOD. SORRY ABOUT CURSING.

LENA: NOT YOUR FAULT.

DANE: I THINK I WAS INVITED TO A POOL PARTY.

Lena frowned and tugged at her lip. She couldn't

invite him to visit this week or next. They would be having Brandon's memorial service tomorrow. Regardless, it would be disrespectful for her to invite her—whatever Dane was—to stay at her in-laws' home just after burying their son.

Lena would settle on her new home in two weeks, and she and Kenzie would be moving. They had been fortunate enough to find the perfect house, and the sellers had already relocated. She had too much going on right now.

LENA: NOW'S NOT A GOOD TIME.

She winced because it seemed rather harsh.

DANE: NO PROBLEM. TAKE CARE OF YOURSELF.

LENA: YOU TOO.

That was it.

And it made her feel like hell.

Chapter One Hundred Four

Two days after getting his hopes up for no reason, Dane hobbled into the task force conference room using the cane Angel had picked out for him. The handle was a pistol grip. She said it was functional *and* cool.

He didn't want to have to rely on a cane, at all, but he was happy just to be walking. Every day he was getting a little stronger.

Thorne sat at one end of the conference table. Sam was next to him on one side, and Angel was on the other. Their husbands took up the other two chairs, so Dane flopped into the seat at the other end of the table.

It was good to see them all outside a hospital room.

He avoided looking at Sam, but when he finally did, he didn't see the same guilt-ridden expression he expected. Instead, she looked happy.

Maybe she'd finally forgiven herself for shooting him the first time. Lord knew, he had. He would have done the same thing in her situation. A stranger had been a threat, and she'd taken him down. He could only be glad she went for the leg.

They spent the next hour going over the brief for their raid on Viktor's yacht. While the prosecutor had been charged with bribery and various other things, they still needed to formally account for their actions.

Thorne was confident it wouldn't be an issue. Once they gave their statements the case would be closed, and everyone could go about their business as usual. Too bad Dane wasn't quite ready for business as usual.

He rubbed his leg and sighed as they continued talking.

When they were done, Thorne thanked them all for making the trip in to town, and suggested they go out for dinner while they were all there together.

Dane left the cane in his car before going into the restaurant. It was a little more of a distance to walk than he was used to, so he was hurting by the time he slid into his seat at the table. He was feeling it, but he'd made it without the cane. Progress.

At the restaurant, they sat in the same arrangement as they had at the conference table. Dane realized it was because he and Thorne were the ones who were alone.

After the orders were placed, everyone fell into silence. He wondered if they were all thinking what he was thinking—about how much their group had changed over the last few years. Justin was gone, and that left a hole in their family. But they'd also added Samantha and Colton to the team.

"Did you see Justin's star on the wall?" Angel asked, verifying his suspicions.

Everyone nodded including him.

He'd worried Justin's star for death while serving wouldn't be awarded since their mission hadn't been sanctioned, but Thorne had pushed that he'd given the order as his boss, so Justin's service wasn't to be questioned.

No one said anything else for a long moment.

Finally, Garrett let out a sigh and shifted in his seat. "We have a bit of good news to share," he said.

Samantha's eyes went wide, and she shook her head slightly.

He smiled. "I know we said we would wait, but I can't hold it in." He turned to the group as he rested his arm around Sam's shoulders. "We're having a baby."

Thorne—normally distinguished and calm in any situation—shouted with joy and leaned over to hug his daughter.

"I'm sorry, Dad. We just found out yesterday, and we *were* going to tell you first," she told him after a mock glare at Garrett.

Thorne waved it off. "It's fine. I don't mind sharing the moment with my entire family."

It was the first time Dane heard his boss admit to thinking of the team in that way. Dane had come to think of Thorne as a father figure—a real father, not a distracted excuse for a father who forgot Christmas and birthdays, and who never realized what a joy Tobey was.

One by one, everyone congratulated the happy couple.

"This means I won't be going on any more missions," Garrett said. "I know I was semi-retired before, but now I'm officially turning in my badge. I promised Sam I wouldn't make her worry."

"I don't want my child to grow up without a father." Sam said, glancing at Thorne. "I had to do that, and even though I got you back eventually, I wish you'd been around when I was younger." Her lip quivered as she spoke.

"I understand." Thorne nodded and patted her hand. "Believe me, I wish I'd been there, too."

Colton cleared his throat and looked at Angel. "We were waiting for the right time, but since we seem to be doing this now," he sighed, "Angel and I are out, too. Officially."

"I never really thought about the danger before," Angel

said. "But now that we're parents we have to consider it. Since Viktor is no longer a threat, Colton will be able to reunite with his brothers and his mother. We just want to be a normal family without looking over our shoulders all the time."

Dane hated the jealousy that reared at the sight of the two happy couples. He'd had to give up on his chance of being in a normal family. He knew he'd done the right thing. Caroline and Tobey were happy and safe.

But sometimes, the price seemed a little too steep.

Thorne nodded and smiled at Angel. "I completely understand. I expected as much. I might look into getting some new recruits…or maybe I'll see what retirement has to offer," he said.

Dane's pulse hiked at that last bit. He glanced around the table and cleared his throat. He might be on medical leave for another month or two, but eventually he would be coming back to work.

Maybe he'd given that father figure thing too much credit.

"You kind of forgot someone, didn't you?" He said evenly.

"Oh." Thorne studied him as if just realizing he was there. "I— I assumed you would be going to make a life with your young lady."

Dane blinked. "Uh, no." He didn't have a young lady. "She… No." Hell, Lena hadn't even wanted to invite him over for a swim, let alone to be in her life.

It was better this way. He still wasn't free to do what he wanted, even if Task Force Phoenix disbanded. Tim Reynolds was not in jail, and Dane was supposed to be dead.

Everyone shifted their focus to him, as if he was their biggest priority.

"Why not?" Angel asked with a puzzled expression. "What happened? I told you to call her."

Dane shook his head. "I left Caroline and Tobey behind so they wouldn't have to live in hiding, afraid of bad guys like Viktor Kulakov coming after them because of me. I'm not going to do that to Lena and Kenzie." He shrugged, just wanting to get this awkward topic over with. "Besides, things didn't work out between us. She moved on. I don't have anything to offer her, anyway."

There was a moment where everyone looked around the table at one another in a stunned silence. Then their gazes came back to rest on him.

"Did you tell her you want to be with her?" Sam asked with hiked brows. "It's important to communicate exactly what it is you want, so the other person knows."

Colton caught his gaze and held it. "Don't be afraid to tell her you want to be with her. Even if she turns you down the first time."

Angel placed her hand on Colton's. "Make sure she understands you're willing to give up the danger to start a normal life with her."

Thorne reached for the sleeping baby in Angel's arms. "You deserve to have something good, Dane. Just because you can't have your old life back, doesn't mean you can't make a new one that's even better. You can have the life you were supposed to have."

"Did you even try?" Garrett crossed his thick arms over his chest.

Dane's mouth had dropped open at all this sage counsel. "Wow. Okay. Good thing you're all off the team since everyone's turned into advice columnists. Bad ones, at that."

"Thing is, you're off Task Force Phoenix, too," Thorne said, patting the baby like a pro.

Dane's jaw dropped even further. "What? Why? My leg will be better in a month or two. I'm already getting around easier. I don't even need the cane." He pointed out how he didn't have it with him now.

"First, let's address the cane issue." Angel held up her

index finger in her standard lecturing stance. "You're *not* getting around without it. You're too damn stubborn to admit you need it. Which leads me to my second point—the woman you're in love with. And how, again, you're too freaking stubborn to admit you need something. Or in this case, some*one*."

Dane ground his teeth. Angel was relentless when there was blood in the water.

"I'm not too stubborn," he insisted indignantly. "She's moved on. She got insurance money and bought a house in Charleston." He may or may not have used some of the skills he'd learned from Angel to cyberstalk Lena. He'd never tell. "She didn't include me in any of those decisions or plans. Which means she clearly doesn't want me involved."

He was happy Lena was nicely set up, but he wished they could have made a life together.

His statement about her not wanting him involved was met with a collective groan, an "Oh, boy," and muttered "Dipshit," from Garrett.

Colton held up his hand in a stop gesture to the group.

Dane gave a weak smile. It was nice to have at least *one* person come to his defense.

"I'll take care of this." Colton turned to Dane and patted his forearm as one might do when teaching something to a child who wasn't getting it. "That's *not* what it means when someone strikes out to make their own life."

Dane didn't respond. Because he had no clue what the hell that meant. He knew someone would enlighten him.

It was Samantha. "It means," she said in a long-suffering tone, "since you didn't *tell* her you want to be with her, she assumed *you* don't want to be a part of *her* life, and she has no choice but to move on without you."

Was that what really happened?

Doubtful.

Lena was strong and independent. Even when she had needed him, Dane knew she wasn't comfortable with that. Her husband had let her down badly. Maybe she preferred to take care of things on her own because she thought she had to. For survival.

"Lena is probably still carrying around a lot of guilt over what happened with Tobey," Angel said. "Maybe she thinks deep down you're still mad about that."

Which would be a very painful explanation. Dane hoped to hell that wasn't it.

"We've all been where you are," Garrett said. "Trust me, I know telling a woman you love her is scarier than walking into a firestorm." He kissed the top of Sam's head and whispered something to her that made her smile. "But once you get through it, it's totally worth it."

As always, Thorne was brutal and pragmatic in his concern. "If Lena turns you down, I'll consider continuing the team just for you. But I have grandchildren to spoil now, so make sure you put some effort into making it work with her."

Dane's head was spinning.

The team dispersed with hugs and plans to get together again soon.

Dane nodded and smiled, but felt completely adrift. He'd already been forced out of the family he'd built with his wife and son. Now he was being forced from the family he'd managed to piece together with his team.

He didn't know if he was strong enough to go through all that pain again.

He and Lena had helped each other through something most people never had to face. They'd shared so much, including their hopes and strength.

But was that enough to build a real relationship? After living through something so extraordinary, how would they handle normal, everyday life?

One thing was certain, Lena had her safe life back, and it made sense she wouldn't want to sign up to live with someone in his previous occupation. He didn't blame her one bit, but was he able to put his heart into having a family again?

Hell, he wasn't even sure if he remembered how.

Chapter One Hundred Five

Lena sat dangling her legs over the edge of the pool in the backyard of the new house as Kenzie splashed around in swimmies and a life vest a few feet away.

Lena knew she was being overprotective. Kenzie could swim like a fish, and she knew not to go any deeper than chest-height. Still, it wasn't the fear of drowning that caused Lena to hover close to her daughter every minute of the day.

She hoped it would get easier. It had to. Soon. She was starting a new job next week and would have to leave her daughter for nine hours a day. Fortunately, Denise and Alan would be watching Kenzie and had promised to text her regular updates throughout the day.

"Come on. It's time for lunch," Lena announced and got up to get a towel. They'd only moved into their new home last week. There were still boxes everywhere, but unpacking the swim stuff and towels had been a priority.

Kenzie didn't complain or whine about having to get out of the pool. She was always on her best behavior these days, which broke Lena's heart. Kenzie's therapist said it was to be expected, considering what she'd gone through.

No matter how many times Lena told her daughter she hadn't done anything wrong, and that Lena hadn't left her behind on purpose, Kenzie was still suffering some abandonment issues. The things Brandon had said to her when he took her from the daycare didn't help, the bastard.

At least with his death, Brandon had provided for his daughter—if unknowingly. Their new home was bigger than what they probably needed. And the pool was a luxury they definitely didn't need. But the house was in a safe neighborhood, and Lena had wanted Kenzie to have the nicest home possible.

The therapist had identified *that* behavior as a manifestation of Lena's guilt over not protecting her daughter better.

Obviously, both she and Kenzie had some things to work out. But they were together again, and that was all that mattered.

Well, almost.

Lena's heart pulled uncomfortably as she thought about the one thing that was missing from the happy scenario.

Dane.

She tried not to think of him. She'd start to get weepy again and didn't want Kenzie to misinterpret.

"You're dry enough to go inside," Lena said cheerfully, ruffling her daughter's hair with the towel. "Do you want PB&J for lunch?"

"Yeah! And can I have a popsicle, too?"

Lena put on her mother face. "After you eat the real food. What color do you want?"

Kenzie jumped up and down. "Red!"

"Red, it is." Lena hung the towels on the back of a chair and followed her daughter inside. She stayed back as Kenzie scrambled up onto the tall stool and took a sip of the water that had been in her cup since that morning.

Making their sandwiches, Lena took care in making sure the peanut butter reached out to every corner. She used to just smear it around the center without a thought. But everything was important now. She cut the sandwich into four neat squares and pushed it across the island to her child. "There you go, kiddo."

"Thank you, Mama."

The doorbell rang as Lena put the jelly back in the refrigerator. "I'll be right back. Stay here."

Lena's pulse took off. They hadn't been living in Charleston long enough to expect visitors. The Scotts always called first, and the cable guy had already been there.

She stopped briefly in her bedroom and pulled her new gun from its safe before going to the door.

Her heart pounded in her ears as she checked the peephole.

And froze in shock.

Chapter One Hundred Six

When the door opened, it took every bit of strength Dane had not to just grab Lena and kiss her. Then he looked her over and decided he wouldn't have been able to stop with just kissing her.

Her brown hair was pulled up in a messy knot on top her head, with a pair of sunglasses holding it back from her face. She was wearing a bright pink bikini top and a pair of black cotton shorts that were on the short side. The *very* short side.

His mouth actually watered.

"Mama?"

He heard a small voice from inside the house. Mackenzie.

"It's okay," Lena called over her shoulder. She turned back to him and opened the door wider. "Come in."

As she closed the door behind him, he noticed a gun in the hand she'd had hidden.

Her cheeks turned pink. "I'll be right back. I guess I don't need this."

It was normal to be extra cautious after surviving an ordeal like she had. He didn't like that she still didn't feel safe. He hoped he could help with that.

He stepped deeper into the living room using his cane to support his injured leg. He was able to get around without the cane, but it was better when he didn't overtax the leg.

He looked around. Her new home was nice. There were still boxes everywhere and the walls were bare, but it had a lot of potential.

"How's your leg?" she asked, hurrying back.

Hopefully good enough to chase you, he thought.

"It's getting better every day," he said. "The surgeon expects it to be as good as it had been in another six weeks. You know, after the other gunshot and dog bite."

She chuckled. "That's good."

He followed her into the kitchen, which was also full of boxes.

Kenzie was sitting at the counter. She turned to face him and smiled. The sight wasn't marred in the least by the jelly surrounding her mouth.

"Dane!" She scooted off the chair and ran to the refrigerator to grab a drawing. "This is the dragon I said I was going to send. But Mama liked it and asked if she could keep it. It was really for you, though. Are you going to swim with me?"

He grinned. "Well, I did bring my swim trunks."

Actually, he'd brought everything he owned. And he'd sold his house. He was making a fresh start.

He hoped with them.

He'd missed Lena. A lot. His team had said he needed to make an effort to win her. That he needed to tell her how he felt about her.

He figured it would be easier to get shot in the leg a third time.

Chapter One Hundred Seven

Lena excused herself for a moment while Kenzie was showing Dane her artwork. She needed a minute to collect herself.

She looked at her reflection in the bathroom mirror, sighed, then washed the jelly off her hands and went back out. There was no use trying to fix herself up. He'd already seen her at her worst.

Nervousness jangled through her. Why was he here? How had he even known her new address? Then she remembered how easy it was for Angel to find someone.

Good grief. Had his team been watching her in the pool from a satellite?

Seeing Dane sitting in her kitchen had the immediate effect of wrecking her carefully thought out plan to get over him. Talk about an impossible task. It didn't matter that she now had a house and a job, and could take care of her daughter and herself very well, thank you.

She still wanted him.

Her heart needed him. Her body needed him.

Maybe she would somehow get used to watching him walk out the door to face a dangerous mission. One thing was certain, she couldn't just give up. That plan wasn't working.

Giving the girls a heathy shove upward in the bikini top, and tucking a loose strand of hair behind her ear, she stepped back into the kitchen to find Dane and Kenzie laughing like old friends.

"Mama, we named the dragon Puffy. Dane knows a song about him. Can he swim with us?"

Lena assumed she meant Dane and not the paper dragon. "Sure. If he really brought his suit."

"He did. He did!"

"Good." Lena smiled at him.

"I hope you don't mind," he whispered as he passed her. "If you don't want me to stay, I could—"

"I do. Want you to stay." *Forever.*

But she couldn't bring herself to say that last word. She had trusted him with her and Kenzie's life. She knew he was steadfast, and he'd saved her in more ways than he probably realized. But she was still afraid to be thrown back into that world of guns and danger.

She knew he wouldn't think twice about walking into fire to save her, but would he be there when Kenzie had the flu? Could she count on him to pick up groceries if she was running late? Could she trust him to keep his job separate from their everyday life?

"I'll go grab my bag," he said. "Where can I change?"

She pointed. "The bathroom is the first door on the right."

She and Kenzie went out to the pool, and she helped her daughter back into her swimmies.

"Can Dane stay for dinner?" Kenz asked excitedly. "I

want him to sing the Puffy dragon song for you. Do you think he likes barbeque chicken? Are we still having chicken, Mama?"

"We'll see." She had to stifle a frown at her daughter's exuberance. While it was wonderful to see her daughter so happy, Lena worried she was getting too attached to Dane.

Hell, she was getting too attached, as well.

He stepped out of the house shirtless and wearing a pair of board shorts that hung low on his hips. Oh, yeah. Hello, all those glorious muscles. The ones she couldn't help thinking about when she was all alone in her empty bed every night.

She swallowed when he winked at her. He tossed his towel on a chair as Kenzie danced around him telling him all the rules of the swimming pool, and offering him a pool noodle.

This was definitely not the way her sexy fantasies had played out, but for reality, this was damn nice.

He squealed dramatically as he was urged into the water. She knew the water was a little chilly at first, but felt good once you were in. "Why is your mama sitting on the side of the pool?" he asked, raising his brows at Lena.

"She always sits there. In case I have a distress," Kenzie said.

Lena and Dane laughed. "Can't have that," she confirmed.

He held his hand up to his forehead to block the sun as he looked up at her with a broad smile. "Why don't you go rest on one of those comfy-looking lounge chairs, and I'll take care of any distresses."

"I'm not going to distress!" Kenzie declared. "I can swim real good. Do you want to see?"

He relaxed onto a float. "Of course I do. That's why I flew the whole way here from Washington, D.C."

Lena bit her tongue when Kenzie tugged off the swimmies so they didn't restrict her movement. She trusted Dane to keep her safe and moved to the chair to relax.

She watched the two of them playing in the pool. She winced as some of her daughter's questions came out sounding a bit invasive. Though she did learn a lot from the interrogation.

She found out he did, in fact, like barbequed chicken, and also that he planned to stay for a couple days, at least. It was the way he looked at her when he said "at least" that made her stomach do a flip.

What was that supposed to mean?

She found out when he calmly told Kenzie that he'd quit his job and was thinking about moving away from Washington, D.C.

She tried not to get her hopes up…but it was much too late.

Chapter One Hundred Eight

Dane taught Kenzie how to play Marco Polo. He'd forgotten how much little kids cheated at games where they were trusted to keep their eyes closed. Tobey had been the same way. Even when he promised he wasn't peeking, he was peeking.

While Dane had spent a lot of time in a pool over the last few months for physical therapy, it was different when trying to avoid getting eaten by a six-year-old shark. Or while dragging her around on her large inflatable dolphin.

He needed a break, and he could tell Kenzie was winding down, as well.

"Look," she whispered. "Mama's asleep. I'm going to go wake her up."

"No," he whispered, and put a finger to his lips. "Let her sleep. She's tired. She's been through a lot."

Plus, he'd seen her face when he'd said he quit his job. That wasn't strictly true, but Thorne had made it pretty clear he should move on. Good thing Lena had been sitting down, she'd looked so shocked.

"Yeah. She cried at my daddy's funeral," Kenzie said.

"I'm sure it was sad," he said sympathetically.

He had seen a short notice about the memorial service in the Charleston paper on one of his internet digging expeditions.

"I'm mad at my daddy," Kenzie confessed with a frown. "Miss Tanya said it's okay to be mad at him because he made me scared and took me away from my mommy."

Dane guessed Miss Tanya was a therapist and knew how to handle such things. He was glad Lena had thought to take her to talk to someone who could help her deal with the experience. Was she also seeing the therapist?

Kenzie took his silence as approval to sneak over to her mother, where she proceeded to drip all over her. But the joke was on Kenzie, because he'd seen Lena's lips twitch while trying not to smile. And as soon as Kenzie got close enough, she jumped up and grabbed her.

The little girl squealed in surprise, then laughed as Lena wrapped a towel around her and pulled her onto the chair next to her.

"Are you two having fun?" Lena asked, giving him a searching look.

"Yes!" Kenzie shouted. "I want Dane to stay here for longer."

So did he.

He wanted to stay for the rest of his life.

Chapter One Hundred Nine

Halfway through dinner, Kenzie's head bobbed twice before it finally rested on her arm on the table. Lena had known it was only a matter of time. A full day of swimming paired with a warm meal had put her down for the count.

With a chuckle, Dane reached over to move her plate away from her face.

"I'll get something to wash her hands," he offered and stood, wincing as he turned.

"I can do it."

"So can I," he said with a wink as he hobbled to the sink and got a wet paper towel.

He took extra care to wash the sauce from Kenzie's fingers and cheeks without waking her. When she was clean, he reached down and picked her up.

"She's too heavy," Lena protested in a whisper.

"I've got her," he said, and shifted Kenzie's weight slightly. Her head flopped against his neck as he walked to her room. He laid her in her tiny bed and covered her with a blanket, and Lena's heart swelled at the sight of the man she loved tucking in her daughter.

She was in such big trouble.

Especially after that bombshell about quitting his job. Her whole reason for not wanting to be with him had suddenly disappeared. Which terrified the hell out of her.

He turned to her, took her hand, and led her out of the room. The look in his eyes made her heart pound even harder.

"Do you want a beer?" she asked, thinking he might want to talk.

He shook his head. "Not what I had in mind."

"We could sit in the living—"

His mouth claimed hers as soon as they were out in the hall and Kenzie's door was closed. With a sigh, she wrapped her arms around his neck, pulling him closer as his tongue delved into her mouth in a delightfully possessive way.

Oh. Okay.

"Your room?" he asked when he lifted his head.

She took the opportunity to fill her lungs with oxygen and pointed to the door across the hall from Kenzie's. Hell, yes.

She was the one to pull him inside. She closed the door and locked it, not wanting any awkward incidents.

He had already pulled off the T-shirt he'd donned for dinner. She untied his trunks and pushed them down his legs as he worked on the knots of her bikini top.

"I've missed you," he said, kissing her cheeks and hair as he worked. "So much."

Joy flitted through her at his heartfelt confession.

"I've missed you, too," she said.

He kissed up her neck to whisper in her ear. "It feels different."

She froze for a moment, unsure what he meant. "It does?"

"Yeah. It feels better. No other worries. No hurry. No panic. It's nice," he whispered, then sat on the bed and reached for her to join him.

With a surge of desire, she slipped off her shorts and—careful of his leg—launched herself at him.

Despite what he'd said about not being in a hurry, she felt frenzied when their bodies touched. He apparently did, too. His hands caressed her everywhere as she reached for his wallet, eager to get to the condom she knew must be inside.

As soon as she covered him, he rolled over her and pushed fully inside. He let out a happy moan, but soon she could see he was struggling.

She used all her weight to shift him onto his back.

"Let me be the man," he said. He'd said that before.

"Oh, you are the man," she assured him with a smile. "Let your woman love you."

His brown gaze met hers, and he smiled back as his hand stroked her hip. "Do you, Lena?" he asked. "Do you love me?"

He'd already opened up. This was her moment. It was time to tell him the truth about her feelings, and see what came next.

She took a deep breath, and said, "Yes. I love you."

She leaned down to kiss him. It had felt so good to say it, and to know she truly meant it. She wasn't afraid to be let down again.

Yes, she was in a position to take care of herself. But she desperately wanted him in her life.

And she knew in her heart he'd be there for her through it all, in both hard times and good.

Chapter One Hundred Ten

Lena loved him.

The power of those simple words nearly made Dane leap off the bed and carry her off to the justice of the peace that very moment. But he knew carrying her wasn't an option… and besides, she was moving on top of him, her heat encasing him in the best possible way. No chance he was going anywhere anytime soon.

He wanted to tell her he loved her, too, but his words caught in his chest when her orgasm overtook her. She tightened around him, and her head fell against his chest.

Using the last bit of strength he had, he pushed up off the bed to release as deeply into her as he could.

It still wasn't enough.

He wrapped his arms around her and smiled. Her heart hammered against his, a little faster than his own. As they relaxed, there were a few times when their heart rate synched up. He thought that was a good analogy for life. Sometimes they would be in harmony, and sometimes they would disagree. But they would always be there for each other.

Together.

"I want to marry you and spend the rest of my life with you," he said, and pulled her closer.

Okay, maybe he should have started with telling her how much he loved her, but he was focused on the next step in their future.

She looked at him in surprise. Not bad surprise, just… uncertainty. "But you hardly know me. The real me. You only know the unstoppable force I become when my child is in danger."

He nestled closer. "I'm pretty sure you face even the minor things with that same unstoppable force."

She made a wry face. "Maybe."

He kissed her temple. "I'm not saying we should run off this instant and seal the deal. I'm saying I love you, and I'd like the chance to marry you after I move into your fancy new house." He winked at her and grinned.

She looked up at him and smiled back, but uncertainty still clouded her beautiful features. "It's not going to be like it was before. I have a child."

"I know. She's great, and I promise to care for her as my own." He swallowed down a twinge of pain for the child he wasn't able to have in his life. "I know what it means to be a parent. I know it's a lot of peanut butter sandwiches, and sex only when they're sleeping. I know it's sometimes chaos and stress, but it's also joy and happiness. And best of all, it's family."

Tears of happiness glistened in her kaleidoscope eyes, making them appear green. "That's…perfect."

He knew he had almost won, so he said, "I love you, Lena. I love Kenzie. Give us a chance to be a family."

The missing piece of their happy future slipped into place when he pulled her close and kissed her neck. Their lives had been completely upturned, only to fall perfectly into place again.

As he kissed along her jaw, there was only one thing left to do to set them on the path to their forever.

She looked up at him and he knew he'd do anything to protect her and her child, and make them happy. With a smile she whispered, "Yes."

Epilogue

One Year Later

Nerves got the best of Dane as the soccer game began. His leg swayed with anxious motion, needing an escape. It wasn't that Kenzie was in danger. At least not from anyone but herself.

She wasn't the most graceful of athletes, despite the hours they'd spent practicing in the backyard. She was, however, as determined as her mother, who was now patting his knee in a calming manner.

Giving up her place, Kenzie ran after the ball and stole it from a frail-looking boy who was shorter than her. Dane clapped and cheered as she dribbled it between her tiny feet down the field. She was quick. He knew the effort was taking every ounce of concentration, as evidenced by the way her tongue was sticking out.

God, please don't let her fall and bite off her tongue.

As if by some kind of magic spell, she glided right up to the net and kicked it past the goalie, scoring like an Olympic star. The look of shock on her face was priceless.

Without a thought, Dane jumped down from the bleachers and ran to scoop her up on the sideline in celebration.

"Did you see that? I got a goal!" she squealed, panting.

"I saw."

Other kids piled around, chattering and patting her on the back when he released her. "Great job!"

"How did you do that?" one of her team members asked.

"My dad's been practicing with me." She looked up at him with wide eyes. "I mean Dane."

He swallowed and smiled to reassure her the slip-up was fine with him.

It was the second time she'd called him dad. The first time, he hadn't known how to handle it. He hadn't really handled it, which was why she probably thought he didn't like it.

In a sense, he was her dad. When he'd married her mother four months ago, it had made him officially her stepdad. But they hadn't taken the next step yet to straight dadhood.

He had never wanted to use another child to fill the empty space in his heart he kept for Tobey. But over time, he realized the space wasn't empty.

His son was happy, safe, and loved by three parents. And Tobey knew it.

As much as Dane loved his son, he found he still had plenty of love left for Kenzie, Lena, and however many more children they might have in the future.

The team ran off as Lena fixed her daughter's loose braid. He remembered the stress Tobey felt over using the title Dad with Randy. Dane couldn't let Kenzie go through the same dilemma. He didn't want another moment to go by without making sure she was completely happy.

He bent down to her level and pulled her close. "Know what? I like when you call me Dad."

She looked to her mother, who had tears in her eyes. He hadn't meant to make the soccer game into something so dramatic.

"Go on. Your team is waiting for you. Remember to have fun," he added, sounding very fatherly.

She grinned. "It was fun making a goal."

"Well, good. Then keep doing that." He winked at her.

She tore off, only to run back and hug him. "I will, Dad."

"I love you, sweetie," he whispered into her hair.

"Love you, too." She was gone in a flash.

He wrapped his arm around his wife to lead her back to their seats.

"So… What would you think about having someone else call you Dad?" she asked.

He stopped walking and darted a look at her. "You want to have a baby?"

They'd discussed it once, and Lena said she wasn't ready. She'd been anxious about what could happen if her attention was divided.

She tilted her head coyly. "Yes, I'm ready now. I think we should start trying."

He wiggled his brows. "I'll give it my best effort."

She snuggled into his arms.

He brushed a stray hair back from her face and kissed her right there in front of all the other parents. "I love you."

She smiled up at him, joy filling her beautiful eyes. "When Kenzie was taken, I thought my life was over. I never in a million years expected to have a happy ending like this."

He rested his forehead against hers. "This isn't the ending, sweetheart. We're just beginning."

About the Author

One very early morning, Allison B. Hanson woke up with a conversation going on in her head. It wasn't so much a dream as being forced awake by her imagination. Unable to go back to sleep, she gave in, went to the computer, and began writing. Years later it still hasn't stopped. Allison lives near Hershey, Pennsylvania. Her contemporary romances include paranormal, sci-fi, fantasy, and mystery suspense. She enjoys candy immensely, as well as long motorcycle rides, running, and reading.

Don't miss the Love Under Fire series…

WITNESS IN THE DARK

WANTED FOR LIFE

Discover more Amara titles...

The Man I Want to Be

an *Under Covers* novel by Christina Elle

DEA agent Bryan Tyke hates weddings. He hates them even more when he's forced to travel to a hot as hell resort to watch his best friends say I do, while acting happy about it. Forever isn't in the cards for Tyke. It hasn't been since he joined the army years ago and lost everything. That is, until the woman he's never forgotten shows up as a bridesmaid and puts herself into immediate danger.

Dark Justice: McCabe

a *Dark Justice* novel by Jenna Ryan

Rowena Connor's ex was a monster. She was left with no option but to fake her death and hide their son. Now he's kidnapped her son and wants her dead—for real this time. US Marshal Ryan McCabe had to leave Rowena to save her. Now she's on the run from the man McCabe has been hunting for years, and her only hope to stay alive is to trust him, dark secrets and all.

Undercover with the Nanny

a novel by Cathy Skendrovich

DEA agent Sawyer Hayes never planned on being so drawn to a possible suspect. How is he supposed to do his job when his growing feelings for her are clouding his judgment? Romance is not on interior designer and nanny Kate Munroe's radar. But her hot new neighbor could change her mind, with his broad shoulders and Southern charm. Too bad his secrets could destroy her.

Made in the USA
Middletown, DE
26 February 2022